20/20

B SHAWN CLARK

 First Run Books™
Englewood, Florida USA

ISBN: 978-1-7343083-0-3 (hard cover)

ISBN: 978-1-7343083-1-0 (eBook)

Library of Congress Control Number: 2019956295

Front cover image is of a wood carving by Evelyn Dales.

Book design by JetLaunch.

Printed by IngramSpark, in the United States (and elsewhere).

First printing edition 2019.

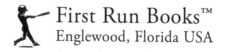

First Run Books™
Englewood, Florida USA

DEDICATION

To the lost peoples of the Calusa Nation.

ONE

Captain's Log
Volume 20/#0001 (Book 48)
Dockside at the Hermitage
(a Tuesday)

Whenthe cock crowed this morning, I paused for a moment. Not that his throaty cry was any more earnest or in tune than usual, as far as I could tell. But I found myself feeling very content. All was right with the world. He was telling me he was full of life, and there was more than enough room for optimism for what the future would bring.

I knew that, more likely, he was just baying away, prompted by some genetic sequence embedded in his soul - if he even has one of those.

These were the thoughts that seeped into my head as I stood there, morning brew in hand, staring out at the dull glint of the morning sun making her way through the haze, reflecting softly off the water that stretched away from the dock and towards the bay, farther off in the distance, where her majesty was poised just above the horizon.

I must be getting old. Maybe I was just in a reflective mood. Maybe the two go together, who knows? But my thoughts drifted back to the first time I heard a cock crow.

That was many, many years ago, back in the year 2020. I remember the year. Who could forget that one? Other things I don't quite remember with such precision - not that that matters too much - I guess. What type of adventure I was on with

Larry and Art on our bikes I don't recall, not that that matters too much either.

But I do remember negotiating through the urban landscape of Miami in what some people gamely called the "Upper East Side."

That probably sounds incredibly dangerous to you: three kids riding their bikes, back in the Roaring Twenties, on the streets of what was then an urban jungle called Miami, replete with busy roads, people with bad intent, and God only knows what else.

Other images pop into my head.

I see the top of my wheel spinning as I lean forward and up on my bike, looking down at the rush of rubber before me, carrying me onward.

Here in the future where I sit now at the dock I train my mind's eye to peer deeper into the distant past, seeing things as they once were, reliving things as they had once happened, feeling what I felt as a youngster so many years ago. I see myself looking down, studying the thin line of black grime in the crevices on the inside folds of my elbow.

Not that I really remember specifically seeing grime in my elbow pits that particular day, but I do know I did at one point or another. I can see that image so clearly in my mind. It's funny how memories can work that way, seeing things in such vivid detail even so many years after the fact. Like I said, I must be getting old.

Anyway, where was I? Oh, yeah, the strange sound of a rooster crowing in the middle of an urban landscape – a landscape that doesn't exist anymore.

Back then, I'm sure I had heard a cock crow on cartoons and animal shows on TV, but that was not the same thing as hearing that distinctive sound live while riding your bike on a city sidewalk. The sound could have just as well come from another planet or floating through the air as a by-product of some weird science experiment in someone's garage.

Somewhere in the midst of the concrete and cars and dingy motels was the sound of an actual *barnyard animal*. How eerie and out of place was that sound, or the sound of any living thing that wasn't human, beyond the occasional shrieks of the green

Amazon parrots who had found their freedom, or the high-pitched call of the squirrels who had managed to find their niche in this world we had created for them.

Okay, there I go again, going off on a riff about the good old days. Like I said, that was quite some time ago, and the days were not that great, to be honest with you.

I was one of those weird kids back then that liked to read the newspaper and watch news shows on the television. There was a constant parade of bad things happening, which I relished for reasons that are not that clear to me. There were the wars in the Middle East, rising oil prices, the runaway budget deficit of the U.S. Government, the "retirement" of what we called "baby boomers" that put a strain on the Social Security system, and pension plans that were either in bankruptcy or headed in that direction. My mom always said the bringers of the bad news were just selling misery. As if on cue the news show would run an ad for aspirin, a stomach antacid or the occasional anti-depressant.

"See, I told you," she would say with some amount of authority.

Merchants of misery notwithstanding, we all knew that life was getting a little more difficult back in the Twenties. Our prospects looked bleaker with each passing day. Everything cost more, and those who were lucky enough to have a good job were hard pressed to make ends meet. People who had a job, or two, discovered that an ever-increasing chunk of their pay went for taxes to pay for the constant wars we were fighting, trying to pay for the upkeep of those too old to work, and, of course, pay the debts run up by politicians, long since dead, who borrowed money on the national credit card.

People who thought they would retire in their sixties discovered that the new sixty was forty, and they had to try and compete with people in their forties (now apparently in their twenties) for a place in an ever-shrinking workforce. Those who worked hard all their lives so they could retire in their sixties discovered they couldn't afford to do that.

They had to keep working until they dropped dead of exhaustion.

Not very many people back in the Twenties were old enough to remember what life was like during the Great Depression of the 1930s, much less the carefree 1920s that preceded it, but many people had an inkling that something was seriously wrong, even while we reprised our own version of the Roaring Twenties a century after the first one.

In hindsight, we know now we were in the middle of a slow-motion economic catastrophe, but at the time we just kept cruising along as if nothing really was wrong with the way things were. I know that is what I did. Of course I did. That is what I was supposed to do. I was just a kid trying to be a kid, cruising on my bike like every kid does.

That is when I first heard the cry of a rooster, beckoning to me. Let me tell you what happened:

That particular day, Art, Larry and I had turned off Biscayne Boulevard, the main thoroughfare that served as the "Great Divide" between our neighborhoods on the "East Side" and the neighborhoods to the west, which were known as "Little Haiti."

On that day's adventure, we were riding our bikes on a street in a quiet neighborhood lined with Art Deco and other houses with architecture from various by-gone eras, most of which were in various stages of disrepair. When I heard the strange sound of that other-worldly creature, I know now that what I heard was probably just Ahab, trying to impress the other chickens in the roost or just doing whatever it is roosters do.

But at the time I first heard him, by reflex I turned in his direction, leaving Art and Larry on the path that had been ahead of us. I followed the sound, and as I traveled I am pretty sure I actually forgot all about Ahab and the other-worldly sounds he had been making as I came to rest on the side of the road. I just sat for a minute on my bike.

Across the street was something that distracted me even more than Ahab's crowing.

There was nothing particularly alluring about the house across the street. Actually, I couldn't see much of the house at all. What I saw was a structure surrounded by trees and vegetation, parts of the roof and a chimney barely visible above the tree line. A rounded structure did jut prominently skyward out of the top of the trees, but that was about it.

Otherwise, the whole thing was shrouded in greenery.

But the place had an aura. A path through the vegetation wound its way through to an iron gate barely visible when I craned my neck to one side. "Keep Out!" was the first thought that came to mind. Yet I was drawn into where that path might lead. As I peered in more closely, I could make out the faint outlines of a masonry wall through the greenery.

The wall extended outward on either side of an iron gate at the entranceway that seemed to beckon to me, yet warned me to stay away.

"Looks kinda spooky."

Larry had pulled up with Art and stopped his bike, leaning forward on his handlebars. I remember his face as sweaty, and he may have been a little out of breath.

Art said nothing, I'm sure. Art didn't say much.

I looked at them as if seeing them for the first time. I had this feeling that they had intruded upon a private discovery I had just made. I wanted to enter into this new secret world, by myself, that I instinctively knew lay just on the other side of that iron gate.

Once inside I would shut everyone else out – including them.

"It's haunted. You must never go near this place again," I said, pulling up on my bike and steering them away from my new secret hiding place.

They followed.

That night, my mom told me the crowing I heard was probably from an animal kept by a Haitian family, or maybe in a *bodega* to be used in a Santeria ritual or something. I know that was not the case because of the discovery I had made that day.

But I didn't argue with her.

That evening we gathered for our usual evening repast. I don't remember what we had exactly. No doubt we had the generic macaroni and cheese with mystery-meat hot dogs and maybe some baked beans. Don't get me wrong. I am not complaining.

I was glad to have it. We all knew my mom worked her poor little fingers to the bone to make sure we had anything and a chance to share whatever that was with one another.

Like I said, I watched the news. Times were hard in those days.

My mom was strong, and I loved her dearly for how she was. Things were bad for all of us, but she always worked hard to keep us together as a family. I know now more than ever what she did and how hard that was for her to do. Even then, knowing what I did, I was more than happy to gulp down the mystery meat or whatever she wanted to call whatever it was she offered to us. She always made sure that dinner was a special occasion, a time when we would talk about the things we did that day, or what was on our minds, as we hunkered over what she presented to us that evening for our sustenance.

One thing we did not talk about was my dad.

With all she had on her plate, having to make her way for herself, not to mention her kids, I know that what she was doing was a hard thing to do all by herself.

She told us that our father was reported as MIA during one of the wars, long before I can remember. At some point I eventually learned that MIA does not stand for Miami International Airport. I think she said that he went missing someplace in the Middle East, but I didn't press for details. I was dying to know more, but I knew this was a sore subject with her – one of the few things we didn't talk about too much.

I remember her being in rare form the night I told her I heard the cock crow for the first time. After stern lectures about *santeros* and other manners by which our souls could be snatched, she told me and my little sister Kate at the dinner table to beware of all the dangers that faced us in the surrounding environs outside our small family circle. My story about what I found that day with the secret garden that no doubt lurked behind the mystery gate just fueled the fire. She told us that what I described was what she heard was the hiding place of an old hermit living in an estate first created back in the old days when people had, well, *estates* that they actually lived in at the time.

"Hermit the frog" came out of Katie's mouth as she hunkered over her gruel.

I giggled along with her.

Undeterred, Mom went on to tell us of the rumors she had heard of the strange hermit who lived at the estate and his odd preoccupations. He rarely left his compound and kept all manner of mysterious and illegal devices and equipment on the premises. He was not "normal" in any sense of the word, and we were to keep our distance from such a strange creature. He also had a strange woman that worked for him, an "Amazon" of some sort brought here from another continent. He was said to have enslaved her.

"Amazon Dot Com," said Kate, still bent over her gruel.

I just smiled this time. She was only five, but I knew that now she was trying to be cute, having gotten some mileage from her big brother out of her first silly comment.

My mom forbade me, not to mention my little sister, from going anywhere near the enchanted estate of old, turned into a compound with exotic animals and an enslaved Amazon Warrior Princess lurking within its walls.

Yeah right.

TWO

Captain's Log
Volume 20/#0002
(Tuesday)

I must have been sitting there on the dock for quite a while, staring off into what had become the sparkling glint from a rising sun reflecting off the water before I became aware of the fact that I had, well, been staring off into the glistening water for quite some time. My mind had progressed from thoughts of roosters giving fair warning to kids riding their bikes in a concrete jungle – a jungle destined to become extinct - to not much of anything worth telling you about, certainly not worth writing down for people to read.

Which reminds me, I should check in the manuals to see if there is much more in there about the economic collapse ushered in by the Roaring Twenties. Heck, maybe they should be called the Whimpering Twenties. Not too much to roar about in that decade, at least not something most people would think of as things to be proud of.

But, in hindsight, I can say there were a few things here and there to crow about.

As I was heading back in, taking my half-filled cup of cold coffee with me, I made a mental note to check the manuals for more about what happened back in the so-called Roaring Twenties, but that would have to wait until later, when and if I had more time.

You see, today was the day for harvesting fruit from our trees. Somewhere in one of the manuals was an explanation of when and how to do that, no doubt along with a lot of other facts and data on the subject, but at this point we all knew what to do and why.

Maybe it seems a little odd at this point in time that there would have been a need to write down things such as how to grow stuff to feed ourselves.

I guess that was an indication of just how far we had come from where we were.

We do have a lot of fruit trees. We have oranges, tangerines, grapefruits, lemons and limes in our citrus department. Then there are the banana, papaya, mangoes, avocado and some other things like star fruit that I'm not so sure merit much mention.

Come to think of it, maybe there is quite a bit more that we really need to keep better track of, but we seem to have fallen into a groove taking care of our trees – or maybe grove is the right word for it - knowing when to harvest their fruit, when to feed the soil around them with our composted, organic material, and knowing in general what to do next. We had learned so much over the years, much of it had now become second nature to us.

This morning I worked the avocado trees with the long fruit catcher, a concocted wire contraption that at the end looked like one of those things lacrosse players use but with wire fingers sticking out to pull the fruit from the trees and gather them into the place where the lacrosse ball goes (or whatever they call that thing they fling around). We had to attach the lacrosse thing to longer and longer poles to reach up high enough to grab the avocados and mangoes, seeing as how our trees were getting so high and all.

Laying the wobbling pole on the ground next to the tree, I drew closer to the trunk for a better look. I found myself drawing within inches, peering intently at the face of her body, and then upward along her trunk to the sight of her branches spreading outward and skyward.

I gently touched her, looking for the inner tree, the one that was there before she had become so majestic. I like to call this one the Sentinel.

This may seem a little strange but there is something about looking at a fully mature tree in all her glory, soaring upwards to the heavens, taller than most surrounding buildings, bearing fruit, providing shade, providing oxygen, doing all the things she did, and then realizing that this very same tree was, when you first saw her, the same weak little twig you had seen sticking out of the ground decades in the past.

I was looking into her trunk to find that little twig somewhere inside of her.

After a while I circled around her and up the embankment towards the road. I consciously left my hand on her trunk as long as I could, sliding through my movements on purpose just to linger and caress her, judging her age as I went.

I wanted to maintain that connection and to get my bearings.

Up on the embankment I looked down the road, first one way, then the other, still trying to get my bearings. I squinted reflexively, maybe because the sun was glinting so harshly, but probably more so because that is what people like me are supposed to do when they are getting on in years. We reflect on how things are now, trying to remember how they used to be back in the olden days. We seem to want to draw comparisons.

I'm trying to fit into this role, you see, of the older guy thinking about how things used to be and how much they have changed.

I'm not so sure I much care for this new role of mine.

In days gone by an old codger would tell a young whipper-snapper how there used to be a dirt road where now, with so much progress, the road had become a four-lane highway. Today is more like the reverse. At one point there was a neatly paved city street right here, where I am standing. Over the years we filled the potholes of the unattended street with crushed shell and other pervious materials to the point where we had made this road into a pathway probably more suitable for oxen and horse-drawn carriages than the cars and trucks it had originally been designed for.

We didn't mind. We had other ways of getting what we needed when we couldn't produce it ourselves. Most of the time we would travel by sea rather than venturing into what the outside world had to offer via the roadways, such as they were.

Squinting westward at the intersection of what had become of our city street with that of another, I pinpointed where I likely sat on my bike the first time I saw the Amazon.

My thoughts returned to that time and place:

Then, as now, I looked for landmarks, trying to find my way back to the enchanted compound with the hermit and his slave woman that my mom had warned us about.

Looking around, listening for the tell-tale cry of the other-worldly rooster, I had paused in my quest, trying to retrace my route from a few days before - you know, when I was on my bike cruising around with Larry and Art.

Then, in the distance, down the road, I saw her.

She was bent over, digging or doing something near the side of the road. I approached slowly on my bike. My eyes were fixed on her as I drew closer, but I could not help but notice the array of freshly planted twigs that marked my path towards her. They were positioned near the road, not exactly pointing in a straight line. They seemed to be strategically placed for some unknown purpose at various points closer and farther along the side of the road in a pattern I was yet to discern. Each little twig with the fragile-looking leaves sticking out of them was surrounded at the base with soil and some other stuff. Some had rocks encircling the base and sticks holding them up.

My pace fell to a crawl as I got nearer to the Amazon. I had to start twisting my handlebars to keep from putting my feet to the pavement until I finally came to rest just a few feet from where she was working. She had laid her shovel down and had just finished filling a hole with water. She twisted the nozzle at the end of the hose that snaked from somewhere out of the dense vegetation behind her, stopping the flow of water that smelled a little funny to me. She then carefully lowered another twig with leaves on it into the hole she had dug. The thing was about three feet high at most.

She continued what she was doing as if I wasn't there watching her every move.

I put down my kickstand and leaned back to regard what she was doing.

"*Whatcha doin'*?"

The words seemed to come out of nowhere until I realized they came out of my mouth. I don't know why, but I felt ashamed of what I had asked her.

She continued, bent over her labor, tenderly tucking the soil around the twig with the leaves on it and then sprinkling some kind of stuff around the base.

She said nothing.

After a while I started to wonder if she heard me - also if I should not beat a hasty retreat. Just when I was about to raise my kickstand and push off, her voice hit me like a bolt of lightning. Okay, maybe it wasn't a "bolt of lightning" exactly, but I was startled when I heard the soft words drifting up from where she was bent over her labors.

"From these trees there is life. This is where they belong." I looked around for a second, trying to locate the nearest tree to which she may be referring.

She must have sensed my confusion. She had finished fussing around with the dirt and the other stuff she had been patting into place around the base of the twig she had just planted. She stood up to her full height, straight and tall just like an Amazon should, towering over me. My mouth probably fell open.

Her skin was chocolate and perfectly smooth, glistening in the early-morning sun.

She wore a brightly colored halter top and cut-off jeans that barely concealed a sinewy physique that likely had not an ounce of body fat included. Her eyes were blue-green and were shaped in a way that, with the shape of her face, looked vaguely Asian. Or maybe Native American. Or something exotic. I wasn't sure.

All I know is that in my eyes she was the most beautiful woman I had ever seen.

She peered down at me, expressionless, from the veil of the straw hat on her head that threw small specks of sunlight onto her face. Now conscious of her stare, her words finally came to me, and I looked at the pathetic twig with the leaves sticking out of it that she had put into the ground. Her eyes followed mine.

She seemed to know what I was thinking.

"Someday, many years from now, she will tower over you," she said, looking down at me as if to graphically bring home the point. "She will bring you life, air, and shade you from the sun. She will provide food to you - all that you can ask of her. And she asks so little in return."

She turned without another word towards her last twig that was sticking out of a burlap sack. The bottom of the sack bulged, holding in the dirt and roots of the sapling she was holding in her hand. She picked up her shovel and headed towards the next space in the pattern, where she started to dig. I couldn't help watching the muscles of her arms and legs flexing through her ebony skin as she bent to her task.

To my young eyes, she was a work of art.

I inched a little closer to where she was planting the twig and took up my position. I resisted an impulse to jump off my bike and help her, although I'm not sure why.

After a while I suddenly felt a presence and looked up to see Mr. Peabody standing over the Amazon, his hands on his hips. I didn't know his name at the time but came to learn who he was later. He had come strutting up the road, but I hadn't seemed to notice.

"I don't know what you think you are doing, but I hope you know those plants are in the city right-of-way, so close to the road." He glanced my way and waited for a response from the Amazon.

She said nothing.

He waited and seemed to become a little agitated at the lack of a response.

"*You* people have to learn that you can't do whatever you want whenever you feel like it. There are *laws*." I could have sworn he was tapping his foot impatiently, but I may have made that part up. But I do know an eternity seemed to pass before

I heard those words drifting softly once again up to where Mr. Peabody was standing.

"From these trees there is life. This is where they belong."

She continued at her labors, gently pushing the soil and that other stuff around the base of her final entry into the Trees of Life.

When she finished she rose again and looked at her handi-work, seemingly ignoring the older white man who seemed to me to grow so much smaller.

"These trees are on city-owned property. The city has the responsibility of taking care of the right of way and can come at any time and rip these things right out of the ground. The government by law maintains the area near the roadway that they have responsibility for," said Peabody, sweat rolling down his nose.

The Amazon looked at Peabody, as if for the first time. She peered down the street going one way, then the other. The pot-holes had already started to form. A speed sign was tilted. Utility poles along the road were skewed in a haphazard pattern from high winds in bygone years and even more years of obvious neglect.

The road for the first time looked to me like an abandoned relic of the past, with overgrowth already creeping into unclaimed territory along the edges.

I don't know if Peabody saw what she and I saw, but she just turned her gaze upon him for a moment after regarding the sight of what the road had already started to become. She said nothing, turning to gather up her heap of empty burlap bags and shovel.

"This is not the end of this!" he called out after her. Then he shot me a final glance and strutted off down the road.

From that day forward I started looking at the world in a different way, starting with the enchanted Hermitage now in my direct path. I pushed off and headed back up the road and around the front of where the Amazon and her supposed master lived.

For the first time I noticed the many holes and imperfections in the road around which I had been negotiating without a sec-ond thought. I slowed down for a moment at the mysterious pathway to the front of the place I had seen before and sought to guard with jealous secrecy from Art and Larry. I made out with greater clarity how the enclave that lay beyond what I now saw as carefully positioned trees and vegetation was surrounded by a masonry wall stretching all along the front and sides of the property.

I steered my bike slowly past the entrance and across the front of the place and turned down the next street, keeping my eye trained on spots along and through the vegetation where I saw the faint signs of the masonry wall peeking out.

The whole place was a virtual fortress. I came to the end of the road that stopped rather abruptly on the edge of Biscayne Bay, near the seawall. I flipped down my kickstand and ventured through the overgrown grass towards the point where I judged the masonry wall surrounding the Hermitage ended and the water had to begin.

Near the seawall I found what, indeed, was the terminus of a masonry wall. Extending out from the edge of the wall was a semi-circular chain-link type fence structure with barbed wire at the edges jutting out from a steel pole placed snug against the end of the wall. I got as close as I could to peer around the edge without falling in the water and held onto the chain links, half expecting them to send out an electric shock. What I saw was more vegetation mostly obscuring my view. I also saw the edges of what looked like some kind of boat house and the dock jutting out into the bay.

From out of the bushes and trees came a sudden high-pitched rapid-fire sound that made me recoil in surprise. For a brief second I was bewildered until I recognized the sound as the bleating of some sort of goat or lamb or some such.

When I heard a rustling near the edge of the wall where I stood, a sound only a dog or other large mammal would make, and some pointedly loud snorting, I decided I had pushed my luck far enough and retreated back to the edge of the road. I 'bout broke my neck jumping on my bike when my foot almost slipped off the pedal, making me swerve wildly to keep my balance. I righted myself and started pumping like a bat out of hell.

I looked back half expecting to see the Amazon running after me, but she was nowhere to be seen. After I put some distance between me and that place with the bleating goat creature and mad dog, the adrenalin started to slack off a little, and I settled down in my saddle, breathing a little easier while I rode my trusty steed back home.

That night my mind was racing with what had happened, but I knew I couldn't say anything to my mom. There was another rolling blackout so we had our meager dinner by candlelight, lending a spooky air to our house that made telling such tales even more out of the question. I remember wishing my dad was there so I could tell him about the Amazon and the weird place with the trees and strange animal sounds and the mysterious hermit.

There were a lot of other things I would tell him.

Katie came to my room afterward. She wanted me to read her a bedtime story to help her fall asleep. Without lights to read, I offered to tell her a story instead.

We went into her little-girl room. While she curled up all snug in her bed, I regaled her with a tale of a little girl and her adventures riding her bike in an enchanted forest filled with strange creatures and an exotic, fierce African princess woman who ruled over the forest, protecting the animals and making things come to life with her magic powers.

I wasn't sure how the story would end - but that didn't matter.

She was fast asleep.

I quietly tiptoed out of her room.

THREE

Earlier today I was out back again, staring at the old dock stretching out into the bay, trying to remember some song from way, way back that was hidden somewhere in the recesses of my old, addled brain. I remember the basic tune somewhat. The words were something about sitting out on a dock somewhere, watching the tide, or something like that. Who was the guy that sang that song? It was before my time, but I seem to recall my dad singing along to that tune at some honky-tonk he took me to, way back when.

Not that I minded. Thinking back on it though, that was probably not the best place for a young boy to spend quality time with his father.

But I took what I could get, I suppose.

I say the dock is old, but it really isn't that old. We had to build it up a good six feet or so not that long ago on account of the king tides they told us would just keep getting more and more king-like. It's all in one of the manuals. I need to check on that. Seems like the tides are getting more ominous, and we may need another face lift on this old girl.

There were some storm clouds at the horizon just beyond the docks; nothing too much to be concerned about. These days we watch the weather sites that are still operating real careful like, to

17

keep an eye on things. Have to. We've got to keep a "weather eye out" in this water world of ours, if you know what I mean.

I did know without having to double-check again that this was just another typical rain storm heading our way, like that one back in the Twenties, not long before The Big One hit us. I wonder if there is something in the manuals about that little storm we had. It was like an appetizer to the Big One, I like to say. I made a mental note to check to see if the Appetizer was mentioned in one of the manuals. Maybe there was also something in there about that song that was just on the tip of my brain, but not quite there.

"Otis" somebody? Nah, I don't think he had an old country boy name like that.

Not sure why that Appetizer storm stuck in my mind. Every now and again images and action would run inside my head about that day, like scenes from an old movie you have seen a hundred times. That is part of getting old I suppose. You remember things many, many years in the past but have to make a mental note (usually scribbled on a piece of paper) to check on something in the manual when you get back to the fort.

Almost forgot what I was supposed to remember . . .

Oh, yeah, the Appetizer.

Come to think of it, I was on a dock that day, fishing with my buddy Art:

Art and I were enjoying a little recreation, fishing off the end of a dock. True, I was enjoying myself, but I was not exactly goofing off. There was no school that day, and, although I didn't say anything to Art, our family needed something a little more substantial to feed ourselves. The idea of having some grilled fish to go with our macaroni and cheese for dinner was like to make my mouth water just thinking about it.

I didn't say anything to Art, nor did he say much back.

Art is not a big talker.

The wind was starting to whip up pretty good in that telltale sign that the storm is near and heading your way. We knew we could linger no more. I shoved what little fish I had caught into my worn-out bait bucket, folded up my fishing rod and balanced my way onto my bike and onto the road with my gear.

Art silently did likewise.

Good thing the wind was at my back as I pumped furiously to beat the storm. "Better hurry," Art managed to eke out, nodding his head in the direction of the storm clouds as he peeled off and headed towards where he lived. I was heading to Mrs. Jacobs' house. She was a nice older lady, half blind. She lived alone and barely made ends meet with the pittance from Social Security and a small amount paid to her from the army. Her dead husband had spent some time fighting some long-forgotten war, it would seem. She was, in a sense, all alone in this world, except for us – and, of course, her beloved cat.

She took pity on us and would watch Kate when she was not in school and mom had to work her second job. Or third. I think maybe the exchange was to the mutual benefit of everyone concerned. She was alone there in her little house in a neighborhood that was getting as old as she was. Things were changing and not for the better. She seemed like she could use the company, and, though she tried not to show it too much, she seemed to really like having youngsters around. She might have been a teacher or librarian of some sort at one time or another. She sure looked like one.

I didn't notice that Kate's bike was not parked out front as I pulled up frantically, like Dorothy in the Wizard of Oz, wind whipping around like a banshee.

"Mrs. Jacobs?" I called out as I opened the front door. I looked around and saw no one, except for her cat perched on top of the couch. After a second or two that seemed to last forever, Mrs. Jacobs came out from the kitchen. "I heard on the radio this was going to be quite a storm. Severe thunderstorm warnings, they said." She looked past me as if she was looking for something – or someone, it turned out.

"Where's Katie?" she asked.

My face must have turned white as a sheet. I am pretty sure my mouth fell open. "She's not here?" I am also pretty sure my words came out in a very high pitch.

"No, I thought she was with you. She left here an hour or so ago and said she was going to this place you had told her about. Maybe she went home." She had a concerned look on her face that grew more worried when distant rumbles of thunder could be heard.

They were so loud I could swear her dishes and ceramic stuff she had hanging on the walls rattled with the vibrations. She cast a wary eye out the window.

"I'm sure she is at home," I said, probably not too convincingly.

At least, I wasn't too convinced.

On the furious ride home, wild thoughts kept racing through my head. There was also more than a little bit of fear. I think what I was doing was something like praying. *Let her be home. Let her be home. Let her be home. Oh, please, let her be home.* I kept saying these things to myself as I rolled into the front yard, letting my bike sail forward towards a crash landing somewhere in the front yard. I had my fishing rod and bait bucket in my hands.

The rain started to fall.

Her bike was nowhere to be seen. Nor was she as I slung my gear on the front porch floor, bursting into the house, calling out her name. The calls came out as screams.

There was no answer.

Fear turned to panic as I went outside and into a space with an increasingly dark, menacing sky. It was the middle of the day. The rain started to come down a little harder.

Not sure if it was nervous sweat or rain water, but I was soon drenched as I found myself pumping like a madman with all my strength, pushing my bike as fast as it could go. The rain started coming down real hard now, slowing me down to a near crawl. By sheer instinct, I guess, I somehow made it outside the Hermitage place where I thought she might be. I peered through the rain to catch a glimpse of her bike. I saw no signs of it or her. I walked closer. I called out in what had to have been a pitiful, woe-begotten wail of a plea for help.

There was no answer.

There was a sudden flash of light I caught out of the corner of my eye. At almost the same instant a loud clap of thunder shook me to the core. I knew enough that the lightning was close enough to strike me dead if I didn't get the hell out of there.

For a good long while I pumped that bike of mine in the face of a maelstrom, spurred on by an occasional clap of thunder that felt like a whip cracking at the seat of my pants. I was awash in rainwater and sweat.

Plus, more than a few tears.

After a while I gave up riding the bike. It was faster to walk it back to the house. The rain was falling real hard, but at least the thunder and lightning were getting a little farther away. *One Mississippi, two Mississippi, three Mississippi, four Mississippi, five Mississippi* I counted before the thunder struck. Three more states away than last time. That means it was moving away from me, and I might just live long enough to get home.

But would my little sister make it?

By the time I got to the front yard I was a wet rag of a boy. I was moving real slow, resigned to my fate, whatever that would be, I guess. If my little sister was dead, I was not sure it wouldn't be just as well I was struck down by lightning myself.

There was a strange vehicle I did not recognize in the driveway. Some sort of jeep or work truck of some sort. I looked at it passively as I continued up to the carport, feeling kind of numb. The rain slowed a little but was still coming down pretty hard, as I recall. I put the kickstand down on my bike and parked it in the carport.

I looked over and passively regarded her bike, there in the carport as well. I was still numb and things were not registering quite yet. As if in a dream I walked back out into the rain. I lifted my head up and saw a flash in the distance. I didn't count Mississippis. I didn't care about that anymore. I went into the front porch and looked up at the giant standing there. She had just come out of the front door. Her chocolate skin glistened. Her soaking wet clothes clung to her body. She had a placid expression on her face.

The front door was still open, and I could just make out my mom standing there, Kate held close to her side. Kate was not clinging to her in the least little bit. She was calm as a cucumber. By golly, she had a smile on her face. I would have wanted to smack her one if I was in any right state of mind - or maybe not. She was there all in one piece, no worse for wear. That was the important thing. My little sister wasn't dead, after all.

I looked up at the Amazon. I am pretty sure I had a blank expression on my face.

I blinked my eyes.

She looked back at me with her classic, placid, expressionless look. Kind of regal, come to think of it. Maybe she really was a princess. She turned her head, regarding the look of shock and awe of a mother, alongside the beaming face of a little girl. She gave me one last look, and then headed out into the rain without the slightest flinch. The rain came down just a bit harder, but she did not seem to notice. She strolled upright and confident towards her vehicle, got behind the wheel and drove off. I stared at the sight, my eyes following her as she splashed down the muddy stream of a road outside our house.

I stood for a moment, just taking it all in. I was emotionally and physically spent. My mom and Kate moved closer to the doorway.

"See, Mommy? I told you it was a real story. There is an enchanted garden with strange creatures and a fierce Warrior Princess right here in our neighborhood!"

She looked down, picked up the bait bucket, looked inside and thrust it towards her mother. "Look, Mommy, we're having fish for dinner!"

FOUR

CL 20/0004
The Hermitage/Thursday

I took another morning constitutional today.

This had to have made six or seven days in a row by this time. I lost count. This is what people are supposed to do when they are getting on in years. Not like I needed the exercise so much seeing as how just getting from one day to the next in these times of ours, here in the future, was pretty physically demanding. But a routine is just what the doctor ordered, if I had one that is. Hadn't seen a real doctor in so long, I wasn't sure I ever did.

Not sure what one would look like to be honest with you.

White coat and stethoscope, I suppose. Not like one of the ladies in the Village that would tend to folks' aches and pains, bandage up their wounds, or give out some herbs or other types of potions and medicines or other such things they kept in their cupboards or satchels. Better to keep your body and mind in tune to ward off the bad things that happen as your body and mind start to get too advanced. I guess that is why I get so much lost in thought as I amble my way around the Village on these morning walks.

Either that or it's early onset of getting a little more demented than I would like to be at this stage in life, especially considering my responsibilities around this place.

I was so lost in thought I had a feeling of actually being lost for a second. I guess I was staring at the ground for so long I forgot where I was going and where I was. I looked up when one of the villagers let out a single word "morning!" to greet me. He was coming out of his place. He has a name, I know, but forgive me, I can't think of it off the top of my head right now. Not like we are not a close-knit community. Have to be in these times. Probably just early-onset, I guess. Oh yeah, Little Freddie. That's his name.

I call him Little Freddie even though he is not exactly little anymore. We go way back to when we were still youngsters, back in the olden days. He is as old as I am now, give or take a few years, but he is still Little Freddie to me. He is one of Old Man Peabody's boys.

He was around during the olden days, back in the Twenties.

Speaking of which (or "whom" I guess is correct English), I came upon Larry as well, my old pal and another of Old Man Peabody's clan. Not sure if he was his boy or his nephew exactly, not that that matters much. Larry looked at me expectantly for a moment – or so I thought. I didn't feel like talking for some reason, so I just gave him a quick nod of the head, and he nodded back before going back to whatever it was he was doing.

I guess I should have stopped and chatted for a while, but he can be a real talker sometimes, and I was not in the mood.

This may be a bad sign as I really am getting to be more and more drawn into myself. I guess I am trying to live up to the image of the Hermitage where I increasingly spend more and more of my time, holed up, away from the villagers and other people out in the real world. But this morning for some reason I wanted to be left alone with my thoughts. Increasingly they turned into more like ruminations.

This is another sign of getting on in years, most likely.

Come to think of it, seeing Larry must have triggered more memories of days gone by, diverting them away from the place those thoughts had otherwise been headed, sending them back down the old rumination highway I seem to be on. The on-ramp took me right to the memory of that incident I like to call the day of the Standoff at the OK Moat:

I can't remember when exactly it was, sometime in the Twenties, but it must have been not too long after the episode with the Appetizer storm. I thought it was only proper and nice to thank the Amazon Princess for rescuing Kate the way she did. Plus I had what looked like a good excuse to pay a visit to her and the hermit and see what was really going on over there. I may have also had somewhat of a boyish crush on her, but I was ill-equipped to know exactly how to show my appreciation in a proper, gentlemanly manner.

I thought of flowers, but that seemed a little too hokey. Besides which, I had no money to get flowers anyway from an actual florist.

Then I remembered the incident with the trees she was planting and had what I thought was a great idea. I had started to root an avocado seed, thinking how I could help feed ourselves better. Long-term planning, it would seem. I read somewhere on the internet how you could stick toothpicks in a seed you got from an avocado (after you ate the fruit, of course) and set the bottom half in water.

Sure enough, after a few weeks I had the thing sprouting up. Seeing those leaves sprout like that made me proud and a little excited, I must confess.

I had actually made something grow. It was like magic in a way.

In my sock drawer was a pair of socks I was still holding on to for some reason. They were riddled with holes and were long past their expiration date. My mom probably would think it was not a waste to forego trying to darn them up anymore. They were threadbare and not worth the trouble, but, as usual, I felt the need to hold on to them.

I couldn't bear the guilt of just throwing them away. Even back then there was a sense with a lot of people that you needed to repurpose things, not just throw them away without giving them a new lease on life – which is exactly what I did.

They were not made of burlap, but by doubling them up they would serve my purpose well all the same. I rolled the doubled-up socks, aligned just so that all the holes were covered up, and carefully placed my sprouting avocado seed into the makeshift burlap mini-sack. On my way to the Hermitage I saw some flowers poking their heads up out of some weeds on the side of the road. In a flash of inspiration I parked my bike and got a handful of flowers and arranged them, so to speak, to accentuate the twig with the two leaves sticking out of the mini-burlap sock-sack. Balancing the whole contraption carefully on my handlebars, I continued on my way to the Hermitage, proud of my clever ingenuity.

Pride turned to anxiety and panic as I walked towards the front gate. What made me sally forth and onward I will never know, but I had the presence of mind enough to put the bouquet behind my back with my left hand, reaching forward with my right to ring the bell.

Only there wasn't one.

I guess they did not have too many visitors and didn't want to give the idea that there should be any. After all it *was* a Hermitage. I looked up and saw there was a camera overhead, staring down at me with what I swear was a glowing red eyeball, like that scene from the movie where the computer took over the spaceship and had to be unplugged.

I forgot the name of that movie. It had to have been close to a century ago.

Anyway, someone did finally creep up slowly on the other side of the gate, crouching slightly as he advanced. He was a black and white border collie. He froze in his tracks and just stood there, staring at me, not making a sound.

I felt a presence behind me even before I heard the words that startled me back into reality and out of all of those visions of spaceships and computer eyeballs and crouching wolf-dogs that seemed just about ready to pounce on me.

"He's not here right now."

I turned around, quickly hiding the bouquet behind my back at the sight of the Amazon Princess. She craned her neck in mock intrigue at what I was holding behind my back, no doubt having already gotten a good look at it while she was standing silently behind me, watching me trying to figure out how to ring the doorbell.

My eyes probably got real wide, both at the surprise and the fact she actually said a whole bunch of words. I swear she had a smirk on her face, but she didn't ask what I was holding behind my back. I swung the crude bouquet in front of me and thrust it at her with both hands. Water was dripping from the arrangement, dripping off my hands.

She studied the offering for a moment.

"It is a tree - a tree that gives life." Not sure where those words came from but they were pretty good. Good enough to crack a smile, even a small one. Heck, her lips even parted a little, revealing the whitest, most perfect teeth I had ever seen. I thought for a moment she might even break into a broad grin, but then the spell of our sweet little encounter was rudely broken by the sound of a voice over a bullhorn.

"Attention! Attention! You people in that overgrown house over there. Come out here and make sure you keep your hands where we can see them."

We peered out through the leaves and vegetation and saw Mr. Peabody standing on the street next to a young guy in a crumpled uniform. The old police car parked nearby was dirty and had more than a few dents. The faded words "Police Service Aide" were etched on the side of the car. The young guy reminded me of a character who played a skinny, inept deputy on an old TV series set in a small town in rural America. I forget the name of the show. "Barn" is what the wise sheriff who ran the town affectionately called him, as I recall. "Barney" (as in "Now, *Barney*, why'd you have to go and do *that* for") is what the sheriff called him when he made another bone-headed move. I saw the Barney Character slap Peabody on the arm and heard him tell him "you can't say that!"

"Well, what if they are armed and dangerous?" Peabody asked.

The Amazon Princess did not hesitate and walked tall and proud out to confront them. They pulled back at the sight of her. I followed not too far behind but not too close, either. She stopped, hands on hips, at the edge of a deep and wide meandering ditch that ran between the road and the wall surrounding the Hermitage.

The ditch was partly obscured by plantings which gave it a pleasant appearance of being a tree-lined stream or babbling brook. I had not noticed it before.

Now that I took a closer look from that vantage point, it seemed like just as much a moat around the Hermitage as it did a serene waterway.

For the first time I noticed there was a figure in the back seat of the dented police cruiser. Then the door suddenly flung open. Out stepped Larry, who was gawking at the Warrior Princess and the stand-off taking place on either side of the moat.

"Get back in the car," said Peabody, waving his arm. "It's too dangerous for you to be out here in the open. You don't know what they might do." Larry looked at him, then glanced in our direction, and then back at Peabody.

He lifted his pudgy arm and pointed in our direction.

"But I know him. He's practically my best friend."

"Nowadays you don't know anybody. You don't know who your so-called 'friends' really are. One day he is your best buddy and the next he's shooting at you and everybody else who happens to be in the schoolyard the day he goes off his rocker. Now get back!"

The Amazon and I exchanged glances.

This was getting surreal.

Larry gave us one last look, frowned, and turned on his heel, walking in the direction of his house. Peabody called after him, "Lock the doors when you get there!"

He then turned his attention back to the two desperados across the moat. His face was red. Sweat was pouring down his face and soaked the front of his shirt.

I remember that guy sure did sweat a lot.

We could hear him just fine but he turned the bull horn back on, probably to better help him emphasize whatever point he was trying to make.

"As the president of the association I am hereby putting you on notice that you are in violation of the rules and regulations by, among other things, illegally installing a water management system in the public right of way." I don't know why, but right at that moment Ahab let out a real loud "Cockle Doodle Do!" His timing was perfect, lending an air of even more absurdity to the whole strange confrontation with Peabody.

"Plus, harboring illegal farm animals in an urban zone!"

The Amazon crossed her arms across her chest and did nothing much else.

Barney the Deputy grabbed the megaphone.

"Give me that!"

"Hey, that's my personal bullhorn, you can't confiscate that."

"I am holding it in protective custody until things calm down a little bit."

He looked back at the imposing figure of the Amazon and the little boy next to her, who by this time also had his arms crossed across his chest. "I thought you said there was some sort of crime taking place over here – an emergency situation," said Barney, turning his attention back to the sweaty association president.

"Don't you know it is against the law to file a false police report?"

"I didn't file nothin', and you ain't exactly the police neither."

Peabody now had *his* arms across *his* chest.

"Truth is, the water management district does have rules about installing water management systems such as this one, but they don't have jurisdiction over city property, and even if they did, this is technically county property, and besides which, I don't see any permit being issued for any of these things these crazy people are doing over there." He jerked his head in the direction of us and the Hermitage, arms still crossed.

Deputy Barney let out a phrase that people were familiar with back then, but I forgot the name of the guy who made it famous. He was a great tennis player who made the phrase famous when he would yell at the umpires calling his shots out of bounds.

"You CAN'T be serious!"

FIVE

Today I found myself marching out to the kayak launch to start the new addition to the exercise routine for this old body of mine. This was to be my maiden voyage, so to speak, nothing fancy or too involved. Just paddle around the series of waterways we had dug out over the years to handle the influx of water from the bay while at the same time creating a "Blueway" – a means to get around from place to place in a way that made things easier and used up less energy – except the human-generated kind, that is.

I figured I could kill two birds with one stone by touring the Village and surrounding areas on the Blueway, making mental notes (yeah, more of those things that I tend to make and then forget) of areas on the canals that need repair or work to keep them up to snuff. At the same time I would be working this old body of mine to get it up to snuff, too. The idea came to me a few weeks back. Now, here I am, manifesting it into reality.

I started ruminating about the standoff at the OK Moat with Peabody and Barney the Deputy, which then led me to start rummaging through some of the manuals in the study at the Hermitage to refresh my recollection on the whole silly incident that happened that day. There wasn't much I found about the incident itself but plenty about how and why the moat was put there in the first place and, later on over the years, the system of canals and the rest of the Blueways that came to be. The journals

30

recorded incidents and information, telling the story of how the Hermitage came about, and later the Village, the Blueways, and a lot of other things that led us to where we are nowadays.

Sort of like what I am doing right now with the words you are reading.

I took to calling the journals the Harrison Chronicles on account of the fact that is the person who was writing them before I took over doing that for him. And maybe for posterity, I reckon. Not that anyone would read them after I am gone.

Not sure exactly when I had seen some of the Chronicles for the first time. That must have been one day not that long after the Standoff at the OK Moat. As things turned out, the standoff was an important turning point in my life:

After that day I felt as though I was welcome into the Hermitage. Not that I was exactly invited over to visit and chit-chat by the Amazon. No sir, she was not the chatty type to begin with. Besides which there was a lot to be done around the place. I knew I would have to either offer to pitch in and help or stand back and get out of the way.

There was no time for tomfoolery around that place.

I was standing in the open area just as you walk in – foyer I guess someone might call it back then, although it did not look much like one to me. There were not too many walls, if any, that divvied up the space that I could recall. Still isn't. It is an open area with a concrete floor that covers almost the entire ground floor. Straight ahead as you walk in is a chest-high bar made of bamboo behind which you could see the kitchen.

There was an old wooden table 'twixt where I was standing and the bar.

That was presumably for entertaining the many dinner party guests that came by, no doubt, although they would have to move those stacks of papers and books piled up on the table. Plus that reading lamp that was there as well.

I was trying to figure out how to communicate with the Amazon and was considering if I should try sign language (I didn't know how to do that exactly) when my attention was drawn towards a spiral staircase I hadn't noticed before and the sound of footsteps being made by boots as they landed on each step.

Attached to the boots a set of legs began to emerge, descending down the stairs, then came a torso. Finally I saw the white-haired head of a very tall man, cutting what to me was a very striking figure, not at all what I imagined a hermit would look like.

Come to think of it, I don't think I had imagined what to expect a hermit to look like.

"What's all the racket down here?" he said in a soft yet commanding voice. I was probably still standing there with my mouth agape when he asked, "Where's that cat?"

"What cat?" I replied once I realized he was looking straight at me.

"The one that has your tongue, young man."

After a pause I think I broke out into a broad grin.

But I said nothing, Amazon-style.

"Well, I see you are starting to turn into a real chatter box. How about if you come into the study with me so we can visit for a while, have some tea, and you can tell me more about what the villagers are saying these days about the old hermit and the Amazon Princess. I hear you and she have gotten to be fast friends, not to mention your little sister - which, hmmm, I guess I just did."

He motioned me towards the double doors leading into the study and smiled.

"But is the Amazon Princess going to join us?" I felt a little uneasy about going into a room alone with this towering man I had just met. Plus it felt like it was the polite thing to do to have her join us. I turned my head back expecting to see her reassuring presence.

She had vanished.

"She may join us afterwhile if she is so inclined. She probably has a few other things to do – maybe she will even bring us that tea I had mentioned earlier." He walked up the few steps into the study which I now realized had been raised up a good four feet from the concrete floor. The steps were tiled and led into a large room with wood floors. Bookcases lined the walls. A desk was positioned so as to face outward and through the large window overlooking a lush garden. The window ran nearly floor to ceiling – if there were one. Up above, the rafter beams were exposed as was the decking for the roof.

The hermit took up a spot on one of the stuffed leather chairs in front of the fireplace. I settled into the other one. The look and feel was that of a parlor, like the ones I had seen on TV, if that's what they call those things. Or a room inside a ski lodge where the skiers sit around in their warm sweaters, sipping brandy or some such while they talk about their adventures that day out on the slopes.

Not like I knew what that was like. Never seen snow before, much less been skiing or seen a ski lodge for that matter. Had an active imagination though!

"She has a name, you know. So do I. My name is Harrison," he said, reaching forward and jutting out his giant hand towards mine. I shook it.

"What is hers?" I asked, not thinking to introduce myself more properly. That didn't matter too much as he was to give me my own nickname I have gone by ever since.

"Well, Captain, her name is Calusa."

"Calusa? I never heard of such a name before."

"She is named for a people, the last of whom were exiled from this land that they had inhabited for centuries. A handful of the last survivors left on a ship bound for Cuba, launched not too far from where we are sitting now. Legend has it that the blood of some of the survivors runs through the veins of their descendants who still live in Cuba, except, of course, for those that found their way back to the lands of their ancestors."

He leaned forward so as to be better heard as he whispered, "They were a tall, proud people, towering over the Europeans who invaded their land, tried to enslave them, and brought pestilence and disease that eventually vanquished their once-dominant civilization. They were a people the likes of which the midgets that came to conquer them had never seen. They were a tall, beautiful, and graceful people – and fierce warriors."

"Is Calusa a descendant of these people?" I asked, also in a whisper.

Just then she came into the room, bearing a tray with a pitcher of iced tea. There were only two glasses so I guessed she wasn't planning on joining us. She gave no hint that she heard what we were saying or that we were talking about her.

"Thank you very much, Princess Calusa. Aren't you joining us?" I asked. She straightened, standing erect for a moment after setting down the tray on the small table between Harrison and me. She did not correct the way I addressed her.

"I will be back later. I am going to catch something for us to eat this evening. Will he be joining us?" She had turned to Harrison for an answer.

"Oh, no, thank you very much, but I have to go home to help my mom make dinner for me and my sister Kate. You remember her," I said.

"Maybe some other time," Harrison said, turning to me. "Maybe some evening we can invite the young man, as well as his family, to dine with us," he said, turning back to Calusa. "That should prove to make for some interesting conversation."

Calusa smiled, nodded slightly, and then turned on her heel to go fishing.

Harrison got up, walking towards one of the bookcases. He brought an extended finger to his lips, scanning the titles on the spines of the books arrayed in front of him until he found what he was looking for, between one called *Black Elk Speaks* and another called *Bury My Heart at Wounded Knee*. He put his finger at the top of a bound study from a couple of professors at one of the universities and gently pulled it forward and out of the shelf.

The title was *Culture and Environment in the Domain of the Calusa*.

"You see, the peoples that came here before our ancestors – the Europeans who invaded this land – could not be defeated even by superior technology and weapons. The genocide of the people who were here first was brought about mainly by the spread of the diseases that the conquerors brought with them. These were diseases brought from a land far away that had before that time never been known in this part of the world. The bodies of the people who lived here were unable to fend off that kind of invasion."

Harrison walked back and took his seat, handing the study to me, almost as a prop. He continued to tell me about the people who were here first but were no more.

"The indigenous people who came here many centuries ago had built a thriving community and way of life integrated into the land, as well as the sea, for those who lived closer to the Gulf of Mexico, the oceans and seas that surround us. They were not at war with the environment. They did not seek to conquer nature. They recognized that they were a part of the way the natural world works, and built their tools and systems and ways and means of living to match up with the ebb and flow of nature – including the tides."

He paused for a moment to pour a glass of tea that he handed to me. Then he filled one for himself. He took a long draw from his glass before continuing.

"We started to dig trenches and water features – such as the one you and Calusa were defending the other day – because we are aware of how Mother Nature is responding to the war being waged upon her by the ancestors of those who invaded this land and vanquished the native people who would never think to provoke her. Many hundreds of years ago, the seas did rise and fall, but the people who made this place their home adjusted to that reality.

"They built canals and waterways and tide pools and areas to catch and store the creatures from the sea that they depended on for survival. They took the shells and other refuse from the things they consumed to sustain them and piled them up, making these huge middens that they used as a foundation for the shelters they built on top of them, rising high above sea level for even the highest of king tides that may come.

"As ironic as it may sound, the invaders destroyed the very civilization and ways that they now need to replicate in order to weather the upcoming storms," he turned to flash a look of grave concern in my direction, "figuratively and literally."

I looked down at the book in my lap, his words sending all sorts of thoughts through my head that I needed more time to process.

"Can I take this book home with me to read later tonight?"

Harrison's eyes got big and his look of concern turned to alarm for a moment before relaxing back down to the calm expression he usually had on his face.

"We don't check out books in this particular library, but I will tell you what I can do. How about if you come back any time you want, and you can read this one, and some of the other ones that strike your fancy, all to your heart's content."

That is exactly what I did.

SIX

CL 20/0006
The Hermitage Study
(Monday)

I went back and took another look at the last journal entry I just made. "Captain's Log" I had started to call them. Communicating with a journal, making entries about things that are happening and that I am thinking about, these are import- ant to someone who is increasingly alone with no one to talk to. Maybe someday there will be another person on the other end of this conversation. They are not able to say anything to me right now – probably never, but they will have read what I had to say.

There was one thought though that was expressed in that last entry. Yes, those things – thoughts I mean – do come into this otherwise cobweb-riddled head of mine from time-to-time. It's not a case of beginner's luck, you know – although sometimes it may seem that way. That little germ of a thought was like to almost escape notice.

I don't know about you, but it did mine, up until just now.

Here it is: A person can manifest something by sheer force of will. I visualized a man destined to paddle around in his kayak to inspect a Blueway that was itself a manifestation of someone's intent. Next thing I know, there I am, marching down to the launch doing exactly what I had manifested myself doing.

While I would like to take credit for the idea that someone could manifest themselves to be a person as they visualized them- selves to be, in a place that they had likewise conjured up inside their head, that distinct honor belongs to someone else. His name was Harrison, and he taught me these things many years in the past – back in the Twenties:

I was in the study, well, *studying*, way back then. I had a history test coming up, as I recall, and was plowing through the text, about to fall asleep when in walks Harrison. His hair was wet. He had a towel he was using to dry his hair. He had on some sort of bathrobe deal. Obviously he had just taken a dip in the natural pool he and Calusa had constructed inside the perimeter of the Hermitage. It was not like a pool I had ever seen.

According to the manuals, they had put rocks at the bottom of it. Aquatic plants were on one end where the water fell off into a lower part of the "pool." The water was filtered through the plants and re-cycled by a pump run by a solar-powered generator. The whole thing was self-contained, fed by rain water. No chemicals needed to purify the water.

We took to calling it the "Lagoon".

Animals watered at the edges and tributaries of the Lagoon. Humans swam in it. Sometimes so did the animals – hopefully not water moccasins or alligators.

"What has your rapt attention so much you look like you are about to take a nap, Captain?" He nodded in the direction of the text book on the desk. I perked up.

"Nothing much; you would hate it."

"How so?"

"I have a history test tomorrow, and they are making me memorize all this stuff about 'Manifest Destiny,' Andrew Jackson, and all that stuff. You know. I am getting to the part where they annihilate the native tribes and push the ones they didn't kill Out West in what did they call it . . ."

". . . Trail of Tears," he said, finishing my sentence.

"Yeah, but don't give me hints. I need to get this down on my own so I can regurgitate it on the test tomorrow. Then I can forget the whole sorry mess the next day."

Harrison frowned.

"I told you you wouldn't like it. It's real depressing."

"You have a point there, but I think maybe it is something we should not be allowed to forget. You know what they say: 'Those who do not learn from the mistakes of history are doomed to repeat them.'"

"Oh wait, let me write that down. I can use that for the essay part of the test." I paused for a moment and put my pencil down. "On second thought, my teacher is not exactly a nice person. He's probably a descendant of Jackson. If I write that, he might mark me down a grade or two – maybe flunk me altogether."

"All the more reason to do it; who knows, maybe he will learn something himself. And *you* would be the one to teach it to him, Captain." He poked me with his finger.

I looked at him like he was a nut job. At the moment he sounded like one – or maybe a mad professor doing weird experiments inside his haunted Hermitage while the villagers were gathering with their pitchforks and torches outside the gates.

"That reminds me," I said, "I ran into my buddy Larry a few days ago."

"Larry?"

"Yeah. He is one of the 'villagers' as you call them."

"Would he be one of the idiot variety or just regular?"

I glanced up and gave him, and his joke, a sidelong glance. "He was out there the day Calusa and I had that Standoff at the OK Moat."

"I see that you and the Amazon are now on a first-name basis which is encouraging to hear. The 'OK Moat'? Is that as opposed to the 'Not OK Moat'? And what moat are we referring to? I told you, that canal is a water management system that helps to keep us all from sinking into water up to our eyeballs. We are not trying to build a moat to guard against the rampaging villagers from storming the walls." He stopped his rant for a second, and I swear I remember he stroked his chin. Maybe I am mistaken. But I do remember him saying "Hmmm, maybe that is not such a bad idea after all."

"As I was saying, my buddy, he has a name you know – it's LARRY – was a little embarrassed by the whole thing, but he warned me that the people in the neighborhood – the 'villagers'

39

as you put it – are a little bit intimidated, frightened even, by you and your Amazon Princess Warrior . . ."

Harrison interrupted, "She has a name, too, you know."

"I'm sorry. I know. But they think of her as some sort of Amazon Warrior Princess under the control of you as some sort of mad scientist living like a hermit in a secret compound doing things they do not understand and are, well, afraid of."

"I see your point, and I do appreciate their concern – somewhat. But there is a moral imperative to what we are doing here. I think you are beginning to understand what I mean by that. This is a question of survival for all of us – including *them*." He motioned with the wave of his hand towards the window overlooking the garden and the "villagers" beyond.

He pulled up a chair next to where I was seated. He bent over, resting his elbows on his knees, rubbing his hands together at first. Then, as I remember it, he struck a pose like that of *The Thinker*, resting one hand on his thigh. The other cradled his chin. He thought for a moment while I studied him. I studied him, there in the study, you might say.

After a few minutes, he took his hand from his chin and motioned towards my textbook. "You can write in your thesis tomorrow about rugged individualism and the American spirit of adventure and exploration, about how the early settlers wanted to do for themselves and not be told what they could and could not do. This is a story of being self-sufficient and living off the land, not of conquest and pushing people off the land so they could set up a factory and churn out things for people to buy. This is a story of people who believed that they should be able to do what they thought was the best for them and their families. People who wanted to make decisions for themselves that did not do harm to others. Live and let live, so to speak. That is all I am trying to do.

"I am manifesting my own personal destiny, not *theirs*."

He looked at me for a beat before continuing. "Put that in your teacher's peace pipe and let him smoke it. You will probably get an 'A' for sure. No need to worry about plagiarism. I didn't make this all up on my own, you know."

With that, Harrison stood up to go get dressed or something. He paused as he was leaving and turned his head around to give me a last look. "You know, the invitation for you and your family is still open to stop by for dinner some evening. You know how we are, nothing fancy, just the five of us enjoying a meal and some light conversation."

I knew better than that.

Shooting back a sheepish look, I started to say something, but he interrupted, "I know, I know, Captain, you have home-work and a test tomorrow. When you are ready and able, I am sure you will work up the nerve to tell your mom all about us and ask if she wants to stop by some evening – with your sister, of course. She has already been here a few times herself. We would not want your mom to think we are brain-washing you into doing some independent thinking on your own and all that sort of stuff, would we?"

I must have stood there silent for a moment, not knowing what to say. I was, it would seem, lacking in social graces I had yet to learn – and maybe never would.

"Here, let me give you something, Captain." He walked over to a cabinet and pulled out a cap. I stood up and walked over to him. It looked sort of like a naval officer hat, but it didn't have any insignia or other stuff to indicate rank or anything like that. It was very plain. Was this a fishing cap of some sort? I was puzzled, and that must have shown.

"You haven't quite reached the level of admiral yet, but I think your studies, here in the study, qualify you to wear, with distinction, this fisherman's cap, rumored to have been like the one worn by the character in the story *Old Man and the Sea*." I must have still looked perplexed. "You know, Ernest Hemmingway? Have you had classes on great American literature yet?" I had a blank expression but was eyeing the cap with increasing inter-est. "Well, someday soon you will – and will know what I am talking about."

He thrust the cap in my direction. I took it.

It fit perfectly.

I put my textbook and gear in my backpack, flung that across my shoulder, and with a salute ventured outside and mounted my bike. I pedaled fast, but the cap held fast to my head despite the wind blowing hard against my face. I pulled up into the carport and parked my trusty steed neatly, next to that of my sister. I walked into the house, all full of myself. "Honey, I'm home!" I shouted to the vacant air.

I pulled the pocket door to one side and entered the "utility room" as we called it. I slung my backpack off my shoulder and onto the small cot where I slept. The room is where the washing machine, dryer, ironing board, cleaning supplies, and other stuff were. It had been converted into a space where I could sleep. A room I could call my own so Kate could have her own little girly room all to herself.

I was very happy with this arrangement.

I came out of my "room" to see where everyone else was. I heard a soft murmur down the hall in the direction of my mom's room. It sounded like sobbing.

I knocked lightly on the door that was ajar. The door pushed open, and I helped it a little with a gentle shove of my hand. "Anybody home?" I asked softly.

She was sitting on the other side of her bed, hunched over a paper that she folded and put into a drawer of the nightstand. She straightened herself up, dabbed underneath her eyes with a tissue, and turned to face me. Her mascara was runny.

So was her nose.

"Hi sweetie. I just came home from work and haven't had time to start working on dinner just yet. I will be out in a minute to figure something out."

"Don't worry about it, Ma. I will rustle something up for us. Why don't you just take a load off and rest for a bit? I'll let you know when dinner is ready."

She smiled weakly and started to protest, but then didn't. She was clearly exhausted physically and could use a break. She also seemed emotionally spent about something, but I was not sure if I should probe any further. I decided I would – just a little.

"Is that news from Dad?" I asked motioning towards the nightstand and the contents of whatever missive it contained that she had been reading. The weak smile on her face vanished, and she drew herself up to her full height as best she could while still sitting. She ran her fingers through her hair as if to spruce it up a bit and make herself presentable.

"Never mind," I said, I think to some relief. I walked over and gave her a hug. I kissed her on the forehead and smiled at her. "Just lie down for a spell, and I will let you know when dinner is ready. You could use a break, methinks."

"What about your homework?"

"All done, Ma. Got some great ideas for the history test I am taking tomorrow. I think I will do just fine on that."

"Were you at that hermit's place again today? Kate keeps talking about it, too. I am worried about them, you know. There is talk in the neighborhood about how weird they are with the hermit guy and that Amazon lady."

"She has a name. So does he." I didn't say it in a mean or defiant way. I was seated next to her, stroking her hair. "Would you like to meet them? They have invited us over for dinner: you, me and Kate. You can get out and socialize a little. It might be fun."

She gazed into my eyes as if she was not hearing anything I was saying. She did some hair stroking and purring of her own, trying to sooth me as much as I was trying to do likewise for her. Then she became frozen for an instant.

"Where did you get that hat?"

"It's a Captain's hat. Do you like it?"

"I like it just fine, but are you sure it's a Captain's hat? It looks more like that milkman hat worn by the guy from *Fiddler on the Roof*."

I must admit I was deflated for a minute, but I dismissed her comment about my new prized possession that I would end up wearing proudly for many years to come.

"Well, that guy must have been a fisherman or sailor because this is a first-level hat worn by people who become sailors, ones who command great vessels bearing passengers and other stuff out at sea. They wore them with great honor and distinction.

"Like that guy – what's his name? Oh, yeah.

"Hemingway."

SEVEN

CL 20/0007
The Hermitage Study/Friday

Out the front window today I saw a ladder propped up against the place and someone coming down it. I went out the front door to see who was climbing around up on the roof. I came out right when one of Freddie's boys had just stepped off the bottom rung. I can't exactly remember his name, but I will think of it if I rummage through my memory a little. This does not mean I am getting demented, I swear. There are a lot of villagers to keep track of, and I was always bad about remembering names.

Probably had a blank expression on my face as Clyde – see, I told you I would remember his name (or was it "Clem"?) – gave me an annoyed look and waved the wires he was holding in his hand. "Came to fix the wind generator that got blown around in that storm we had the other day, Cap'n. Remember? Just some loose wires, but I replaced 'em as these were getting a little ratty. You should be good to go now."

"Thanks, matey." I decided to go generic instead of actually taking a stab at his name and getting it wrong. "You're a good man; I don't care what they say." He gave me a smile, and all seemed forgiven as far as not knowing his name and all. Maybe he thought I plumb forgot all about the wind damage from the storm the other day or that I had asked his pa to send someone down to check it out – *which I did not,* by the way.

In fact, I was just looking over the manuals on generating power here at the Hermitage and in general when I saw Clyde (that is his name, I am sure) clambering all over the roof. I just got a little sidetracked reading over something in one of the journals.

Like many older people, my long-term memory works a lot better than those short-term ones. I remember things so much better back when I was a young man:

I am able to picture in my mind that day, or really night, back in the Twenties when I was laying in my makeshift room, reading a book Harrison had actually let me check out of the library. It was literature of some sort – not sure which, maybe Swiss Family Robinson – and, although he dearly loved them, I think he thought they were not as important as some of his science books and other things he really needed in order to be a good survivalist.

That's what he called it – being a survivalist.

Being the geeky kind of kid that I was, I had the radio on, tuned to public radio, of course, and a small reading light on so I could see the words printed on the pages.

There was a light knock on the pocket door as it slowly came open. My mom poked her head in and gave me a sweet smile. "I saw the light on under the door. I thought you had gone to bed already. Are you still studying?"

"Not really, I'm just doing some reading and listening to the radio. Not really required reading, but maybe I will get extra credit or something."

"Well honey, I know we are not having a rolling blackout right now, but we need to save as much electricity as we can. It is really expensive these days, and I am not making as much as I would have liked at work, so things are a little tight right now."

I didn't budge from my comfortable position I had gotten myself to. I nodded in the direction of the light. "Oh that? It doesn't cost anything to run. It's running on electricity that is free for everyone to use if they just make the effort to generate their own." I nodded towards the radio, "Same with that. It doesn't cost us anything."

She tilted her head and looked at me with a quizzical expression.

"There's a battery down there in a little contraption I made that gives enough juice to run the light and the radio, plus a whole lot more." I was still in my comfy position, but as it turned out my explanation was not enough to placate her.

"Sweetheart, we have to save the batteries for an emergency. We are already in hurricane season, and we have to be prepared in case something happens."

At this point I realized I needed to focus more on this conversation. I put a bookmark in the book I was reading, closed it up, and sat up straight in the fold-up cot that served as my bed. I reached over to turn off the radio and turned to give her my full attention. "But I'm not using up the energy in the emergency batteries. I am generating electricity and using that as a power source. Here, let me show you."

I got up and folded half the cot into an upright position. I reached down and pulled the cover off the contraption I had made. Wires were feeding into and out of the box. At the bottom of the box were two 12-volt marine deep-cycle batteries that had wires connected to them. She looked down into the box.

She didn't know what to make of it.

"You see? I built a wind generator from some old parts I got. It's in the backyard on a pole with blades that turn as the wind blows. I also got a little solar panel and mounted that back there as well. Between the two sources of power, it generates enough power to flow into these batteries that we can use to run small things that pull a small amount of energy, like this light and that little radio over there, plus more."

"Is that safe? How did you figure out how to do such a thing? Did you get this idea from those strange people you have been hanging around with? You know I don't like you going over there. They could be dangerous people. I have heard what people have been saying about them in the neighborhood. They're *weird* and have weird ideas."

I decided to tell a little bit of a white lie. I didn't want her to bar me from going over to the Hermitage. "Oh, no, this is a science project for school. It's all perfectly safe and legit. You can ask my teacher. He wouldn't let me do something dangerous."

I didn't tell her my teacher was actually Harrison so that part really wasn't a lie.

"Where did you get the money to buy the parts for this project of yours? We can't afford to be spending money on experiments at school."

"It didn't cost anything. I got the parts from stuff people threw out on the side of the road and garage sales and so on where people in the neighborhood took pity on me and let me have stuff for free." This was technically true, but Harrison actually gave me almost all of the parts from when he upgraded his own wind generator and gave me parts from the old one. He did take pity on me and wouldn't have taken money for it even if I had it to give to him. "So long as you don't charge me to haul it away" is the way he put it.

"You wouldn't be telling me a story, would you?" Her eyes narrowed.

"Would I ever lie to you?" It was a clever response that evaded the question. Fact is I would lie if I had to. Harrison had become a very important person in my life, same with Calusa. I learned a lot of stuff from both of them – important stuff.

My mom probably knew that I was not telling the truth, the whole truth and nothing but the truth, but for reasons yet unknown let me slide – for the moment.

"Okay, smarty pants, but did you check to see if this is even legal? We can't afford to have Mr. Peabody coming around here and making life miserable or getting us fined."

This part was a little bit trickier.

While he was breaking down parts of the old wind generator and solar panel at the Hermitage, Harrison did tell me the story about the problems he had with the "villagers," one in particular. You can take a wild guess who that would have been. He warned me that I may run into trouble as well. But the parts he gave me and the installation of them at my house was perfectly legal, he told me.

"If you look closely, you will see that there are no power lines from the poles on the street into my property. They were disconnected a number of years ago when we went off the grid. That raised the ire of some of the neighbors."

"What do you mean, 'off the grid'? What does that mean?"

"The power company generates electricity by various means, including nuclear power generators that are not that far away from where we are standing. That power is carried into people's homes by these lines you see on poles all over the neighborhood. There is one at your house, too. The power company makes money off of people by selling them the electricity that they are using, but if a person is able to generate their own energy without using the electricity from the power company, they are not making money off of that person anymore. So they don't like it. But there are laws that force them to accept energy produced by a house. That energy is sold back to the power company when the house passes its electricity through the wires connected to the house back through and into the wires that are strung up all along the side of the road. Those wires are part of the grid."

"You mean, if the wire to your house is connected to the wires on the pole, you can sell energy you produce back to them and make money yourself. Is that what you are saying? Why wouldn't you do that? Then you can make money yourself."

Harrison smiled as he paused for a moment in his dissertation to detach some wires from the wind generator. "Ah, yes, Captain, but there always seems to be a catch. The rules for how much to charge for electricity are controlled by a government agency which is, in turn, controlled by the power company. They do this by providing information to the government agency that sets rates about the cost of producing electricity, including the maintenance of their poles and wires and other things that are part of the grid, plus other stuff like the cost of maintaining those really expensive nuclear power plants."

"This is very confusing," I recall saying, although that exact phrase was not in the journal entry Harrison made on the day he was replacing his old wind generator and little solar panel. I must have said that because I *was* confused. Still am.

He stopped what he was doing, standing up straight, hands on hips. He may have let out an audible sigh, but I may have made that part up to add a little drama to the scene.

But the next thing he said I remember as if it were yesterday.

"Think of it this way: When you see those wires attached to your house, there are also strings attached that come along with them. You have to play by the rules of the grid whether you like it or not if you are connected to the grid. When there is an emergency and the power from the grid is cut off, your power is cut off, too. That makes perfect sense, because you don't want to be feeding live juice through the system when there are workers trying to fix the lines and poles holding up the grid. They would get fried to a crisp.

"That is on the one hand. On the other is the fact that there you are, able to produce your own electricity, but you can't use it when the power goes out. Why? Because you are hooked into the grid, and that is part of the rules of the grid."

"Oh, I see. You are off the electric grid which means you are on your own, but so are the people who are on the grid when they shut it off. You get to do your own thing. You are not reliant on the system provided by the government and the power company. You are self-reliant. I think I have heard you use that term before: 'Self-Reliant.'"

He seemed to be pleased that the little grasshopper had finally caught on to what Harrison was all about. "Yes, but going off the grid is not just about electricity. It means using resources, like water, for example, without relying on the government, or other people or businesses, to provide them for you. It is a way of thinking differently about things, and doing things in a different way than what your neighbors are used to."

"Let me guess. Peabody freaked out when you disconnected from the grid and called to get you in trouble for that and tried to stop you."

"You learn quickly, Grasshopper."

"So what happened? Did the police come to arrest you?" I called law enforcement "police" and other polite terms such as that in those days. "Cops" seemed a little like something an outlaw would call them, and I was anything but.

"Government types – we used to call them 'G-Men' – accompanied by law enforcement came and tried to get me to let them in and take a look around to see if there was anything they could use to give me a citation or cause some legal trouble."

He gave me a sidelong glance before continuing.

"I politely declined the invitation."

So when my mom asked if it was legal to set up the generators to run little tiny lights and appliances off the grid, I was pretty sure the answer was "yes." But the part about whether or not my little science experiment might engender the wrath of people like Peabody, the answer would be "yes," if he was told about it, otherwise "no."

I gave my mom the most serious expression I could muster and said with the most serious tone my young mind could come up with:

"Mom, do you really think that my teacher would let me do something that would get us all hauled off to the hoosegow?"

EIGHT

CL 20/0008
The Hermitage Lagoon
Wednesday

From my vantage point floating in the Lagoon, I could see the skiff pulling up into the canal that ran out into the bay. I figured it was one of Art's boys. I had seen their schooner coming in from the bay towards one of the docks while I was out in a kayak, getting my weekly exercise and inspecting the Blueway. Today was a little hot, so I decided to float around in the Lagoon to cool off when I climbed out of the kayak.

The skiff pulled up alongside the edge of the canal. Sure enough, it was one of Art's boys. His name was easy to remember because Art, always a man of few words, named his boy Art, who in turn named his boy Art. Family tradition, I guess. One for which I am eternally grateful because I can't go wrong calling out his name. This one was the youngster so I knew he was technically Art, the Third. When people in the Village were referring to an Art, they would say "Art Number Two" or "The First Art."

Otherwise, face to face, the one word salutation worked just fine.

"Art!"

"Ahoy Cap'n. Got suppun' for ya."

"I see that."

What I saw was a goat, standing on rigid legs, most likely about to topple into the drink. I figured it was from Kate's farm over on the Gulf side.

I figured right.

"That's not all. I got a message from your sister." He held up an old corked-up wine bottle. I could not tell from that distance, but I knew there was a rolled-up message in it.

Yes, that's right. My kid sister liked to send me messages in a bottle.

Plus, on occasion, a kid, it would seem.

Number Three did not have time to linger for chitchat, not that he was inclined to do such a thing. He had to get back to the schooner and help his pa unload the shipment of stuff they got from Kate's farm and the other stops they made on their voyage. There were closer places to do trading for the things Kate had on her farm, but they had other stops near where her village was on Pine Island, and, of course, she was family.

Here's what her note said:

My dearest brother, the Captain: What news is there from over there on that side? Is there a Tennille yet to go with the Captain?

I have resigned myself at this point to being a non-aunt, but at least I could take comfort in knowing there really is a first mate in life out there for my big brother and that you have found her. If not, there are a bunch of island ladies here that are just dying to meet you.

How about paying a visit to your little sister? The Arts are fine and all, but they are not the best of conversationalists, to say the least, which, come to think of it, is exactly what they do: say the least they possibly can.

I would love to see your smiling face on the next ship that pulls into port from your neck of the woods.

Have one of your tech-savvy villagers send an RSVP the old-fashioned way.

You know, email. Remember that?

No Kidding,

Your kid sister, White Feather

I had to smile as I read her note. I decided I had been cooped up long enough and should get out and explore a little more. Besides which, aside from the natives in her village she had in mind for me, no doubt wearing few clothes and some war paint, the island where her village is has the remnants of the capital of the long-lost tribe that had once dominated the peninsula just a few hundred years ago. There were huge shell middens still standing, and the ancient canals were restored to their former glory.

I had that little girl in the Village – don't ask me her name – send a message to Kate the "old-fashioned way" to find out when her next harvest festival would be. Somehow we still had some semblance of an internet, despite all that happened with the Great Crash, but I had long since gone off the grid anyway, and that included doing email.

Later the Little Girl told me Kate was very excited to hear that I would be paying a visit. It would be "just like old times" she said. She also said to take good care of Kid Carson (the goat she sent me), and she would be good to me. By that I am sure she meant she would produce plenty of goat's milk, a family favorite, so to speak.

That story dates back to the Roaring Twenties. Probably 2020 if I recall correctly. It was before the Big One, I know that much. I know it was on Mother's Day. Like most of my memories of the long-term variety, I remember it like it was yesterday:

My mom had been working herself to exhaustion. She got a decent job as some sort of Candy Striper I think they called it back then. It didn't pay very much, but it offered some benefits from working at the hospital. Getting decent health care was getting harder and harder in those days, and she could not afford to get sick or hurt, or have her kids go down for the count. We would go under for sure if that happened, she had told us.

She had worked the graveyard shift the night before and was still in bed around the crack of noon when we knocked gently on her bedroom door and quietly came into her room. She was a real light sleeper and looked up at us, propping herself up on an elbow.

"What time is it? Heck, what *day* is it?"

She was pretty groggy.

"It's Mother's Day!" Kate exclaimed with a broad grin.

"Come on, we are making brunch for you." I held out my hand to help her up.

"Brunch? But we can't afford something like that," she said, as she made her way into the small dining area in our little house. Places had been set, juice was on the table, along with some cheese, bread, and, of course, a vase filled with wildflowers. I quickly excused myself and went into the kitchen. I had omelets on the stove.

She loved omelets.

"What is all this? This is way too much. Where did you get the money to get all this stuff? I appreciate the gesture and everything, but . . ."

Kate pulled out a chair, and our mom sank down into it. She was in some sort of stupor. Kate poured her some juice and offered her some bread.

"It didn't cost anything, Mommy. The cheese is made from some goats, and the eggs we got from the chickens. The bread is homemade out of a bread machine."

Mom absent-mindedly chewed on the bread and sipped from the juice, trying to take it all in, trying to wake up a bit more and figure out what the heck was going on.

"Here's your omelet. Just the way you like it. Cheese with veggies. The cheese is from the goats, and the veggies are fresh from the garden." I put the plate in front of her. She looked down at it like it had landed from outer space or something.

"But we don't have goats – or a garden."

"But they have them over where the Amazon Princess Lady lives. Here, she made this for me. She told me I could offer it to you as a Mother's Day gift if I thought you might like it." She reached down to grab a wood carving with some crude bows on it and a card Kate had made that said "I Love You, Mom" on the cover. Inside were stick figures that were supposed to be me, my mom, and Kate standing together.

Off to the side was this giant stick figure of a woman drawn with a dark crayon.

The carving was of a Native American woman wrapped tightly in a blanket that opened at her shoulders to reveal a child poking her head out of the blanket. The child was being carried on the woman's back, "Indian-style," I guess you would call it.

"She said she saw some sculptures by a lady from the Hopi Nation in Arkansas that showed how the squaws were very important to the tribe with all the things that they did with the children and a whole bunch of other stuff. She liked what the lady artist did and carved this herself. I think she may be part Indian or something."

Mom looked at Kate with a blank expression.

"The lady artist is from her own mom's clan who are called Bamboo. Her father's clan is called Coyote," Kate explained to her mom with some gravity.

"Well, that is very thoughtful of the Amazon princess. Maybe someday soon I will have a chance to thank her in person, maybe chat more about the Bamboo people, the Coyote people, and maybe a few other things I would like to chat about."

"That sounds great, Mommy, but she really doesn't talk a whole lot."

"So I gather. She didn't say two words that time she dropped you off here at the house when you got caught out in the storm that one time."

"Here, I got something for you, too." I slid into a chair next to my mom with the book I had in my hand. It was another loaner from Harrison. I gave it to her.

"What's this? A book? I hardly have time to read, but maybe I can find time today to read it. It has been awhile since I took time to just sit back, relax, and read a book. What kind of book is it?" She probably wanted to know why I would give her a book to begin with and why I thought she should read this particular one.

"It's called *1984*. This is the famous book by George Orwell. You know how they sometimes say something is very 'Orwellian'? That's where that saying came from."

"Thank you for the literary lesson, my son. I do seem to recall learning about Orwell and his book about the future. I did take some college courses, you know. I never did read the book itself, so now I can catch up with what all the fuss was about, I suppose."

"I think you might like it, but my teacher said the book was written in 1948. Orwell switched the last two digits and called the book *1984* sort of as a joke." I didn't dare tell her that my "teacher" was the hermit she was so suspicious of.

"What do you mean?"

"The way it was explained to me is that, while the story in the book was about a world in the future where all these 'Orwellian' things were happening, the book really told the story of what was happening right then when he wrote it – in the present."

"Don't spoil the ending, but what sort of 'Orwellian' things were happening in 1948 that were predicted to happen in 1984? And did those things come true? I don't recall the world coming to an end in 1984. That was over 35 years ago, and we are still here."

"My teacher says *1984* – the book, not the year – is about a world that is destructive to a free and open society, where there is brutal and draconian control using propaganda, misinformation, and 'double-think,' which is when the society is brainwashed into denying what the truth really is. They even have what they call 'unpersons' – people whose past existence is erased from public records. The memory of them disappears."

"Hmmm, I don't seem to recall any of that happening in 1984, and I wasn't around in 1948 to be able to say one way or the other. But it sounds like a very interesting story. I like science fiction, and that sounds like what this book is. I am sure I will enjoy it."

She set the book aside and smiled at me sweetly. I decided not to try to convince her that the book was really about things that happened in the 1940s, the 1980s, or in the present – today – any day that a person just happened to be reading *1984*.

How would a person brainwashed into thinking that reality wasn't really real be able to tell if the things depicted in the book, like double-think, existed now or in the past?

I doubt she actually ever read the book. A few weeks later I found it on the bottom shelf of the bookcase at our house. I returned it to the library in the study.

"Well, how did you like it?" Harrison asked.

"I thought it was great. I gave it to my mom to read."

"And?"

"She didn't get the ending."

NINE

CL 20/0009
The Hermitage Study
Sunday

During my morning constitutional I made a point to take a route past some of the corn fields and other fields with crops we had been growing in the Village. This whole morning routine has worked out pretty good, and I am very happy with myself for sticking to it. In fact, the times I have taken a day or two off – mainly when it is raining – I notice the difference when I start back up again. At my age you have to be consistent and consistently get a good workout, or your body will quickly turn to mush.

At the rice paddy field I paused for a moment. I didn't need to take a breather, but I was, as usual, in a contemplative mood. I leaned forward and rested my arms against the bamboo fence constructed around the field with the grasses poking up in what amounted to little more than swamp water. Bamboo is what they probably would have called this place if we were an Indian tribe, seeing as how we used so much of the stuff. It grows really fast, thrives in this environment, and makes for very durable lumber.

But if we were going to be called a bamboo tribe, we would have had a lot of company. Many of the villages all over Florida found out about bamboo and how to make good use of it. I know Kate's farm did. That led me to thinking about her invitation to come out to her place for their upcoming harvest festival.

Funny how the mind works like that: you start out looking at crops, and then the next thing you know, your mind wanders to Indian tribes, bamboo, and harvest festivals.

Thoughts of space aliens would be next, most likely.

I took another look at the rice paddies. I know in the manuals somewhere there is an entry from when Harrison first started trying to grow rice in this environment. He had found some seeds from an ancient version of a rice grass species that was known to be tolerant of salt water. It did not thrive exactly, but with practice and experimentation we were finally able to get some decent crops in water that was what we call "brackish," meaning saltwater would intrude from the bay into the fields, but it was mixed with measured amounts of the precious fresh water that we allowed into the mixture.

We had a series of canals and irrigation systems and whatnot that kept our crops alive. Each villager also had their own small plot that they tended to, offering their excess to others who needed it when they harvested and canned the rest for later.

One of the things about this part of the world is that the growing season really stretches out over a long period of time, unlike up north where, from what I am told, even though the weather patterns have now made their growing season a lot different than in the olden days, they still have some sort of winter during which they can't grow much of anything. Besides which, they get these really bad winter cyclones where the cold air from what's left of the Arctic combines with the hot moist air from down here in the southern latitudes. Those storms tear up a lot of ground when they hit – not to mention gardens.

Those winter cyclone storms started coming on a real regular basis starting, oh, I'd say back in the Twenties. I made another mental note – or at least tried to – to look that one up in the Harrison Chronicles once I got back from today's morning stroll.

These random thoughts wandered into and out of my mind as I left the rice paddies and continued my morning walk, and sure enough, they somehow led my crazy brain back to Kate and the invitation to her shindig. I stopped for a second outside a little village cottage, trying to remember what it was I was trying to remember about Kate's invitation.

The cottage was Maryann's, a sweet lady who still wore her hair in pigtails now and again like that character in an old TV series I used to watch in my youth, back before I went off the grid and stopped watching TV altogether. I had been watching what they used to call "reruns" of a show about people stuck on an island trying to survive, driving around in makeshift golf carts made out of bamboo and straw.

Before you know it, my mind started drifting off again, wondering if you could actually build such a contraption with some of our bamboo.

Now where was I? Oh, yeah, I was staring at a painted sign with a bunny rabbit on it that said "Happy Easter," and somehow that got my mind back in gear.

When are people supposed to harvest their crops?

Things had been laid out on the subject in the manuals a long time ago, but harvest time had become so routine we scarcely thought about it anymore. Plant during the growing season in a staggered pattern, so to speak, so that there was a continuous harvest of crops pretty much throughout the year, trying to avoid the worst parts of the storming season and, although few and far between these days, periods of frost.

But over at Kate's village, they did things a little different. They did have a more frequent incidence of cold weather than we did, but that is not the reason they made a conscious effort to have a grand harvest time just before winter. It sounds a little pagan if you ask me, but they wanted to inject a little celebration into the harvest time, to honor the earth that we all knew we relied upon so much to sustain us. We still had holidays in our village like Easter and Christmas, and we did have a Thanksgiving, which turned out to be one of the most important holidays, but we just did not focus as much on the celebration of all that the earth and sea gave to us, like they did over at Kate's village.

Hard to imagine it now, but way back when, people had lost their connection to the earth and had forgotten where their food and sustenance came from, and how to cultivate the dirt and the water to get enough to fill their bellies and their family's belly.

Those days were so long ago, but I still remember how it was back then:

One day in particular I remember. It had to have been in the year 2020 or thereabouts. It was before the Big One, I know that for a fact. It was in the evening time, and Kate was at the kitchen table doing her kiddy homework. It was already getting dark, and our mom had not come back yet from the job she was working that day. I was in the kitchen, cutting up some vegetables to make a salad, boiling water, and getting some fish ready to stick in the oven. Calusa had given me some leftover fish she had caught.

"Hi, Mom," I heard Kate say.

"I am so sorry I am late. I had to close the store, and these people just would not *leave*." She worked at one of the many thrift stores that were everywhere in those days. Things were very harsh back then, and people needed to scavenge for what they needed at stores like that, or at garage sales or estate sales that seemed to be popping up everywhere all the time with more and more frequency.

Times were hard for everyone, as I think I already mentioned.

"Oh, my gosh, I forgot to pick up something for dinner. I am so sorry." She slumped down in a chair, looking defeated. She did not seem to notice that I was busy in the kitchen, already rustling up some grub. I knew that she would be tired and under duress by the time she got home. That was happening more and more frequently these days. I wanted to take a load off her and make dinner so she didn't have to worry about it.

Dinnertime was family time. I knew that was important to her.

"Not to worry, I have everything under control. Just relax and take your shoes off, Mom. Dinner will be ready in a jiffy."

"What do you mean? We have no food in the house."

"I found some leftover rice in the cabinet we can have with the other stuff."

"What other stuff?"

"We're having a fresh garden salad to go with the rice and broiled flounder. Here, have some bread to tide you over until the rice is done simmering." I handed her a bowl covered with a napkin. Inside was some bread I had baked earlier in the day with a bread machine Harrison had given me. Calusa also gave me some eggs, goat's milk, and some yeast, plus a recipe on how to make a loaf of bread in a bread machine.

"Where did you get *this*? Is this from those weird people again? I told you I don't want charity from the neighbors, especially not those people. And didn't I say I didn't want you two going over there so often? Sounds like you practically live there. From the sounds of it, maybe you would rather live there than here." She seemed a little hurt, but she tore the bread in two and started eating it. She was probably starved.

"Hmmm, this is not half bad; tastes almost like it was fresh-baked."

"That's because it is. I made it all by myself." That wasn't entirely true, but I didn't think she would want to know where I got help to bake the bread she seemed to be enjoying so much. I didn't want to spoil the experience for her.

"How did you do that?"

"I made it from scratch with a bread machine someone gave me. Excuse me for a second; I have to stir the rice." I got up and went into the kitchen while she was still chewing and unable to ask who gave me the machine, not to mention the other ingredients I used to make the bread. I put the fish in the oven to broil and brought out the salad.

"Where did you get the money to buy all this?" She looked down at the salad bowl with skepticism. I dished some out onto her plate.

"Mom, it came out of the ground. We didn't have to pay for it."

She started to open her mouth to say something but didn't have a chance.

"All done," Kate said with some flare. She turned off the little battery-powered reading light and folded her fingers, steeple style, in front of her. "I did all my homework, and I am all ready to have our usual family dinner, just like always."

Her timing to say just the right thing at the right time was perfect sometimes.

"Excuse me, I need to check on the flounder."

"Found time to go fishing, too, I see. What about your homework: did you have time to do that yourself, young man?"

I didn't feel the need to correct her about the flounder for some reason. She didn't need to know Calusa had given it to us, and that didn't seem the best time to volunteer the information. She had already been agitated enough about them and was beginning to calm down. She looked like she was on the verge of enjoying her dinner.

"You know I always do my homework ahead of schedule," I said, cleverly avoiding the fish issue and turning to a safer subject.

"Yes, you are a studious lad and a good son."

"Mommy, we're growing vegetables in the back yard."

"Oh? When did we start doing that?" She shot me a glance as if to say *what will this child imagine next?* She was in a good mood, and I didn't want to spoil it.

"Nothing major, we just have a little lettuce and some tomatoes, some cucumbers and later when it gets cooler, we might do some broccoli. I know you love broccoli." I put my arm around her and gave her a little peck on the forehead. That seemed to divert enough attention away from the subject, at least for the moment.

She didn't think to ask where I got the seedlings and other stuff I needed to start the garden, and I was still not in a mood to volunteer a whole bunch more information.

What started out on shaky ground ended up being a rather pleasant evening having a nice family dinner. It was a good feeling to eat food that we had gotten out of the ground nearby and from the sea just down the road. I think my mom even ended up laughing a time or two at some of the silly things Kate had to say.

I wanted to ask my mom if she had heard anything about my father but didn't want to spoil the mood. That was not the time or place to bring that up. She had been under a lot of stress and was working herself towards a physical and emotional collapse. At that moment though, she was where she liked it best: at home with her kids, enjoying a meal together with her little family, letting the world outside spin whatever web it was destined to spin, leaving us alone to enjoy each other's company, at least for the moment.

She deserved to have that experience, if only for a little while.

TEN

CL 20/0010
The Hermitage Study
Monday

Maryann showed up at my front door. I figured she had seen me lingering outside her place the other day and was wondering what was up. She timed her visit to just after my morning constitutional which sort of gave me a feeling she was keeping tabs on me.

Either that or maybe paranoia is another symptom of old age.

Not that I am *that* old. Oh, don't get me wrong. I don't really think about age that much or at least not until more recently, but seeing a woman Maryann's age standing in front of me with what I swear was an earnest expression on her face sure did drive the point home. I don't have many mirrors on the walls in this place and am not the sort that would stand around staring at my countenance for hours on end even if I had some, but I did start to wonder what she was seeing as she stood there, gawking at me like that.

She presented me with some fresh-cut wildflowers. She said something about the place needing a woman's touch. She looked around for a vase to put them in. I fetched one of those large mason jars I was saving for something – hadn't decided what just yet – so I thought it could serve just as well to hold flowers. She looked at the jar and then back at me for a second or two. Being as how that was the best I would be able to do, she shrugged her shoulders and took the jar, heading to the sink with the jar and the flowers.

My eyeballs probably got wide when I saw her heading towards the kitchen sink and realized what she was doing. Potable water from that sink was for just that: po-tating. Reclaimed water was what to use to water plants. I got there just as she had nearly filled up the jar, and then reached past her to turn off the spigot. She looked up at me with a quizzical expression and then realized the error of her ways.

"Oh, I'm sorry, I just forgot." She looked at me with a sheepish smile. I could have sworn she was batting her eyelashes at me, but that might have been my imagination.

"Why, Maryann, I am surprised at you. You know enough not to waste water, especially here at the Hermitage. We have to set a good example here for the rest of the Village, and besides which, you know how important these issues are to me."

"Well, I don't see anybody around looking at what we are doing."

"Don't include me in what *you* decided to do. Besides which, that is not the point. I don't waste water because it is wrong. Our survival depends on everyone playing by the rules. One of those rules is to not waste water. C'mon, Maryann, you know that."

I felt bad seeing the deflated expression on her face. She was about my age and still remembered the way things were done in the olden days. Maybe old habits really are hard to break, even after all these years of doing things differently. I reached out to her and laid my hand gently on her shoulder. "Why don't you show me where a fine woman would put this fancy vase full of beautiful flowers in a man cave such as this?"

That brightened her mood a little, and she proceeded to set the makeshift flower arrangement near the big window up in the study. "There. Now you can be reminded about the way a woman sees the world while you are here, looking out that window and figuring out what we should all be doing to keep it from spinning out of control again."

She sat down in the desk chair. I sat across from her.

"Angela said you were planning a trip to the west coast for their harvest festival."

"Angela?"

She stared blankly at my blank expression for a brief moment.

"The 'Little Girl' I think you call her? She's in her twenties, you know."

"Oh, right – Angela. Now I know who you are talking about." I was trying to evade where this was leading.

It didn't work.

"Mind if I tag along for the ride?"

"These voyages are no place for a lady. It can be rough – and dangerous – as you know. Besides which, it will be harvest time here as well with a lot going on. I wouldn't want to be selfish and leave the Village short-handed by having you come with me on a pleasure cruise out to the wild lands where my sister and all those natives live."

"You mean those half-naked island girls your sister is trying to hook you up with?"

I paused just for a second.

"Maryann, I think you should go."

Her eyes got real big, and it looked like they were about to fill up with tears. I gave it one more beat. Then I motioned back behind me with my head, towards the big window. The room was going dark, and it was early afternoon. She hadn't noticed, but I knew what she would see if she glanced past my shoulder and saw what was going on outside.

"That storm is going to be here in about 20 minutes, and you need to get home to batten down the hatches. It is going to be a rough one. We can talk about this maybe later when I have more time to explain it to you better. Right now you need to get a move on to make ready, and so do I." That seemed to do the trick.

She offered up pursed lips at the front door, but I knew better. I brushed my cheek up against hers and gave her a nuzzle and a warm smile as I pulled away.

"Be careful. I wouldn't want anything to happen to you."

"You, too, el Capitan. We don't want to lose you either."

Not that I wasn't fond of Maryann, or that I would mind nuzzling more than just her cheek. But I didn't want to lead her on, thinking I was able to give her what I am pretty sure she wanted, which was a lot more than I was able to give. Plus, the invitation to engage in hypocrisy over wasting water did not set well with me, to be honest with you. I really mean it when I say not wasting water is a matter of survival, something we are all too familiar with, given the environment in which we find ourselves.

But I came to that conclusion well before water conservation had become, quite literally, the difference between life and death in this day and age. I had been shown the handwriting on the wall way back in the day, when I first started getting off the grid.

Things started to change, at least for me, back in the Roaring Twenties:

Back then our back yard had become much more than a series of science experiments, what with the wind generator, the solar panel and the organic gardening taking up more and more space. Luckily we had a high fence to keep prying eyes from seeing what was going on. They probably would have put a halt to it if they knew.

But *why?*

I guess I started to get some clues when my mom came home early one day. Seems she had lost one of her jobs and was sent home. Economic reasons, she said.

I stood up when she came through the back door and into the yard where I was tending to the plants. It was a cloudy day, so I was wearing my captain's hat instead of the wide-brimmed shade hat I would normally be wearing whilst farming on a hot sunny day in South Florida. She stopped and saluted a greeting.

"Ahoy there, Captain! Need a first mate? Looks like I'm in need of the work."

"Uh oh, that don't sound so good."

She looked around, scarcely recognizing her back yard with all the rows of plants and tubes and wires all over the place. "Well, you have quite the operation going on here. Maybe we can turn some of this green into green so we can pay some bills."

"In a way, I suppose it does already. Our electric bill is a little less, and our food bills are less. So we may not be making money, but we are saving money." I reached down and picked up the pail of water next to me to finish watering the plants.

"What about that?"

"What?"

"That water." She pointed at the pail in my hand. "That costs money, you know. Don't you know we have to pay for the water we use? Have you seen the water bill?"

I looked down at the pail. "Oh, this? This is not city water we had to pay for."

"What are you talking about?"

"You see those rain barrels over there connected to the gutters, and the tubes running down to the plants? We are catching rain from the sky and using that to water the plants and clean tools for our garden. This water is from Mother Nature. She doesn't charge us to bring it to us like the city does. She delivers it for free."

This irritated her to no end.

"You sound more like an Indian chief than a captain – not any son of mine. I know where you learned to talk like that. And don't try to tell me that this is all part of some sort of science project at school. I wasn't born yesterday, you know. I know who your teachers really are. They are not teaching things like the rest of us were taught."

"How so?" She was right about parroting things that I had learned from them, in particular the Mother Nature stuff that came right from the Amazon Princess.

"Look here, young man." She had her hands on her hips. I recall she started wagging her finger at me, but that may be my imagination filling in details again of things that really did not happen that way – but just as well could have.

"You are living in a fantasy world." She pointed outward, in no direction in particular. "Out there, in the REAL world, people have to work at a job, maybe two or even three, all day and all night to scrape together enough money to pay for everything

– everything – in this world, including the basics of life like food, water, and electricity."

"And cell phones and TVs?" I could tell this really made her angry. Not sure why I said it. In retrospect I can say I was more than ready to jump off the grid, but I was also feeling that sense of defiance and rebellion against the way grown-ups said things had to be. It is a common feeling among youngsters in that time of their life. Especially for a kid like me, forced to do more parenting than I should have been doing, growing up a little too fast.

Besides which, was I really the one in a fantasy world? Maybe the truth was that I was being more realistic about the future than the grown-ups. Sure, I was more idealistic than people like my mom and the neighbors. Maybe "optimistic" was more the word for it. Surely a young man bravely facing a new world might think of that world as a place that was not as dreary and hopeless as how my mom saw it.

"As long as I am the head of this household, paying all the bills, you have to do as I tell you, Mr. Captain Corn-on-the-Cob." She flicked the hat off my head. I reached down slowly and picked it up. I calmly put it firmly back on my head.

I looked at her serenely, quietly saying some words that I wish I hadn't.

"Does that mean Dad is not coming home anytime soon?"

Her face fell. She stepped back. She suddenly looked a hundred years old. She seemed like she was about to stammer something else, but nothing came out of her mouth. I trained a steady gaze on her. Somehow I seemed to know what I was doing. I looked up at the black clouds rolling in. I felt the cool air that started to whip up.

I motioned skyward with my head, cap and all, and then, again, towards my mother.

"Best you get back into the house. A storm is brewing."

ELEVEN

CL 20/0011
The Hermitage Roost
Wednesday

Angela showed up at the front door today. Yes, you read that right. She has a name, and I do remember what it is, although I have a nickname for her I want to use instead, just not sure she would appreciate it yet. I may try it out and see what happens. Little Girl is apparently not acceptable but is quite apt. She is a very petite young lady with long blonde hair she usually wears in a ponytail that is about as long as she is tall. She has a cute pointy little nose that gives her kind of an elfin, look especially when she is wearing that impish little smile of hers that makes her eyes twinkle. She reminds me of a pixie.

Not that I noticed all those details. Well, I guess I did enough to write all that down. I seem to be a little taken with the young lass – not all that sure why exactly.

She started showing up on a more and more regular basis, usually on one pretext or another. I got the feeling at first that she was spying on me for Maryann, but I dismissed that paranoid nonsense after spending a little time with her. She reminded me a lot of me, in a way, back when I was just a young lad myself, curious about things, liking books more so than I did people, until I met Harrison and Calusa, of course – that was different.

Heck, *they* were different.

This was not entirely a social call. We had some business to attend to. I buzzed her through the front gate when I saw her on the video screen where I was, up in the "Roost", as we started to call the observatory at the top of the tower built onto the main structure of the Hermitage. I knew she would head to the study to look for me, and I didn't feel like clambering down the old spiral staircase to invite her up.

"I'm up here!" I shouted down to her when I heard the front door close. "Come on up, I need to show you some things." I was going to add "Miss Pixie" but decided not to.

She emerged quietly, a look of wonder on her face as she came up to the landing and then up and into the Roost, a cylindrical room with impact-resistant windows all along the curved sides of the walls. They were designed to withstand high-velocity winds of over 200 miles per hour. There were also, I came to learn, slats outside operated either by a motor or hand crank that would seal up the windows in the event of a major wind event. "They may withstand wind speeds thrown off by tornadoes and hurricanes but not projectiles hurled at them in a major wind event," I was told by Harrison when I myself first entered into the Roost with as much awe as my new friend.

I'm sure I appeared to her much the same way as when I saw Harrison that first time, back in the Twenties. The half-circle counter that ran along the wall just below the windows allowed the captain of this ship to monitor the, well, monitors strewn in an array on the counter top. At the same time, we could observe real-time conditions from the perch sitting atop the Hermitage, overlooking a panorama of Biscayne Bay, the surrounding Village, trees, roads, and even, off in the distance, the Atlantic Ocean.

I especially enjoyed watching the sun rise. That little cot in the corner is there for a reason, you know. It may not seem comfy, but it always felt comfortable to me.

I guess maybe it reminded me of my days on the cot in the utility room where I got to lay my head at night back in the Twenties. Back then we were still living in my mom's little house a few streets over from the Hermitage.

The view was not as nice, of course, but I didn't mind so much.

Today's lesson was rather important because there was a storm that had emerged off the coast of Africa that looked to be heading our way. One of the few things that the national government had managed to do right was maintain the satellites and equipment that monitor developing storms. We could all keep track of climatic conditions and weather patterns so as to accurately predict when we were most likely to be hit and how hard we would get lashed by the high winds and walls of water that would eventually come our way.

The powers that be, wherever they were now, apparently thought many years ago that it was important to maintain weather monitoring systems for use by the military. There were a lot of military operations back then. There were lots of wars. There were more than a few dead people blown to bits along with the buildings and other stuff that those people used to live and work in, much of it leveled, cutting a large swath of destruction through civilizations around the world, including here in North America.

I remember Harrison giving me this really old book, along with a really long lecture, about this reverend called Malthus.

Malthus wrote some things back even further in time, during the turn of the eighteenth century into the nineteenth one – that would be around 1800 if my math is right. The good reverend believed that human breeding would run out of control if not for things that kept it in check like disease, starvation, war, and other catastrophes.

These disasters, manmade or otherwise, would return the population of the world to more sustainable levels. I don't know if his beliefs were right or wrong, but there was a chilling way in which his ideas seemed to be playing out when it came to what we used to call "global warming" and "climate change."

I found myself repeating the same lecture to Miss Pixie in the same space where this whole thing was explained to me many years ago.

"We have reached a tipping point," Harrison had said, sitting at the command post in the Roost, swiveling in his chair, motioning at the screens behind him. "In a mindless pursuit of power and wealth, humans engorged themselves with the bounty that Mother Nature had to offer, stuffing as much as they could into their mouths and leaving nothing for their children – or as their legacy – except for a barren wasteland.

"But eventually, the industrial revolution that gave humans the power to commit these crimes against nature also gave them the power to so degrade their environment that these crimes themselves, in essence, became a form of suicide. The ravenous appetite to take more and more, giving nothing back, saving nothing for our children, was not sustainable. That is why we see the world today teetering on the edge of economic ruin."

Harrison proved to be right, but it was too late for those of us who were destined to live and survive in a world as it was now, after the industrial revolution had run its course and things started to fall apart. The wars, destruction, and suffering corrected the imbalance of nature because the humans could no longer sustain its assault upon the planet.

We were broke.

Ironically, we could no longer afford to pollute the environment to cause more climate change than we already had, but by the time this started to happen, it was too late. A tipping point had been reached. Mother Nature began to respond to what we had done to her. In the wake of her onslaught, we were forced to retreat to a world much like our ancient ancestors who lived in a feudal system known as the Dark Ages.

The way of life we live now, here in the future, probably seems primitive by the standards of people living in the past. Even in the Twenties many people still clung to their fancy devices and cars and other emoluments of excess even as they toiled among the disintegrating vestiges of the corroding industrial revolution, soon to become ruins of a civilization that could not be sustained.

When the wars came, I guess the idea was that this was a last gasp where one group of industrialists made a last grasp for the stuff the other ones had. In the end they pretty much managed to blow each other up, in a grand Malthusian mopping-up exercise.

They were mopping up after the industrial revolution, a thing that had run its course and now was over. It was then time to start over and do something different.

Be that as it may, or may not be, the fact is the military needed to know about the climate and the weather, and so at least they left us with the means by which we could keep track of these things. They made it so we could plan ahead, batten down the hatches, and hunker down when we had to, and build things that wouldn't get washed away in the next storm that came along, like a house of cards collapsing into a heap of rubble.

We had learned our lessons the hard way, and now we knew better.

"You see these screens over here, Miss Pixie?" I motioned towards them.

"What did you call me?"

I had a sense the new nickname would not go over very well. I pushed it anyway, hoping she would not know what a pixie was, and I could make it sound better.

"You remind me of those wonderful creatures known in ancient times as pixies that roamed the forest and delighted the ancient ones with their mirth and merriment."

I smiled at her warmly for added effect. In my defense, since I am such a loner and hardly ever talk to people, what precisely do you expect? I was doing the best I could, given limited resources in the ways of talking to people, especially young people. Who were girls. Young, girl-like people who looked to me like pixies.

My smile was frozen on my face for a good long while.

"Oh, brother." She said. "Okay, so this is like a term of endearment you have decided to call me when we are working here in the Roost and you are feeling squishy or something like that – when there is no one else around. Is that what we are doing?"

I think the smile slowly evaporated from my face.

"Sure. But you can call me 'Captain' anytime, day or night, in front of people or here when we are cloistered in the Roost, going over weather charts and talking about Malthusian theories of population control and stuff like that."

"But everyone calls you 'Captain' anyway."

She had a point.

"Okay, great. I will try to come up with a better nickname for you. But in the meantime, come over here and spread some of your pixie dust on this machine because I don't think it's working right."

"What is it?"

"There are a series of weather stations here and around – well, pretty much around the entire world. We are part of a network connected to what is left of what they used to call 'the Internet' back many years ago. This Web of Underground Weather Geeks . . ."

"What did you say?"

"It's a Web . . ."

"No, I heard that part. But you said you were a – a what? A 'geek'? What is that? Some form of a pixie spreading dust all over the place?"

I looked at her for a second. My eyebrow probably went up a little.

"'Geek' is a very old-fashioned term for a really smart person that reads a lot of books and knows a lot about machines that process information. 'Computers,' we used to call them." We still call them that so that last comment may have come off a little sarcastic.

"May I continue?" She furrowed her brow somewhat and was thinking. I didn't want to get into any more conversations about old names people called people back in the Twenties, which turned out to be not so bad after all. Heck, calling someone a "geek" was a real compliment after it became obvious that our species really needed smart geeky people around to help us solve some of the problems we were having.

"You know, Angela, I used to be known as a 'geek' when I was little."

She ignored the word little and seemed to brighten when I called her by her actual name. I have to make a mental note of that – if I could remember to do it.

"Instruments outside are connected to this machine" – I tapped the top of the monitor connected to the machine that was connected to the instruments connected to the building outside – "that allows us to take measurements and report into the system what those measurements are and what we observe from our location so that other people in the Geeky Web of Underground Weather Bugs out there can see what is happening here, and we can see what is happening where they are."

"What sort of data are you collecting?"

I didn't have to answer. She practically pushed me aside and took up a position in my command chair, looking at the screen, tapping on the keyboard, looking around at other screens, thinking so hard I could almost feel her thoughts humming in her brain.

Couldn't help but smile at that.

TWELVE

CL 20/0012
The Hermitage Roost
Friday

I think I am beginning to understand why I have been in such a reflective mood lately. For some reason the revelation came to me while sitting in the Roost, calmly doing and saying and thinking all the things I have been doing, thinking, and saying in situations such as this, as a matter of rote more than anything else.

There were two storms heading in our general direction, each from opposite sides, plus another one brewing down south, off the coast of South America. Back closer to the turn of this century, they still used to give them names, although I can't remember why they did that. Maybe back then they were thought to be rare occurrences, sort of like a bad relative that came to visit once in a while but would eventually leave, hopefully never coming back. A quaint practice developed to give them pet names, I suppose, pretending they were just a happenstance that occurred every once in a blue moon.

They were things we thought of as being a curiosity, such as in "Wow, look at her go!" instead of a deadly feature of the permanent landscape that had come to visit, but never intending to leave for very long. They would be back again, and again and again.

These days they came fast and furious. They stayed for a good long while during a storm "season" that kept getting longer and longer over the years, so much so that it took up most of the year. There were so many we didn't go by names anymore. How quaint. We of the Weathered Underground took to identifying them by number, or sometimes a nickname if their pattern took on a distinctive shape. I was real good at coming up with nicknames, in my humble opinion: "Fishook-25." "Spaghetti Western-15." "Buzz Saw-18." Those were all mine. I was good at nicknames for inanimate objects.

Maybe I was not so good at the animate ones.

We should maybe have called ourselves the Weary Weatherheads Hunkering Under Ground, or somewhere else good to hide. The Florida peninsula juts out right into the middle of Hurricane Alley: Gulf of Mexico on one side, the Atlantic on the other. Sometimes it seems like Mother Nature purposefully made us into a big middle finger sticking straight out of the mainland and into harm's way, daring her to take her best shot:

"Oh yeah? Is that the best you can do? Is that all you got? Thank you, ma'am; may I have another? We are ready and waiting for you."

A little bravado always brightened the mood right before we got slapped silly again, got up, dusted ourselves off, and got ready for the next one.

Can't say we didn't deserve it after all we did by disrespecting her all those years. Our comeuppance was more than overdue. She sure did oblige.

But what about young folk like Angela – the Little Pixie? We were used to weathering the storms, and we had it coming to us, but she didn't deserve this. Yet here she was, gamely working the machines and watching the monitors and reading the dispatches from other stations in our region, already starting to post some of her own from ours. She was intent on the missiles being shot all around us, judging if they would hit us directly, graze us with a passing shot, or fly right by us with nary a scratch to show for it.

Her time frame was short, as was ours. It had to be to deal with the immediate threats that might be coming our way. We had to prepare for the wind and the rain that would be coming and know how strong the impacts would be. We had to know so that we could take measures to protect ourselves and our village from getting washed away. But from my vantage point, I could see a longer time frame, a bigger picture.

We had settled into what was, at first, a constant state of emergency when this whole thing about constantly being under assault all started, back in the Twenties. But looking back, things are actually much calmer today. Back then, we were told what was happening to the climate and why our own pollution was the cause of these Malthusian disasters, but we had to start living through them to really understand what it was like to feel the full brunt of the consequences of our collective actions. Our way of living had caused our way of living to radically change, and now, well, we had to learn to live with it.

But we hadn't done that yet, so we were not prepared.

Eventually, when the immediate dangers passed and I had a moment for calm reflection, I would explain to Angela the way things were, why they were, and the way things most likely would be in the future, just like Harrison did for me.

I remember so clearly what that was like, so many years ago:

We were up in the Roost. He was showing me the monitor that was tracking the path of some storm that had formed off the coast of Africa. They eventually gave it a name; I don't recall exactly what. Mario? Marco? Something like that.

It was what we call the Big One.

"Human pollution released into the atmosphere over the many years of the industrial revolution has a price tag that comes with it that has yet to be paid. There are consequences when you mess around with the environment to that extent. Remember that old television commercial where the angry lady, dressed in a flowing gown and standing next to a tree looks at the camera and says 'It's not nice to fool Mother Nature' right before she sends down a bolt of lightning?" He turned around to look at me.

"I don't know what you're talking about. Besides which, you don't even have a TV. You have been off the grid for how many years now?"

"Never mind. That was way before your time. Heck, almost before mine. I was just but a wee pup when I saw those commercials, but they stuck in my mind."

He turned back to the monitor. "The last time I saw a storm with these same data points was a few years back. At the time it was the strongest storm to hit the mainland. People had never seen anything like it. They were unprepared for how strong these things can really be. There was a lot of destruction and devastation. The whole fabric of society fell apart, and things got very ugly for a good long while. Then they put the pieces back together again, not that much different from what they had done before."

"Maybe they didn't think lightning would strike twice."

"Then they forgot about that commercial. There were several versions, and they played it over and over again until people got the message. Of course, the message was to go out and buy something, not do something to stop polluting the air."

"What could they have done differently?"

"For one thing: prepare." He motioned to the screen again. "With what we know today the probabilities are that this storm is going to make a beeline right for us, just like that other storm that knocked this place for a loop. Only this time, the waters in the ocean are warmer and the conditions right for an even stronger storm than last time – or the times since. This is going to be a big one, Captain. You need to get ready for it."

I looked up and through the windows of the Roost, letting my eyes pan across the horizon with the trees gently blowing in a soft breeze. It was a beautiful, sunny day with hardly any clouds in the sky, very peaceful and calm. Harrison must have been watching my eyes and anticipating what I might be thinking.

"Nice day, huh? It's the calm before the storm."

I flew home and went straight to the back yard. I took down the contraptions I had attached to the house and moved them and everything else I could identify as a flying object into the shed. I mean *everything*. Then I tied down the shed itself as best I could with some rope and tent stakes. It may not hold, but at least I did something.

Next I went around the house and closed the shutters over the windows. They were the old-timey kind that folded out to decorate the house, but folded in to cover the windows when there was a weather event in the offing. I cleared the front porch and the carport of any flying objects and stacked them inside the little tool shed or inside the house.

I checked our battery and candle supplies. I put the little gas grill in the house and was glad to see we had some gas left in the canister. We might need that. I also got the camping stove out of the shed. We might need that, too. I was filling up every bottle I could find in the house with water when my mom came home and saw Kate and me going about our preparedness. "What's going on?" she asked.

"We are updating our hurricane plan like the people told us to," Kate told her. I did not want to frighten her by telling her a massive storm was headed right for us. I told her we were just updating our emergency preparedness, just in case.

"That's nice," said my mom. She looked at me. "Can you help me with something for a minute?" She turned back to Kate. "He'll be right back to help you."

In the living room, out of earshot, she looked at me with an expression of concern but not panic. Ever since the "Captain Corn Cob" incident things had changed between us. Maybe she thought I was now the man of the house. I don't know. But her attitude towards me had changed. We had become more like partners than anything else. Her attitude towards Harrison and Calusa had changed also.

She did not embrace them and their *weird* ideas, but I think she did give me more credit in judging the character of the people I carried on with.

Could be she also gave them a little more credit in that regard as well.

"Is that storm something we should be concerned about? The weatherman on the TV at the hospital said not to worry about it. You know how I feel about the news people. They usually hype stuff, making things seem more frightening so they can sell more aspirin for people and their headaches. If he said nothing is wrong, then . . ."

"Which weatherman was that? Which station?"

"I don't know. That bald-headed guy. Channel 10 I think it was."

"Oh, *that* guy. He is notoriously bad at predicting weather. He is not a Chicken Little that will tell you the sky is falling but then the next thing you know, frogs will start falling down on your head – or maybe a sleet of hailstones."

She did seem to appreciate the humor. Then she asked, "What is your opinion?"

"My sources indicate we are going to get hit hard - *real hard*. It will make landfall near here in about three days. We may have to evacuate."

"Do your sources indicate whether this house will stand up to the storm? Everything we have is here. We can't afford to get wiped out."

She knew who my "sources" were but didn't seem too concerned about it.

"We have battened down the hatches, Mate," I said with a salute. I called her "mate" to lighten the mood a little. "All the potential projectiles are stowed away. I double-checked, and we have straps on the roof beams so the roof won't go flying off the house. We have provisions to last a good month or so without electricity and running water. We have done everything we can do to protect this house. I think she will do just fine against the winds. We might even be able to ride out the storm here, as far as that goes."

"But? I sense a 'but' here."

"It's the water. If this is a wet storm there could be flooding from the rain and then, of course, there could be a big storm surge."

"How big?"

"Real Big. Maybe 15 feet. Maybe more."

"When will we know if that is going to happen?"

"I think we have to assume it will happen; it's just a question of degree. Depending on which direction the storm goes, it will either be a not-so-bad event, or it could be a really not-so-good event. We will know more as it gets closer. But the bald-headed guy won't know until right before a wall of water smacks him upside the head. We should be looking at the Internet sites like the National Weather Service and the Hurricane Center that will be tracking the storm. They have some really good models that are pretty accurate."

"Do you think we will have to evacuate? I really don't want to leave the house like that with all our stuff here. Our whole life is wrapped up in this house."

I didn't agree with her but didn't say anything.

"The hospital has a designated shelter in the next-door building. I will ask around during my next shift to see what is going on with them and what kind of accommodations they will have. They were making ready in the event there is a surge of patients, but I did not hear anything about evacuations. If we have to leave, we will just have to do that and hope the house is still standing when we get back." She shot me a weak smile.

I put my hand on her shoulder. "I know this house is important to you. We won't leave here unless and until we absolutely have to."

"What about Mrs. Jacobs? Son, could you please stop by and check on her? She is getting on in years and might be a little stubborn about leaving."

That was an understatement.

"I can't leave here. This is my whole life, my whole world. If God is going to wipe it off the face of the earth, He is just going to have to take these old bones with it." Her big Tabby jumped up on her lap as if on cue – either to try and coax her out of her decision or to stand by her side and go down with the ship – I wasn't sure which.

"And what about Tabatha? I know they don't take pets at that shelter, and I am not going anywhere without her. She is as much a part of me as my arm."

It wasn't as if she had not been through this sort of thing before. She knew the drill. She did have flashlights, batteries, a radio, and storm shutters. At least she did let me put those up for her. She was about as safe as she could be within her little house where the world revolved around her and her cat. I told her if things were looking too dicey, maybe she could hunker down at our house. She promised she would consider it.

But I knew she wouldn't.

THIRTEEN

CL 20/0013
The Hermitage Roost
Sunday

By midday Storm No. 12 had pushed itself off the Yucatan and was heading north by northeast over the Gulf of Mexico. The track most likely had it curving in a more northerly direction after a day or two, most likely adding to the massive bayou that had become southern Louisiana. Or maybe it would revisit the Big Houston Swamp. It seems like they have not had a turn for a while. Either way it looked to rake the coast of Florida with wind and rain. Kate and her people would have to take measures.

After No. 12 passed her by, she would not be out of the woods. Neither would we. Lucky 13 was not looking very fortunate. It was the one that was born off the African Coast with a trajectory taking it too close for comfort.

I really don't care for those ones.

Art 2 and 3 were in the Roost. Angela was at the helm looking at screens and checking her data. We needed to decide if the larger vessels we had in our fleet should be put out to sea before Lucky 13 got much closer and things would be too rough to escape. The little storm (14) to the south looked like it would not amount to much. Probably head over Cuba and follow in 12's footsteps. If things didn't change by the morning, the big boats would go out and head south until 13 passed through.

Maryann was there as well for some reason, invited by the Little Pixie.

"There's something about Lucky 13 that really gives me the willies," I said to no one in particular. Maryann walked over to stand next to Angela. She bent down to look at her screen, likely not knowing what she was looking at.

"Is that it there?" she asked, pointing. "That pinwheel?"

"Yes, that's the one. Cappy says 13 reminds him of this storm that hit here back in the Twenties. A real nasty one that hit this area real hard."

Maryann straightened up. "Cappy, eh? Well, I see you two are more or less practically on a first-name basis." She looked over at me with a sly grin on her face. The two Arts didn't seem to react. They looked at me. They said nothing.

"*Real Hard*," I said, ignoring the playfulness.

This was serious business.

Lucky 13 reminded me of the Big One that hit us so hard, back in the Twenties, the one that changed everything. My intuition told me this was another one of its evil twins. The storm track looked eerily like the Big One, glowering at me like a haunting from the computer screen, my memory of it being almost identical to the one I saw so many years ago right in this very room. I'll never forget the day Harrison showed it to me:

"This storm is a Category 6," he said. That was back when they had categories. We really didn't find that useful anymore. We just needed to know the sustained winds, gusts, rain field, and other data related to a storm, not a catchy name for it or a "category."

"The category doesn't even matter. What matters is the strength of it and the speed. This one is a killer, and we need to brace ourselves for it. It's coming right at us, and it is a monster. For our sake, I hope it veers north of us so we catch the weaker side of the storm, but even then, this is going to hurt. It's going to hurt *bad*."

"What about the people to the north?"

He swiveled around to look me in the eye. "I feel for them. I feel for everyone who is going to have to live through this.

But it is someone's turn to take a direct hit. I really hope it is not ours. Have you made ready? Maybe you and your family should evacuate. The hospital should be safe. Why don't you take them there?"

"What about you?"

"Calusa and I are more than ready. This place is built like a fortress. Even if there is a big storm surge, the worst that can happen is some flooding on the ground floor, which is designed to accept that even as close to the bay as we are. We have ways the water can go around us, and we can withstand even a 15-foot surge or higher. The same cannot be said of other places around this neighborhood, including yours."

He had a look of concern on his face. I assured him that we had made ready. I was monitoring the storm's progress on the official weather websites, staying away from that one bald guy. If it looked like we were taking a hit or the storm jogged south, we would evacuate and head for the hospital. We should be safe, I told him.

Harrison did not look too reassured when I left to go home. I am pretty sure the guy really cared about me, maybe even my mom and Kate, even being the loner he was. When I got home, the rainbands had already started up. I shook off the rain from my oversized raincoat that kept me real dry even in a driving rain like this.

Harrison had given it to me.

My mom and Kate were playing some sort of card game. The lights flickered for an instant but stayed on. Mom had a stiff smile on her face, trying to keep up appearances. Between the dark skies and the boarded-up windows, the house looked like it was the dead of night, not the middle of the afternoon. Kate seemed okay, but I noticed her giant yellow ducky was right next to her. The thing was almost as big as she was. I hadn't seen that thing for a good long while. He only came out when she was feeling insecure.

"Can we light a candle now?" Kate sounded a little excited about the whole adventure. She couldn't wait for it to start.

She was unaware that it already had.

"Honey, I know it's raining right now, but could you go check on Carol for me? I am really worried about her." I must have had a quizzical expression on my face. Then I realized who she was talking about.

"Mrs. Jacobs? Oh, yes, I just stopped by her place. I tried to get her to come with me and hunker down with us during this storm but she would not budge. She said she wouldn't leave her house and certainly not her cat – storm or no storm."

"She can bring the cat with her. We have plenty of room, and like you said, we have all the hatches battened down and are snug as a bug in a rug."

"Yeah, I know, but she still wouldn't budge. I don't get it really."

"She is stubborn and set in her ways, that's for sure."

I didn't tell her the whole story of my visit with Mrs. Jacobs and her cat. She was not just stubborn and unrealistic about her predicament. She was fatalistic. I had stopped asking and cajoling her to come with me and started to plead with her.

"You can't stay here alone like this. It's not safe."

"I know that. The officer tried to order me to evacuate. Said he would take me into custody if I didn't come along peacefully and go to the shelter. But I know better. I know my rights. This is my home. It is my castle. I may be old, but I am old enough to take care of myself and decide for myself how I want to live out my life."

"What do you mean?"

She leaned forward slightly in her chair, bringing her face closer to mine. She spoke in a whisper. "Look here, young man. You have your life ahead of you. You have your mom and your little sister. You have each other. You have many years still left to live your lives. The three of you, together, need to go to a shelter if that will keep you safe."

"But we want you to be safe, too. We want all four of us to be together." I leaned forward myself a little. Our faces were so close I could smell the coffee on her breath.

"That's very sweet of you. I have enjoyed taking care of your little sister, and you, before you grew up to be such a little man, but I know I am not really part of your family. My family is long since dead and buried. I am now all alone in this world. I am not sad about that. I have lived a good long life. I have no real complaints. I am very happy and comfortable right here, in this spot." She leaned back and patted her chair.

"If the good Lord has decided it is time for me and my house to be swept up and taken up to the sky like Dorothy in the Wizard of Oz, who am I to argue with Him, or tell Him I am not ready to go? When it is your time, it is your time."

"What about her?" I motioned to her Tabby.

It was worth a shot, but it didn't work.

"She's coming with me, just like Toto and Dorothy. We're inseparable. A package deal you might say. Where she goes, I go, and we are not going anywhere."

I was thinking about what she said later that night. The winds were howling, and the rain pelted the sides of the house. We had lost our electricity. I tried to monitor the storm by the radio after I lost the connection to the Internet. I could not tell if it was going to veer north or south or hit us straight on. We seemed to have reached a point of no return. That point was hammered home when the announcer over the radio advised people to stay put if they had not evacuated already, as it was getting dangerous to go outdoors.

The three of us were huddled together in the living room, debating about whether we should go into the bathroom or a closet where it might be safer. I wondered about Mrs. Jacobs and if she would even bother to at least hide somewhere safer inside her house.

She was ready to meet her fate as ordained by the God she prayed to, whatever that would turn out to be.

I also thought of Calusa as I was leaving the Hermitage earlier that day. She was burning something and waving the smoke with her hand. She was in a circle she had made out of stones. I think I heard her chanting or something. I stood there watching her for a while, saying nothing. The wind was blowing against her face.

"If you ask, sometimes the spirits of the earth, the sky, and the wind will heed your request to spare you from the anger of the Great Spirit. If our grandmother is not too displeased with what we have done, she may ask him to give us mercy."

She looked at me, and then continued what she was doing.

A sudden, loud pounding on the door startled me out of my thoughts of Calusa from earlier that day. I pulled the door open. Calusa was standing there, tall and proud as ever. The wind whipped her wet clothes. The rain subsided for a moment, as if on cue.

Apparently the Great Spirit was not going to extend any mercy to us.

She looked at my mom and Kate.

"You have not left. Now you must come with me. You are not safe here. Come, come." There was very little protest.

"Let's get going!" I shouted. We grabbed the bags we had already packed. Kate grabbed her duck. Calusa looked at it, then at me. It wasn't exactly waterproof and of little practical use, but she seemed to sense why the duck had to come along.

We piled into her vehicle. Another rainband struck, pounding us and the windows of the truck. I don't know how Calusa could see out the windshield, but she knew where to go even in the pitch black monsoon we were driving through. She pulled up and into the grounds of the Hermitage through a side gate. Harrison was out there. He closed the gate.

"Wait! We have to get Carol!" My mom was trying to be heard over the din of the rain and the wind and the trees swaying violently back and forth. A tree branch broke off with a loud crack and fell to the ground. Harrison looked at me, then at my mom.

"She's our nanny. She won't leave her house."

Harrison looked back at my mom. She looked at me.

"You have to save her. You'll never forgive yourself if you don't. Nor will I."

"Take them inside," Harrison said to Calusa. "That includes *you,*" he said, looking through the rain straight at my mom. "You, come with me." He was looking at me.

We got back in the truck and headed out into the maelstrom. He didn't say much.

"Which way?"

"There, turn down there. Here it is. Stop here."

I got out of the truck and ran towards her front door. I didn't notice the very tall tree that had toppled over and onto her house, crushing her roof. I finally forced the door open and flung myself into her house. The rain was still pelting me. I was inside her living room. There was a giant, gaping hole where the roof used to be. I could see the massive tree trunk running across the expanse of her little house. The end of one of the branches had been sheared off, making a spear that had descended from 30 feet in the air.

It pierced straight through her chest and down into the floor boards. The look on her face was one of surprise, looking skyward. Her mouth was open.

I gasped at the ghastly sight. I will never be able to get it out of my mind.

I looked around frantically, unsure what to do. I saw Harrison at the doorway, staring at me, then her, then back at me. "We have to get her out of here!" I shouted. He made his way to me through the debris, death, and destruction that her living room had become. He laid his hands gently on both shoulders and looked deeply into my eyes. In my mind's eye I can still see him: the water streaming down and into the crevices etched into the intense expression on his face.

"Son, she is not going anywhere. But WE have to. *Now.*"

I was too much in shock to cry although I feel like I am about to burst into tears just playing that scene over again in my head. I looked around more. On the floor next to her chair, I saw the cat cage box she used to move Tabby around in. She was in it, apparently all set to go somewhere, or maybe she was seeking shelter.

Harrison followed my eyes. He bent down to take a look. He closed the door to the little cage, grabbed the handle, and picked it up before heading towards the door. He paused at the door, held up the cage, and took another look inside.

"Looks like you were all set to go somewhere. Need a lift?"

He looked at me with the faintest of smiles. I smiled in spite of myself.

We made it back to the Hermitage right as another rainband hit us real good. We made it inside with the bags and the cat cage. I grabbed the duck.

My mom looked around us and then through us as we walked in the door. We set the stuff down on the floor. We shook the water off our raincoats.

"Well, where is she?" I looked at her. Tears were welling up in my eyes. I really did not know what to say, much less how to say it. I heard a voice give her an answer.

"He was right. She is in that house and isn't going anywhere."

FOURTEEN

CL 20/0014
At the Old Wooden Table
The Hermitage Foyer
Wednesday

Out back this morning I boiled some water on a wood stove and sprinkled some coffee on it. The coffee was courtesy of Art's latest trading venture. Not sure where it came from. Maybe it was Jamaican Blue Mountain coffee.

It sure did smell good.

Don't know why I felt like doing coffee caveman style. This was very primitive. It tasted a little harsh to boot. But I poured some Kid Carson milk in it to take the edge off. That is not exactly cheating when it comes to true jungle living – but close. The milk comes from our own animals, so under the Man Cave Rules I decided it is okay to sweeten up your hard-boiled coffee with some goat's milk.

So long as you are the one milking said goat.

What probably set me off was good ole Lucky 13.

That thing would most likely send us back to the Stone Age if it weren't for the fact that we were pretty much already there, more or less. I remember back in the olden days when after a storm, and we had no lights and no water for a month or two, we had to improvise. That included cooking things on a gas grill or wood stove.

Things like coffee.

I could hear the branches and leaves of the trees rustling already, getting more pronounced with a sudden gust that sent them really whooshing and whishing all over the place. To be honest with you, the sound made me calm for some reason or another. I knew these were signals of some much stiffer winds that were on their way, heading right for us, which were not so pleasant and calming. But they were not here quite yet.

Except for the wind gusts, this was actually not such a bad day.

Calm before the storm, as they say.

A few guests would be arriving later in the afternoon. They would be checking in for a day or two. Not that they had to, really. The villagers had been through this so many times before. They knew how to batten down the hatches, secure their animals, get identified flying objects in a place they would not fly, board up their homes and barns, secure their kayaks and vessels, and do all the other things they needed to do to make their places safe and able to withstand whatever rains, wind, and even storm surges that would be coming our way from Lucky 13. Those too close to the bay or in low-lying areas would evacuate inland, either to the hospital or friends or relatives that could put them up.

My guests would be securing their places and coming to the Hermitage to ride out the storm with the Captain and his stories and his books, just like in olden times.

In a way this was a little bit fun, at least for the younger folks who thought of it as more like an adventure than a real-life scary story. I guess we had made things seem more routine and safe when these real bad storms came calling.

The youngsters didn't know better, it would seem.

In the so-called foyer I stood looking up at the rafters high up in the roof we had to raise a few years back. The ground floor was bound to flood once or twice a year during a big water event, even though we raised that, too, but that was okay. It was designed to take water that intruded through the water management systems we had in place.

We kept the living areas in lofts up on the higher floors, along with the stacks and stacks of books and manuals and other parts of the Harrison Chronicles kept in glass-enclosed shelves to keep them from turning into molded bundles of smelly paper and runny blue ink. From the foyer you could look up and see the whole elaborate mess, designed more for books than for people, rising up to the top where, in the daytime, sunlight peeked through the cupola at the apex. By no small coincidence, the effect was like the old Guggenheim museum that used to be in Manhattan.

That place ended up under water from what I was told.

But at least the art they had on the upper floors should have stayed high and dry.

This will sound crazy, but that old wooden table is still here, in the foyer. That thing had to be a hundred years old when I first saw it. It's still here. I must confess I did make sure I took real good care of that thing. Wiping and polishing it – but not too much – and just keeping that old girl in shipshape. Not that we didn't use her. No, sir. A thing that lasts is not meant to just sit there and not be put to use. That is the whole point.

This was not a museum piece any more than I am.

I ran my hand along her smooth, worn surface. Soon there would be people sitting around her, telling stories and sharing things that come out of a person when they are hiding in a dark, candlelit place, the howling winds and gusts of rain pounding violently outside, lashing the walls and doors and windows, unable to get at you. If we had a Ouija Board, we maybe would have pulled that out or done a séance. But we really wouldn't need any of those props to get a sense of how small we were in comparison to the might and majesty of Mother Nature when she was on another one of her rampages.

We knew all too well how insignificant we were in the grand scheme of things.

That point came home in no uncertain terms on that night in the Hermitage, on that day so many years ago, the day Mrs. Jacobs willingly forfeited her life to the elements.

I thought back to that day as I prepared for a reprise of the same scene later tonight:

"Let me show you to your quarters," Calusa said. She was gesturing upwards towards one of the lofts, coaxing my mom and Kate, holding a candle. A more complete explanation for what happened to Mrs. Jacobs had yet to be forthcoming, but Calusa probably had a good idea of what had happened. My mom probably did, too.

"Where is Mrs. Jacobs, Mommy?"

"She is at her house, sweetie. But, look, she had us take Tabatha for safekeeping. Do you want her to stay with you in your room with Mr. Ducky?"

Good move, Ma. Real smooth transition there.

There was a real Dr. Frankenstein atmosphere later that night around that 100-year-old dinner table. There were winds howling and rain slashing outside but peace and quiet inside. Calusa played the part of Igor. The cat was some sort of familiar from some other movie, like Dracula or something. Lightning, the border collie, took his usual crouching stance, eyeing the cat carefully, probably trying to figure out how to herd her.

There was an old, uh, what do you call it, candelabra in the middle of the table that lit the place up somewhat but cast these shadows on everyone's faces and across the room, giving it a real spooky sort of feel. Looking towards the head of the table, I noticed Harrison's face, his torso rigid in an upright position.

He had cleaned himself up real good for some reason. He may have even shaved. I figured he finally got the dinner party he was always talking about and now finally had a chance to show his best china and maybe his other best stuff for his honored guests.

At the other end of the table, there was my mom. I could swear she was wearing some kind of make-up or something.

How did she think to put something like that in her survival bag?

"Thank you all for braving the weather and joining Calusa and I for this modest dinner engagement, somewhat thrown together at the last minute as you might imagine." He nodded towards Calusa and tilted a glass of water in her direction. She, of course, said and did absolutely nothing in response.

"Forgive me, but we have yet to be formally introduced."

It was my mom.

"Ah, the forgiveness is all mine to give. Allow me to introduce myself. I am Harrison, and this is Calusa." He motioned towards her. She did not flinch.

"Is that Mr. Harrison?"

"No, just Harrison."

"I see. And is this Mrs. Harrison?" She nodded towards Calusa with a smile.

Calusa suddenly got up. "Should I open a bottle of wine?" she asked.

"I would love a glass. What do you have?"

"We have some old vine Zin," Harrison interjected. "Shall I go fetch that?"

"I'll deal with this," said Calusa.

Not sure if that had more than one meaning.

"About your friend, Mrs. . . ." Harrison began.

"Carol. Carol Jacobs."

I saw how the conversation was cleverly swerved in a different direction and made a mental note of it, one that stuck for quite a few years, even after I wrote it down in one of my own journals I had already started to keep.

"Yes. I think an explanation is in order, but I am not sure if the setting is quite right at the moment to do that." He looked over at Kate. Her duck was wedged next to her in her chair. The cat was on the floor, about to jump up on the table.

Lightning kept his eyes on the cat.

"She's dead, isn't she?" The words, coming from the mouth of babes, fell like a shroud over the room. A clap of thunder boomed outside.

The cat jumped on the table.

We were in a scene from an old Frankenstein movie.

Then Calusa walked in.

"I found this. You will no doubt be delighted by it," she said. She busied herself uncorking the bottle while everyone looked on in silence. She placed a glass in front of my mom and poured a wee bit into it. She got no reaction. Calusa picked up the glass and stuck her nose over the top of it. She swished the contents.

"An excellent bouquet. It has kept well. Please let me know what you think." She bent over and handed the glass to my mom, watching her expectantly.

Then there was another clap of thunder. Then there was the sound of chickens clucking. Maybe Ahab was among them. A goat bleated.

My mom nodded her approval. Calusa poured her a tall one. She would need it.

"She was already gone when we got there." I heard myself say these words.

"How did she die?" Kate asked.

"I think her heart gave out. That was from the looks of things." It was a little bit of not the whole truth, but it wasn't exactly a total fabrication either.

"You mean she is still out there, all by herself in this rainy weather?" Kate asked, her eyes getting wide as a look of concern spread her face.

"She is where she is supposed to be, where she wanted to be." Harrison had come to the rescue to try and explain things. "We could not move her for reasons we cannot explain right now. Your brother was very brave. He wanted to do something for her, but there was nothing anyone could do. Except . . ." he motioned towards the cat.

"Well, at least *she* made it out alive." She said, stroking the cat.

The cat purred.

Lightning watched.

Calusa brought out food.

"Oh, I am so sorry. May I help you?" My mom offered to help but did not budge from her chair. Calusa did not notice.

"No, I am able to manage quite well, thank you," she said.

I never heard her use so many words, especially so many in a row.

The next day we learned that the storm did, in fact, veer off just a bit to the south at the last minute, as if in answer to a prayer. The storm surge was, as a consequence, not nearly so bad as it might have been had the eye wall made landfall right where we were, but there was much damage we would have to survey the next day and the days to follow.

That night, we all repaired to our rooms after a most enlightening dinner engagement. Harrison regaled us with stories of survival and lectures of how man had polluted the environment and was now being held to account.

As for the ladies, well, that was a different story altogether.

FIFTEEN

CL 20/0015
The Hermitage Roost
Friday

The way I woke up this morning was by violently thrashing my arms. I was having a dream. I don't remember all the details, but I know that in the dream I was trying to put my foot on the ground or maybe it was the floor. It gave way, and I started to fall. I guess I was trying to reach out for something to catch my balance. More likely I was just flailing. That is why my arms started to match up the dream with reality and woke me with a start.

Where was I when I started to fall? Heck, where was I when I woke up? That was the first thing I tried to figure out. Oh, yeah, I was in the Roost. That happens sometimes when you sleep somewhere other than your usual bed and wake up not really sure where you are. I slept up in the Roost last night and gave up my usual bed to Maryann. I think she would have been okay if I stayed there with her last night, but, like I said before, that is not a very good idea, even though the idea was appealing, if you know what I mean.

Once I knew where I was, I tried to remember those vivid dreams from last night – at least they seemed vivid while I was having them. Where was I in those dreams?

My mind reached out and tried to replay one segment, something about being in a house that was floating in the air, but then I walked through a door and found myself in a castle with walls made of stone and torches on the walls, and, well, the images disappeared like wisps of smoke before my conscious mind could get a real good grip on them.

You probably have had that happen to you and know what I am talking about.

I scrambled out of the cot, still a little groggy, and sat down at the command center console, pulling out my daily journal. My pen hovered over the blank page of the journal as my mind tried to focus. So did my eyes. None of them seemed to be working right.

"Good morning, Captain Courageous. Or can I call you 'Cappy'?"

Maryann came up the spiral staircase. She had a coffee mug in each hand. The one she handed over to me was the good stuff, made the usual way. It tasted great.

She reached over and gave me a smooch on the forehead.

"How'd we do last night?"

"Let's find out." I pushed the button, and the slats covering the windows receded, letting in light, but not too much sun. "So far so good. The electricity is still working, at least up here, and the windows held up. Not sure about out there." I stood up and leaned forward to peer out the windows. I looked around. It was a mess. Maryann leaned forward to look, too. She gave out a little gasp and put her hand to her mouth.

"I know it looks bad, but it could have been worse. The storm veered north right at the last second, so we got the less intense side of it. Last report had the eye wall making landfall about a hundred miles north of us before the thing started cutting across towards Kate's neck of the woods. I am waiting to hear from them to see if it has emerged on the other side yet and how they fared. It was looking pretty strong even though it was passing over land, but it should be a lot weaker on the other coast than it was here."

"I hope they are going to be all right. Are you still planning to visit?"

"Right now we need to just take a look to see how bad our damage is and start cleaning the place up. Later, I may head over there if she needs a helping hand." This time Maryann didn't ask to tag along. She knew we would be having a big mess to clean up, and Kate would be doing the same thing. It would be no vacation cruise.

Angela came up, and we looked at the path of 13. It had been lucky for us but not so much so for the folks just to the north where the eye wall came ashore. The pattern looked eerily familiar. I was beginning to have a better understanding about the dreams I was having last night. Lucky 13 looked a lot like the Big One that struck back in the twenties.

Since then we have made the Village a lot more resilient and ready than things were back then. I knew once I got outside and looked around, checking on the villagers and their places, things would not be as bad as they might seem at first blush.

Not nearly as bad as the way the place was after the Big One.

That is a whole different story to tell:

Then, as now, I woke up in the Roost on the morning after. Harrison let me sleep on the cot up there. During most of the night we watched the feeds showing the track of the storm, the wind patterns, and the storm surge. The storm missed us – but not by much.

I, for one, was not prepared for what greeted us when we went outside.

Harrison shook me awake. He was standing there in wet-weather gear.

He had most of mine in his hand.

"Is it over?" I rubbed the sleep from my eyes. He tossed my gear on the cot.

"I would say it is just now beginning." He cranked open the shutters on the windows.

Outside it was gray and still windy, but the rain had stopped. He had gotten up earlier, letting me sleep in while he and Calusa went out to survey the damage. What I saw outside was a place I had never seen before. I did not recognize what I saw as the neighborhood I had been growing up in. What I saw was unrecognizable.

From the vantage point of the Roost, I could see water mostly, with some twisted, leafless trees tilting out of rivers and streams that flowed all around. The Hermitage itself emerged from the rippling waters as if it were an island. It had been built up enough that the waters flowed around its protective walls for the most part and into the moat and other low-lying places where gravity took them. In the distance there were patches of earth with roofless, concrete walls rising up into the air, places where houses used to be.

Here and there they could be seen scattered about my field of vision, like an archipelago of new islands bearing monuments to a failed civilization.

Downstairs we met up with the others in the foyer. The floor glistened with moisture, but at least it was not filled with water. My mom looked at us. Her eyes were wide.

"What happened? Is it over?"

Harrison looked at me. I think he didn't feel like repeating himself.

"The storm has passed by us, so that part is over," is how I started to explain things to her. "But it still looks a little scary out there."

"What do you mean? I'm supposed to be at the store today to work the afternoon shift. I need to get home to get dressed and drive to work."

"You won't be able to drive anywhere for a day or two, maybe longer. But even if you could, I doubt that store where you work is open. Maybe not for a long time. Maybe never." The words came from Harrison who had moved closer to the door. I think he was expecting me to follow so he could take me outside to see what he was talking about.

My mom held up her phone.

"I guess that's why I haven't heard from them, although something seems to be wrong with your cell phone service. Maybe I can go outside and try to get a better signal."

"I don't think this place is causing the problem with your phone. From the looks of things, this is one of the few places left standing. I wouldn't be surprised if most of the cell phone towers in the area have been washed out to sea or turned into twisted metal."

"Well, I can at least try, can't I?"

Harrison stepped away from the door and came a little closer. Calusa came into the room from one of the side entrances. She was muddy and sweaty from doing some sort of work outside, probably tending to the animals. Harrison turned to her.

"Calusa, why don't you take a break for a little while? Maybe you can show her and the little one around the kitchen and storage area so they can help themselves to some breakfast and get something cold to drink. I am taking the Captain here out to show him what we will be contending with in the next few days. We'll be back in an hour or two."

He walked over to the kitchen area, pulled some bananas off the stalk hanging there, and threw a couple towards me. I caught them and started to peel one. He did likewise, putting one in his mouth. His mouth was full, but he kept talking, after taking a swallow.

"When I get back, I'll have the Captain here take you out, and you can see if you can get a signal with that phone of yours." He nodded with what seemed like contempt in the direction of the device she was holding in her hand. He didn't like cell phones much. I think he thought they were too much a part of the grid.

"What do you mean, 'take me out'? Can't I just go on my own?"

"Not without a boat."

We walked out, my mom's mouth still agape as we closed the front door behind us. We sloshed through the walkway in near ankle-deep water and out the gate. His gheenoe was tied to a speed limit sign that had been bent over by the high winds. The water was getting up to my knees when he told me to stop where I was. He sloshed forward, untied the boat and sent the aft back my way so I could climb in. Then he pulled it towards him.

"Why don't you get to the bow? I'll steer from back here, if that is all right with you, Captain." Once I got situated, he aimed the boat towards what I guess was the street and pushed off as he got in, sending us into what was probably the swale.

Hard to tell, exactly.

"Watch for power lines in the water, although I don't think there is any power going through them. Won't be for quite some time to come, I suspect."

We made our way under and around downed trees and debris that were strewn in all different directions. The roofs of houses stuck up out of the water, those that still had them, that is. Harrison told me to make note of landmarks so that I could find my way around when I came out with my mom later. He was trying to get us to our house, but it was a little hard to figure out which way to go to get there.

Most of the street signs were gone.

Up ahead there was a house with people sitting on the roof. They started to wave at us frantically. They were shouting. "Over here! Over here!"

It was Peabody, Larry, and Little Freddie.

Their faces fell when they saw it was us.

"Ahoy there, mates!" I called out. Larry smiled back weakly.

"Avast there, Captain," he rejoined.

"This is no time to be sunbathing. Besides which, it's too cloudy."

Larry smiled. So did Freddie. Peabody, not so much, as I remember.

"We need help; we're stranded. Maybe you can send the Coast Guard."

Harrison couldn't help but get a dig in to Peabody. "Are you sure you want to send in the authorities? It doesn't look like that house of yours is up to code, at least the part I can see that isn't underwater. They might give you a citation. There are laws, you know."

"Very funny. Ha, ha. I suppose that crazy place of yours that you built is high and dry, with hardly a scratch." Peabody sounded as pathetic as he looked, perched up there on the top of his roof, hands on hips, sweating as usual.

"Oh, somehow we seemed to manage. When we see some-one, we will send them back to fetch you." Harrison apparently decided not to rub it in. Maybe he was afraid they would want to climb aboard or – perish the thought – even camp with us at the Hermitage.

"You make sure you do that, and *pronto!*"

"Aye, Aye, Skipper," said Harrison with a salute. He was muttering something under his breath. I think he said something about "Gilligan's Island," but I'm not sure.

We met up with some deputies from the sheriff's department and told them about Peabody being stranded and needing some help. Harrison made sure to tell them there was no hurry to pick up Peabody and his boys. I also told them about Mrs. Jacobs. I gave them her address, so they could find her house on their GPS devices – if they were still working.

I explained to them what to expect once they got there.

Later I took my mom on a ride out to the house. She was silent most of the way except for an occasional "Oh my god" and "I can't believe this." I have a feeling that as she was looking at all the other houses under water, the ones that had not been completely flattened, the realization had not quite dawned on her about what we would see when we rounded the bend and pulled in front of the place where her house used to be.

In her mind she probably was expecting to see what her mind's eye had told her would be there. The image of the house she always knew, there in her memory like a photograph. I know that is what I was thinking before I saw what I was about to show her. Like me, she didn't believe what her eyes were telling her brain when I stopped the boat.

"Why are you stopping here? Aren't we going to the house?"

"That is the house."

"Where? I don't see it."

A slight wind pushed the top of the water, sending ripples towards us. They carried debris that had washed out of the bombed-out structure protruding from the waters that surrounded what used to be our home. My mom looked down, scarcely recognizing the jewelry box she kept in the nightstand by her bed, the one she would put letters and other things into that she never let me see and never wanted to talk about.

The jewelry box floated, as if on purpose, up to the side of the boat, along with other debris, right next to where she was sitting.

She reached down and fished it out of the murky water. She had tears in her eyes. She put the jewelry box in her lap. Her body crumpled over it. She started to sob.

I said nothing, knowing I had to start to paddle back to our refuge.

It would be dark soon.

SIXTEEN

CL 20/0016
The Hermitage Study
(Thursday)

I set out today on what I guess would qualify as my usual morning constitutional, although there was not a whole lot usual about it, seeing as how I would be surveying the damage from good old Lucky 13 that came through the night before. I made a mental note to swing by the spot where the house we lived in back in the Twenties used to be while making my rounds. That mental note was sure to stick this time.

Another one was to check on that old avocado tree that was planted so many years ago, just outside the Hermitage. She was still there, rising tall, reaching up to the sky like she always has, standing up like a sentinel watching over us, still bearing fruit.

That is why I call her the Sentinel Tree.

I couldn't help but to stop and regard her again for a good long while. Then a thought occurred to me: She is just a few years younger than I am. We have both been hanging around together all these many years since the day she was first planted.

Standing there this morning, staring at that tree for so long, I must have looked like one of those demented people you probably have heard about. Maybe there was a little bit of that going on in my brain. Certainly there was a lot of déjà vu all over again.

I couldn't help but realize that I had stood in more or less this same spot, looking at the place where the Sentinel Tree was planted all those many years ago:

A few days after the Big One slammed into us, I ventured out of the Hermitage with my mom on a mission to see what was going on with our house. The waters had receded enough that we were able to walk there without need of a boat.

Harrison sent Bolt along with us.

That is who he called Lightning.

He said he wanted Bolt to herd us in the right direction, but mainly I think he wanted an added measure of protection, probably more so for my mom than for me.

Better safe than sorry, as they say.

Calusa was already outside, tending to the row of trees she had planted in the city right of way that Peabody had complained about so much back then. A lot of the trees ended up growing into a forest of fruit-bearing trees that helped to feed us for many years to come. Or maybe that would make them an orchard. Not sure exactly. I would have to research the manuals and get back to you on that one. It's sure to be in there somewhere.

Where was I? Oh, yeah, the Sentinel Tree.

Miraculously, some of the trees Calusa had planted had not been washed away or blown away by the storm. She had shored up the ones that were still standing along the embankment where they had been planted, and secured them with rocks and hard debris to help keep the erosion at bay. She was working to plant another little tree in a spot that was elevated enough to avoid flooding and, as it would later develop, would be shielded from stiff winds by other mature trees and the walls of the Hermitage.

Kate was sitting next to her, helping out with the planting.

Ducky was nowhere to be seen.

"Look, Captain, we're planting that avocado seed you were growing. We thought it would be OK, since you did give it to her as a present that one time."

She looked up at me, her hand shielding her eyes from the morning sun that lit up her face. Calusa looked up, too. She had the slightest hint of a smile.

"That tree looks to be in the most capable of hands. All four of them, I might add. Carry on," I said with a salute. I turned on my heel and extended an arm to my mother.

"Shall we proceed to our own castle, milady?" Her look of puzzlement at the whole affair about the avocado seed dissolved into a sweet smile at the antics of her children. She did a quick curtsy and took my arm. "Why, I would be more than delighted to be accompanied by such a fine gentleman on our journey, my good Captain."

With that, we proceeded, like a scene from the Wizard of Oz, in the general direction of our house, a dog walking along-side, of course. I could hear the sounds of giggling behind us, as my sister and Calusa finished planting what was to become the Sentinel Tree.

Our smiles soon faded once our arms unlocked, so we could better make our way through the thicket of fallen trees and debris scattered haphazardly all along and on the road to our house. Here and there were more orderly piles stacked up near the road, outside what used to be people's houses. But for the most part, there was very little discernable cleanup activity going on in what looked like a war zone.

I was later to discover that more than a few people had given up and abandoned the place altogether, never to return again.

We stood for a moment outside our own wreckage of a house, taking the sight in, now that the waters had receded to reveal what was in store for us. The straps did hold the frame for the roof onto the concrete walls of the house. That was the good news. The not-as-good news was that the plywood tacked to the framework had been ripped off by the winds, except in a few places. We had been left with a skeleton of wood beams lashed, quite securely, onto concrete walls that encompassed a hollowed-out structure.

Most of the windows had been blown away from the inside out.

Bits of drywall, concrete, furniture, papers, and a lot of other junk which did not look like much of anything, that had been tossed about from inside our house, were strewn everywhere.

Debris from our place and other houses littered the inside of our house, our "yard," and throughout the rest of the neighborhood.

After a momentary gasp and look of shell shock, my mom bravely ventured into the mess, climbing over one thing and then another to make her way towards the interior of the house. I followed her. So did Bolt.

We were like Billy goats, clambering over rocks and hard surfaces on a mountainside, looking to see if there was anything of value amongst the rubble.

I helped clear a path for my mom so she could make her way through more easily. We cleared a spot to stack things that looked like they were salvageable. Things that were not were put into a pile outside. Bolt sniffed through the wreckage as well, turning up his nose at most things, some more than others. It was a very hot and humid day, and the air clung to our skin and seeped into our lungs like an enveloping mist.

My mom was rummaging around, trying to make her way to a filing cabinet with papers and documents, hoping they were still intact. She also had a little fire-proof portable safe with really important documents that she was trying to find. I left her on her quest and made my way to the back of the house to see what had become of my experiments.

By some stroke of luck, the shed was actually still standing. It was dented up pretty good, and there was a small tree lying on top of it, but it was still there. My guess is the tie-downs actually kept it from going airborne, and the tree helped to weigh it down. Had there been a touchdown of one of the tornadoes thrown off by the storm in our yard, nothing would be left. We appeared to have dodged that bullet.

Other houses were not so lucky.

Inside the shed most of my stuff was in salvageable shape. The water level did not go high enough to corrode the batteries and other more sensitive stuff piled up higher from the floor. I would be able to reinstall the solar panel, wind generator, and the rain barrel systems, once I could figure out how to put a roof back on the house.

The plants in the ground were a lost cause for the most part after the high winds and salt water flooding took their toll, but the potted ones in the shed were still viable, as were the ones that I had just started to grow hydroponically. They were all pretty banged up. If plants really do have feelings, they had to be traumatized. Surely they were in shock, but it could have been worse – a lot worse. At least they were still alive.

That was more than what could be said for Mrs. Jacobs.

The thought created an image in my mind of her face, smiling at Kate, that look of concern when I went to her house looking for my little sister during that one storm, the Appetizer Storm I told you about. Those images of her face were replaced by the one I could see now in my mind as she was lying prostrate in her chair, impaled by a tree limb, a mask of horror and death, her mouth having fallen open, her eyes looking heavenward.

Not sure why I started thinking of her, but the images started to push tears through my eyes, which had been sealed shut, real tight, as tight as I could make them, trying to keep them in, trying to keep a lot of things in. That technique did not work for very long. The waterworks started, and I just could not stop it anymore. It was like a geyser.

Finally, I let the tears and all the emotions go. It was a real good workout for my tear ducts, I can tell you that. Maybe clear some stuff out a little. My body shook with waves of sobs. Lots of sadness poured out, uncontrollably. So much I got frightened. Then I think I felt just a little bit of what felt a lot like anger coming out. I looked up at the sky.

"Where are you, Dad? We need you." I said out loud.

Notice I said "we" and not "me" for some reason.

I put some of the plants in a good spot with not too much sun and left the other stuff in the shed. Obviously they would continue to be safe and sound until I had a chance to come back the next day and set everything up as they should be. I had to think about a plan first and maybe check in with Harrison before deciding what to do next.

I found my mom sitting on a kitchen chair among piles of stinky clothes in one spot and ruined books in another. Now

I was really getting depressed. I hope there were no loaners from Harrison's library in that pile. I would go through them later to see if any had made it through the storm without being completely ruined.

I scanned the wreckage and spotted Bolt, who found a place where he could keep an eye on every move my mom made. He looked up when I climbed into the house.

I saw my mom had given him water in a plastic bowl that had made it through the storm intact. It did not look familiar. Probably flew in from a neighbor's house.

"Well, I found the deed and the insurance papers," she said, "and, of course, the *mortgage,*" she said with some amount of scorn, holding up some papers without looking up. Not sure how I am going to make mortgage payments if the places I used to work don't exist anymore, and the house I am paying on is one I can't live in." She visibly slumped again, looking all around at the disaster zone her home had become.

"I am sure we will be able to figure something out," I said, pulling up a chair as close to my mom as I could. Sunlight was pouring through the rafters.

She looked up.

"At least we now have skylights. That should add some value to the place, except when it starts to rain, of course." She looked at me and smiled.

I laughed.

"We should be able to scare up some usable sheets of plywood or some such to cover up some of the holes in the roof. They give out blue tarps in situations such as these, from what I recall. I think we can make the place water tight to some degree at least for the time being while we wait on help to arrive." I was trying to make things seem more manageable.

She glanced up at me before standing up.

"I am not sure it is worth it anymore, but let's get going. We should check on my car before it gets dark, and we have to head back to Harrison's."

At least the car situation panned out. We were clever enough to move my mom's car to a parking lot in a nearby shopping center, where there was higher ground and some protection of a building and some larger trees. Some of the trees were still standing, and those that were not had managed to not fall on top of the car.

"I'll ask Art and his dad if they can come out and take a look at it. They are real good at boats, cars, and engines."

A few days later, Art eventually made it over to the parking lot and worked on the car. By some miracle he got the engine to turn over. My mom would be able to use the car after all – if and when we were able to find any gas to put in it.

Later on, after that first day of venturing out to take stock of the damage to our house and car, we were having what turned out to be regular nightly dinners around the old wooden table. I told Harrison about my stuff that had survived the hurricane. I left out the part about the books or, I should say, *his* books.

"I guess the insurance people will be sending out contractors to restore the house to its former glory, but in the meantime we need to get some wood to cover up the holes in the roof and put up some of those blue tarps to keep out the rain," I announced.

"I would not be that confident in the insurance people coming to the rescue, certainly not anytime soon," said Harrison. "This was the largest, most powerful storm to hit the mainland in recorded history. It left a huge swath of destruction stretching for hundreds of square miles, much worse than the last time a major storm hit this area. Back then, it took months just to clean up the mess and years for the insurance people and construction crews to work their way through things."

Harrison paused for a moment and then looked at my mom before continuing.

"I don't want to cause alarm, but there are some serious doubts that the insurance companies will be solvent enough to pay for all of this."

"But they are backed by the government," my mom said plaintively.

"Given the way things have been with the economy and huge deficits and the wars raging all around the world, I would not count on the government being solvent enough to pay for this either. You may be waiting a very long time before your house is ever restored back to the way it was before, if that is what you wanted to do."

"What do you mean? Of course I want it put back to the way it was before."

Harrison looked back at me and then turned to my mom.

"Look at this place." He glanced up, and our eyes followed his. "I do not have insurance, and I do not need it. Why? Over the years, this place has been rebuilt in a way that is different from the way your house and all the other houses around here have been built. This place is built to be resilient in the face of a changing environment, an environment that other houses were not built to withstand.

"The most severe storm we have seen in over a century came and went, and we are still standing, continuing to function within this sanctuary, unlike what is out there." He motioned with his head to the darkened world outside the safe confines of the walls of the Hermitage, where my mind's eye imagined people huddled around by candlelight in roofless houses, wondering what is to become of them.

"But we are not as lucky as you," my mom said. "Our house is in shambles. Our lives are in shambles. We don't have electricity and food to survive like you do."

"All the more reason not to build another house of cards like you did last time." Harrison tried to soften his expression as best he could. "I understand why you did what you did, just like almost everyone else in the world. You were doing what you were told to do. Building a house and a home that could not sustain itself, could not remain standing in the face of Mother Nature's wrath, a wrath visited upon all those whose ways of doing things defied her, gave her no respect. Now she is returning the favor."

He paused for a moment, looking serene and thoughtful.

"If you rebuild it as you did before, it will just get knocked down again."

SEVENTEEN

CL 20/0017
The Hermitage Study/Friday

On this morning's constitutional I paused for a moment halfway up the narrow roadway made of shell, water on each side lapping up close to the edges, but not too close for comfort. I looked into the swirling water at one point. There must have been a drainage hole of some sort there – I don't recall exactly. I could check one of the manuals later if I had a mind to. But in that moment the thought occurred to me how far we had come that I could even have a morning constitutional just two days after such a big storm as Lucky 13 without use of a boat, like back when we had the Big One.

The system of canals and waterways worked very well, well enough to handle most of the water even during a big storm surge such as what we had last night, not to mention the king tides that made regular appearances. Even places that were inundated by water fared pretty well, such as that barn across the way from where I'm standing. Like almost all structures in the Village it was built up – way up. The sea levels were rising, but so were the houses, barns, sheds and anything else anyone with half a brain wanted to build.

I did recall that mental note of mine I had made earlier: to make sure to walk past the old house we used to live in. Boyhood home, I guess you would call it. Place I grew up. And boy, I sure did have to grow up fast in those days – maybe too fast.

To say the place where our house once stood was nothing like I remembered it would be an understatement, to say the least. That house was long gone, as were almost all the houses in the village – as were, just about, most of the memories of them.

Just about but not quite, as I well remember how I rebuilt that house of ours:

After the Big One the words of Harrison echoed in the back of my mind while I was struggling to get the place back into some semblance of what it once was, always questioning whether it was all a big waste of time. I did manage to find pieces of plywood and planks of boards enough to cover up most of the holes in the roof. Art and Larry helped me to hoist them up and nail them down, when they didn't have to help with their own places or other neighbors who were still around and needed a helping hand.

I guess the place was starting to turn into sort of a clubhouse for us. Barely fit for human habitation, it was straight out of that *Robinson Crusoe* novel – or maybe more like that really old book called *Lord of the Flies*. We had a tarp that we got from the emergency management people who seemed to really make themselves as scarce as water and gasoline had become, but they would show up from time to time to give out bottles of water, really crappy food, and things like, well, blue tarps. Then they would beat a hasty retreat.

Seems our area was not much of a priority. There were some stories I heard on the radio that where we lived, even though it was hit about as bad as anywhere else by the Big One, was not getting much attention. Other places had people that were – how should I put this? – a little more well-to-do than folks where we lived. Funny, I never really thought of ourselves as poor, but I guess that is how people looked at us at the time.

Soon I was to find people who were looked down upon even more so than we were.

I did heed the advice of Harrison and lectured my two friends about how to be sustainable and build things that made a person more self-reliant. I sounded like a mini-Harrison probably. We had the wind generator and solar panel running and the batteries charged up. Even got a few more old motorcycle batteries, wires, and other stuff Art's dad had lying around their shop. We used them to set up an even grander experiment than what I had going before. We also salvaged a few solar panels from the wreckage that was our neighborhood, and even found enough of a rooftop hot water system that we could heat water, collected from rainbarrels.

We managed to piece together a crude cistern system for some of our water needs.

We still had to boil water for drinking and other po-tating, but that was not hard to do. We had scrounged together propane tanks to run the grill and, of course, had plenty of things to use as firewood. Cooking utensils were not hard to find. There was so much of that sort of stuff scattered around all over the place, we started to stockpile it to give out to other people who had a need. Larry in particular turned out to be a real hoarder.

He always wanted to have a garage sale to raise money.

But we didn't have a garage, nor a big need for money, except for getting gas to run my mom's car or our collection of chain saws. We did need to get supplies from time to time, but it turned out – much to our surprise – that many of the people in the neighborhood threw money at us when we came to help them haul debris away from their house or cut down trees and tree limbs from their yards. We were accumulating most of the stuff we were hauling away. At the time I was not sure why, but I knew we needed to salvage things and not throw them away. "Salvage Operation" is what Art called it.

I found out later why we were salvaging what other people considered trash.

Every once in a while, Larry would say something like "We can't do that; it's against the rules," or "We are going to get in trouble for that if we aren't careful." I would usually give him one of the lines I learned from Harrison about becoming self-reliant and "off the grid" – which meant we were not part of the rules anymore. The only rules were the rules of the jungle. This was survival, and we didn't see anybody coming to enforce the so-called rules, nor to help us do what we needed to do to get by, permit or no permit.

"I hereby grant a permit to permit myself to make the club-house water tight and cook our food and boil our water so we can drink it," I said one time. I found a pencil and a piece of scrap paper that I used to scribble nonsense on for better effect. We had an old beat-up desk and "Captain's" chair that I used to preside over the proceedings.

Art and Larry actually took the whole thing rather seriously.

One day we were cooking some weenies over a campfire in the front of the house. We thought we might have to eat them before they went bad. Not sure of the expiration date, but it was a fine excuse to cook them up and eat them with a can of pork and beans we had also salvaged from somewhere – not sure where exactly.

We salvaged so much stuff from all sorts of places. Canned food was good.

We had a can opener.

"Mmmmm, that smells good. What is that you cook, little boys?"

All three of us looked up in unison. There was a gang of about a dozen or so boys standing in the road looking at us and our lunch. Most of them were our age and even younger. The leader who was doing all the talking looked to be a lot older – and bigger. I could tell, mostly by the way some of them were dressed, but also by the hint of an island accent in the leader's voice that they were Haitians from the other side of the big Biscayne Boulevard that had for many years separated our two communities.

Poor whites, it would seem, on the one side, people of color on the other.

The boulevard served to become the "Great Divide", you might say.

"We would share with you, but we don't have enough to feed everyone," I called out.

"Who said anything about sharing?" The leader drew a little closer and had a stern look on his face. His gang members gathered closer behind him. Someone in the crowd said something in Creole, and he smiled a wicked smile. There was some murmuring in the crowd that I did not understand exactly, but I had a pretty good idea what it meant. The gang had grown together into a tight ball but then fanned out as they all edged closer.

Their leader with his two main henchmen walked right up to the edge of the yard.

I started to feel a strange feeling in my gut that ran up from my spine and into my head. This was a new feeling I had not experienced up until that moment. I had felt fear before, but nothing like this. My mind was reeling. My heart was pounding. I was trying to find the right words to defuse the situation, preferably in Creole. Art drew closer and set his jaw. Larry just stood there, his face looking even whiter than ours.

Just then a vehicle pulled up right between the three of us white boys and the mob of very hungry boys of color who did not want to share. The driver's side door opened, and a beautiful, tall ebony woman rose up from the seat in the car. She closed the door and walked slowly to the front of the car. She stopped just a few feet from the leader of the pack, towering over him. She glared at him in that way of hers.

She said nothing.

The boy looked down, unable to hold her gaze. He turned around and motioned to the gang, saying something in Creole that I did not understand. I had an idea of what he meant but didn't know enough Creole to say for sure. I only knew a few words. They turned around *in masse* and headed back towards the other side of the boulevard.

A few of the younger ones looked back in awe at the Amazon who had come to our rescue. They all soon disappeared from view.

The Amazon kept glaring at the spot where they had just been, as if for emphasis.

"Come on, we're going shopping. Wanna come?" It was Kate calling to me from the back seat. Calusa finally stopped staring and looked over at me, saying nothing.

"Well, I am a little tied up right now. Did you say you were going shopping?"

"They will not bother you again." The words came from Calusa. "Here, we have something for you that will protect you."

In the back seat was some sort of African-style mask carved from a piece of wood with two eyeholes cut out and painted to look like an Indian warrior or something. "We made them yesterday. They are dry now. Calusa says they are like the ones that were found on one of the islands a hundred years ago left by a tribe of Indians." Kate handed the mask to me with a cheery expression on her face. She seemed to have no idea that we were about to have a riot, and a crisis had just been narrowly averted.

"Put this up where they can see it. There will be no more troubles," said Calusa.

I handed it over to Larry. He stood there speechless, gaping at the legendary Amazon. "Tack this up over yonder where everyone can see it. Don't worry about the rules. We are playing by a new set of rules from now on."

"Don't worry, we will stand guard until you get back," Art said. He bent down and picked up a baseball bat, tapping it into his palm.

"What about all our stuff? What about the weenies?" Larry asked.

I looked at the wreckage of our house that now seemed a little sad and pathetic but was something worth fighting for, it would seem. "I think we will be safe for now. Put the mask up, and if anyone says anything about it, just say some gibberish in words that sound sort of like French, and then tell them to get lost before the Voodoo hex gets them."

I offered a bowl of beanie weenies to Calusa who demurred. Kate took a bowl and so did I. We had our lunch, to go, in the back seat as Calusa headed to Little Haiti. True to her word, Kate got out with Calusa and headed into what looked like a flea market from a third world country. Not that I had ever been to one, but I had seen pictures.

Plus, I guess by that time we were all living in a world blown back into the Dark Ages.

They got some provisions, and we got back in the car, heading deeper into Little Haiti. Kate was playing with some sort of creepy-looking Voodoo doll she got at the market. She was talking to it in what I could tell was a fake French language she had apparently made up probably on the spot. Calusa said nothing.

We pulled up to an old Spanish-style house. I could hear chickens clucking and then a rooster crowing in the back. Calusa turned to Kate and me sitting in the back seat.

"Wait here," she said. She got some things she had gotten at the market and went into the house. She was there for a good long while. It was sweltering. Kate got tired of talking her gibberish language to her Voodoo doll and started trying it on me. I gave her my best mangled phrases in Creole I could come up with. She pretended to understand, gesturing with her hands and flailing her doll around.

"Who were those boys at the house? Are they new friends of yours?" She finally started talking in regular Kate English.

"Not exactly."

"Calusa says we have to try and make friends with the people who have skin that is the same color as hers. They live over on this side of the boulevard. They need our help, and we need theirs, too, she said."

"So far they are not acting too friendly, but we will see. We have the mask hanging outside the house so they will leave us alone."

"I think the mask is supposed to mean that we are like them and are part of the same tribe. That is what Calusa said. We are all part of one tribe."

At dinner that night Harrison explained things better.

"We are in an enclave where the villagers, as I like to call them, are not that much higher in social standing than the folks who live across the boulevard. Our skin colors match up better with the people in charge of things, but our economic standing is not even close. We are not much higher on their list of priorities than the communities that you went to visit today and that came to visit you. That is why you do not see much effort from the relief workers and government agencies to try and help us. But while we are getting next to nothing from them, the folks across the Great Divide are getting even less."

That night I decided to venture out from the Hermitage and spend the night at the clubhouse. Harrison sent Bolt to herd me in the right direction.

Art was already there, stoking up the campfire. Larry showed up later. We toasted up a bag of gooey marshmallows and washed it down with some soda pop. I think we had somewhat of a sugar high. Art started howling at the moon. We all smeared leftover beanie weenies and some yellow chalk on our faces like war paint. Bolt looked at our strange faces, tilting his head to the side quizzically. We must have been some sight, howling at the moon, our painted faces lit up by the flames of the fire.

Suddenly, Bolt started, jumping up and peering out into the dark. I swear I could see a pair of eyes glowing in the dark, not far from our fire.

"Who goes there? Friend or foe?" I called out these words to the glowing eyes.

Out of the blackness emerged the Haitian boy, who had been the leader of the pack earlier that day. His two lieutenants were right behind him. We were not afraid.

Neither were they.

EIGHTEEN

CL 20/0018
The Hermitage Study/Sunday

This morning I had my regularly-scheduled Blueways jaunt. Good thing I did, because it looked like a follow-on storm to Lucky 13 was brewing. That happened every once in a while. One would come and hit us hard, and then another one would come not long after.

I hate when that happens.

I headed out again in the direction of where our old house used to be. I guess I wanted to see the thing from the other, seaward point of view, so to speak. Eventually, the Blueways had ended up extending about a block or so towards the back of the land where the house used to sit, snaking back westward towards the big Haitian village that adjoined our own before turning northward towards the Little River.

The place looked as strange and foreign to my memories from the back as it did from the front. Sometimes, when a person visits a place from their past, it looks a lot different than it does in the picture you have of it in your head. Usually, if your memory of it is a thing or place from your childhood, it looks a lot smaller. That is probably because you were a much smaller person than you are now, all grown up.

Back then, as a wee tyke, you looked up at things. They towered over you in many ways. Now, as an adult, you are much bigger. So those things don't look so tall after all.

Gee, there I go getting all philosophical again.

One thing is for sure: What I was looking at was not something as it was in the past that only looked different now because I had a distorted memory of it as a child. Back then, this whole place was a whole different world we lived in as kids. Everything has changed in radical ways except, of course, the Hermitage.

It is still more or less the same.

Looking back on it, as you can tell I do a lot of these days, we all started doing things quite a bit differently than we had back before the Twenties. Some people did not understand completely the how and why of it. I do now but can't say I was a genius and knew all about what we were going to have to do and how to do it back then.

I learned as I went along, just like the rest of us, except, that is, the ones that clung to the past. Harrison once told me what he said was the definition of insanity: "Doing the same thing over and over, each time expecting a different result."

That is in a manual somewhere, I am sure. Not sure which one. I may dig that one out. See if there is also something about my "eureka" moment back in the Twenties:

I had finally figured out why we had been salvaging things and stacking them up in the place next door to the clubhouse. Maybe instincts told me not to just throw things away like most people used to do back before the Twenties. My mom told me about how her grandparents used to lecture her about growing up in the Great Depression when people had to scrimp and save and conserve and reuse everything because you were never sure where your next meal would come from or if you had a place to live or not.

My "eureka" moment came as I was in the study at the Hermitage, poring over books Harrison let me read about Native American tribes in Florida and how they had lived and built their communities in a more natural way. Their ways seemed primitive to the fancy-pants ways of the Europeans who conquered them, but like Harrison would point out, who really was the more advanced civilization? The ways of the tribes were more in tune with nature, which is to say, more resilient in an environment the Europeans arrogantly thought they could control, even shape, only to find out different.

I asked Harrison about my idea to use the felled trees to build around our bombed-out house, then attach a thatched roof and siding with the palm fronds stacked up higher in piles than I was tall. He looked at me with an almost-startled expression.

I think he was impressed.

"Calusa is the one to ask," he finally said. "She knows people who would know."

"You mean the people from Little Haiti across the boulevard?"

"No. Their island was deforested in a desperate bid to survive, sort of like the story of Easter Island. Their half of Hispaniola became a disaster waiting to happen with every passing storm. They came here and took up the lifestyle of the slum-like areas allotted to them by the ancestors of the Europeans that originally enslaved them. They need to relearn things as much as the rest of us." I was okay with the lecture. Even repeated it myself, a bunch of times. But I had thoughts running through my head and wanted answers to some questions. I needed more concrete answers – figuratively and literally.

"Have you seen Calusa?" I asked Kate, who was sitting in the foyer, playing with her cat and her Voodoo doll. The cat was swiping at the doll, and she would pull it away. Bolt was keeping an eye on them, having apparently herded them into place.

"She is over at your friend Art's place. She wants to get a boat to take her to an Indian village out in the Everglades." She looked up at me. The cat noticed she was not paying attention and grabbed the doll. Bolt raised his head to watch but didn't flinch.

"Why do you guys call Art 'No-Ha'?" I suppressed a laugh and then knelt down beside her. Kids say the darnedest things, I thought to myself. I got that saying from an old television show – one so old I could not even begin to tell you what it was.

"I think he got that nickname on account of that story in the Bible about the guy who built that really big boat and put a bunch of animals in it before the flood waters came. Those big boats were called 'arks' and the guy's name was Noah. Because Art and his dad are so into boats and boat engines, the name sort of stuck."

"No-Ha is Art?"

"Yes. 'Noah's Ark' translates into No-Ha in Creole, apparently. We call our best Haitian friend 'Cousteau.' His real name is Jacques, but because Art is teaching him how to go out into one of the boats and fish for food, we call him Cousteau."

"Why?"

"That was the name of this famous scientist who went out on the seas in his boat called 'Calypso' to explore and do experiments."

"Why?"

I could see the conversation was going in circles.

It happens with kids her age.

"Did you say she is going to visit an Indian village? How's come?"

"She's going to take me there. She says the time has come for me to go on a vision quest and earn my Indian name. Maybe it will be 'Calypso.'"

"Well that is a catchy name. I'm sure they will come up with something fitting."

When I finally caught up with Calusa, she told me she would ask the medicine man at the Everglades village about what I was going to be doing at the clubhouse.

His name was Mick Jagger.

I'm not kidding.

She told me she would ask for his guidance but more so his blessing.

That was good enough for me. I started to work, enlisting the aid of Larry and Art. Larry, of course, said what we were doing was probably against the rules for the neighborhood, and we would get into trouble for sure. I wrote out one of my "permits" for the work we were doing. "The thing we are building is an official structure of the Native American tribes, all being done with the blessing of their medicine man," I pronounced, reading from the paper I held up in official fashion. "As such, by law, it is exempt from the rules of the neighborhood association, known as the Peabody Rules."

"Really, you got a real Indian guy to say this was okay?" Art asked.

"Yes. That is in the works even as we speak."

"What's his name?" Larry asked.

"Mick Jagger."

"Oh, brother." Larry was skeptical, but he went along with it.

We dug deep holes all along the perimeter of the clubhouse, evenly spaced, all in a circular pattern, each spaced out about 20 feet apart. I had a sketch that we would consult to make sure they were put in the right spots.

Calusa helped me with it.

She was much better at drawing than I was. So was Kate, who also helped.

Cousteau and his buddies eventually showed up to help us dig and plant the larger tree trunks into the holes. The poles were secured by bits of concrete and other hard debris thrown into the holes and then covered with dirt.

We were all learning how to do this at the same time.

The tops of the tree trunks were sawed off with chainsaws so they would all be the same height. Then we lashed thinner poles made from tree branches or the trunks of smaller trees, to link the poles to one another horizontally, like the books I had read said to do. It was all in the series of sketches that Calusa and Kate had drawn up.

People walking in the neighborhood would stop and stare, pointing at the sight of a group of white boys and black boys working like a construction crew, erecting these tall totems on the site of where the remains of my mom's house stood. When we started to thatch the roof, the onlookers, who became more numerous and sometimes would bring lawn chairs to sit and watch, realized we were making a giant chickee. The thing was encircling the house and providing protection from the sun and the elements.

By the time we were done, the driving rain would no longer splash into the house or fly in through the openings where the windows used to be. The sun would no longer be beating down on us mercilessly. The circular hole at the apex of the chickee would allow smoke from the fire pit and other fumes to exit out of the house and the chickee. The poles of the chickee were placed on ground that had been built up hopefully high enough to keep out all but the highest of king tides and storm surges that came our way.

Not all of the onlookers were appreciative of our work.

"What the hell do you boys think you are doing?"

It was Peabody.

He stood on the street, hands on hips, sweating as usual. Larry was up on the roof with Cousteau and one of his lieutenants. Merci, I think his name was, on account of how he was always saying "thank you" over and over again for the same thing. The three of them were finishing the thatch work up there, making sure all was tight and secure.

Art – or No-Ha, I should say – was at ground level doing the same thing with the thatch there. He and a few more of the boys from Haiti, plus a few girls even, were making sure thatch on the sides, which came up about 3 feet from the base of the supporting poles, were secure and mudded in real good. We would eventually shore up the sides with more debris and other materials on hand to create a berm around the chickee.

Everyone stopped what they were doing and looked at the old white guy on the street who was yelling at them. Then they looked at me.

Peabody noticed the mask that had been tacked up on one of the poles. He pointed at it. "And what the hell is that supposed to be? Not a permit, I can tell you that! This is not Sub-Saharan Africa, you know, although from the looks of things you could hardly tell the difference. What are these, these *people* doing here anyway? Don't they know they are supposed to stay on *their* side of the boulevard?"

"They are helping us." The words drifted down from the roof of the chickee. "And I guess that mask is a sort of permit. We have permission to do what we are doing."

Peabody squinted, his hand shielding his eyes from the bright sun beating down on them. He looked up in the direction of the voice he heard. "Pudge, is that you? What are you doing up there, hanging around with these spear-chuckers? Didn't I tell you to stay away from them and this nigger-lover?" He nodded in my direction.

The words hit everyone like a ton of bricks.

They were met by stunned silence.

"You need to get your fat ass off that thing you are standing on and get home. Maybe get some religion while you are at it."

Larry stood stock still for a good long while. He was anything but a "Pudge." All the work we had been doing in the wake of the Big One and building a huge chickee in the hot Florida sun over the past few days had him well on the way to becoming the bear of a man he would someday be. I think I saw him flex his sinews for a moment as he stood there, shirtless, skin darkened from the sun, not quite defiant – but almost.

"I promised I would do the work as agreed and as an honorable man would do according to the scriptures. I have to finish what I started just like I promised. Isn't that what you have always been preaching about all this time?"

"Don't sass me, boy. You have to mind your elders, too, you know. That is in the scriptures as well. And don't think just because you are family that we will be letting you slide on this crazy African thing you and these miscreants are building. That Voodoo mask over there ain't no legal permit, and I am sure interested in seeing whatever paperwork you have that makes any of this legal. Now, I suggest you come down from there, after you help clear up this big mess you and your new jungle-bunny friends made of the place."

Peabody turned away and stalked back down the road. He probably was thinking he would need some reinforcements. The onlookers did not seem too happy about what they had just seen and heard. They glanced back and shook their heads as they left.

"Merci! Merci!" Someone called out from the roof. "Merci, monsieur!"

There was a murmur of chuckles.

Then everyone looked over at me for another minute or two. Then we all went back to work.

NINETEEN

CL 20/0019
The Hermitage Roost/Monday

Just as I figured, that system that had been brewing out in the Atlantic was turning into a follow-on storm to Lucky 13. Angela and I were looking at the thing up in the Roost, but my feeling that this would happen was more instinct than science. After a while I guess you sort of have a knack for these things, but this was more a lucky guess than reasoning.

Luck of the bad variety, unfortunately.

"Are you going to go ahead with the big powwow today, or should we start making ready for this next storm?" Angela asked.

"Both. We might as well kill both birds with one stone."

"What is that supposed to mean?" She was a bird lover – lover of wildlife in general actually. She especially liked the parrots that still fill our skies with their presence and their distinctive voices, here in our world of the future. They are the ancestors of the parrots, mainly green Amazons and African Greys that had been kept as pets by humans several decades ago but were turned loose or escaped from their cages.

They usually fly in pairs, but sometimes you can see them with a third adult flying alongside two others. They mate for life, you know. Apparently, some are allowed to tag along with a matched pair when their own mate is nowhere to be found.

"It's an old expression. Come to think of it, not a very good one. We will meet at the Convention Center to give a briefing on the cleanup from the last storm and talk about the next one.

Two subjects covered at the same meeting. Sort of like talking about two problems at the same time, solving both."

"What does that have to do with killing birds?"

"Never mind; it's just an old expression. Sort of like a joke. If you have to explain it, then it is not going to be funny."

"Well, there is nothing funny about killing defenseless birds, that I know of," she sniffed, turning back to her computer screens to track that new storm.

Later that night, we convened a big meeting at what we call the "Convention Center." It was an old term that they used to apply to big places downtown where all the bigwigs and other dignitaries would meet to think deep thoughts and say big words. Sounds like a big waste of time to me. But nowadays we do things differently than the way things were done in the olden days. Then, as now, there is a need for a central gathering place where people can meet and commune with one another.

But in today's world (that, for you, is tomorrow's) our meetings are a world removed from the way things were done back in the Twenties. Today, our meetings are more like group therapy. Back then, they were more like the Inquisition.

In the olden days we did not have meetings in a village square or at gathering places like the Convention Center. Heck, we didn't have villages. What we had was more like big meeting halls for the inquests, a place where people were hassled by leaders of the villagers that seemed more to me like village idiots than people who made any kind of sense.

The irony was not lost upon me as we held our meeting to discuss the aftermath of a big destructive storm like Lucky 13 and had a follow-on storm heading right for us. It was like déjà vu all over again. We had a meeting on a similar occasion back in the Twenties, right after the Big One hit us so hard but before the Little One came our way.

The two meetings were anything but similar:

Back then, I remember the nightly dinner we were having in the Hermitage, a few days before the big meeting. It was just me, Mom, and Harrison, with Bolt herding us into place around the table, as usual. Calusa had left with Kate to visit the Indian village in the Everglades. Probably seems strange looking back on it that a mother would let such a young girl go out to a swamp with an Amazon Warrior, on a vision quest, to discover what her true Indian name was. But things had progressed to the point where there was a lot of trust involved when it came to little Kate and the big Amazon.

Calusa and Kate had become very close, and with mom gone most of the time, working long hours over at the hospital mostly, the two of them had become inseparable.

Plus, we all knew Kate was safe when she was with Calusa.

"How are things coming along over at that clubhouse of yours?" Harrison asked. "Looks like another storm is coming our way. Is that thing going to stand up to it?"

"From what I read in those books of yours, it should stand up all right. Maybe lose some thatch here and there, but if the water does not rise too much, we should all be safe there until the storm passes and be able to function afterward – as much as we are able to, anyway – with the way things are. Art and Larry are there now with Cousteau and some of the others. They seem to feel the need to guard the place for some reason."

"Not from the natives but from the Peabodys of the world, I presume? Looks like those people are more likely to tear that thing down than the storm at this point."

"What do you mean?" I asked. My mom answered.

"Son, I got this notice from the association today," she said, holding up a piece of paper. "It says the chickee you built is illegal and goes against Association rules. They have called a meeting to make you take it down, or get fined $200 a day until you do. They also said you have illegal wind-generated electricity and solar panels that you are using to power the place, and you don't have proper permits and so on and so forth."

She handed me the paper. It looked about as official as one of my "permits."

"200 bucks a day? That's crazy. I'm sorry, Mom; I didn't mean to cause you all this grief over another one of my stupid experiments."

"Don't worry about it, sweetheart." She smiled at me sweetly. "It really doesn't matter much anyway. I can't pay the mortgage on that place, and the insurance company went bankrupt. I don't know when, if ever, the government is going to pay for the insurance or, if they do, we will get the money soon enough to stop the bank from foreclosing on it. There are a lot of people in the same boat. Most of them have just given up and moved away. It's not worth it. Not worth the headache."

"But you always said you love that place. Your whole life was wrapped up in it."

"That is not our place anymore. I hardly recognize it, and that's not because of all the things you and the other boys have done with it. That place disappeared when the Big One hit, and I know now things will never be the same." She glanced over at Harrison and then down at her plate. "Excuse me." She went to fetch a pitcher of iced tea. Harrison started to get up, but she motioned for him to stay put while she went into the kitchen.

We took turns serving. Tonight was Calusa's turn, but she was not in attendance, so my mom was next in the line of rotation. I would be cleaning up.

"Why, I think she is downright proud of what you and the boys have been doing over there at the Chickee Clubhouse. So am I." Harrison smiled at me reassuringly. "Let's see how that thing holds up in the storm as compared to the other villagers, and the idiots that are leading them over the cliff – reminds me of that story of the Pied Piper. The whole town followed him blindly and ended up drowning when they tried to double-cross him."

"So we should call our village 'Hamelin'?"

"I see you have read the story."

"Yes, but the piper lured the children away, not the adults."

"That is true, but in one version of the story, he lured the kids away to a promised land where they lived happily ever after, away from the scoundrels who ran the village."

"Does that make you the piper?" my mom asked pointedly. She had returned and was pouring Harrison a glass of tea, eyeing him carefully.

"Who, me? Certainly not; I have enough on my hands just trying to be a good little hermit, staying off the grid, minding my own business. I have no desire to clear the rats out from under the feet of the villagers, even if they paid me in gold, which they would not do anyway if the story of the Pied Piper is any indication."

"And what about the children?" my mom asked. "Seems like you have lured at least some of them away with all your ideas about being off the grid and doing your own thing." She was looking at me while she filled up my glass of tea.

"He has a mind of his own, and he is able to make it up as he sees fit.

Isn't that so, Captain?" He looked over at me with a big smile.

"I am the captain of my own ship, that's for sure."

"Well, I suppose that is as it should be. His father went away when he was young, and he has had to learn how to be a man mostly on his own." She sat down and looked over at Harrison with what seemed like a very tender expression on her face.

"I'm glad he had someone to help him along the way."

The next day we got some relief supplies sent down by the military. My mom had convinced Harrison to help. She also got Art and his dad to go down with one of their bigger boats to the port where the big navy vessel was docked. They managed, with Harrison's help, to get the navy guys to load provisions onto their boat to bring them back up the bay to where we were. There was more crappy food and paper products and, of course, more blue tarps. There was also bottled water – lots of it.

Harrison hated bottled water.

Art and his dad, with Harrison aboard, brought the laden boat back to the dock behind the Hermitage where they unloaded it into vehicles to take to the hospital. The storm was still way off in the distance, but the telltale signs that it was on its way to greet us were there. Not sure how to explain that exactly. It was just a feeling, prompted mainly by a sudden gust of wind and a light shower or two.

They were not the rainbands that would come later, but there was a palpable sense that something was coming, and we needed to get ready for it.

Some of the relief supplies were taken to the community center building where the homeowner Association usually met. They were supposed to distribute them to the villagers. Harrison also had Art and I deliver some of the supplies to the clubhouse. He told us to make sure to give it to Cousteau and his gang to take into Little Haiti.

It didn't amount to much, but at least it was something.

The next day was the big meeting at the community center building. The winds were starting to gust just a wee bit more than they had been, and there was fear in the air. Somehow, my mom convinced Harrison to go with me and her to the meeting.

It was the last thing he wanted to do, but he went along with it anyway.

The "community center" was actually the ground floor of a high-rise condo building set right at the edge of where the land ended and the bay began. The place had been flooded by the storm surge and reeked of mold. The AC was still not working, and it was sweltering, even with the doors flung open and the fans blowing. There was no electricity, but they had a generator to run the lights and keep the fans blowing.

The room was filled with anxious people, furiously fanning themselves with plastic fans, magazines, newspapers – anything handy that would make a slight breeze to brush the hot air away from their faces. At the head of the room was a table with Peabody sitting in the middle; two other older guys I recognized as being from the neighborhood sat on either side of him. There was also some sort of coast guard or other guy in a uniform standing almost at attention near the table. I wondered how he could keep his composure in that straightjacket, boiling in the heat. Deputy Barney was also there.

"This meeting will now come to order," Peabody said loudly. The room became silent. "I first want to thank the United States Navy for bringing in more relief supplies to our community. The gentleman here today is not from the navy, but he is a volunteer with the Coast Guard Auxiliary. He assures me that we have not been forgotten in our hour of need and that the U.S. military has been called upon to help our community recover from this awful hurricane that swept through here. All hands are on deck, I am told."

"What took them so long just to bring some bottled water and toilet paper?" someone shouted from the audience. There were some grumbles from the crowd.

"When are we going to get electricity?" someone else shouted.

"A lot of people have abandoned their houses. They are a mess, and we have not had anyone from the city come and pick up the debris strewn everywhere."

"Now, now, one at a time, please. I am told that the armed forces have been called in to meet the needs and are doing the best that they can with limited resources. FEMA is stretched thin, and they are coming to the rescue. They have a lot of ground to cover. We are not the only community that is suffering, as you may have heard."

The Coast Guard guy remained at attention and said nothing.

"There are a lot of downed power lines. The electric company is working around the clock to restore power, but they have to get power running to vital areas first, such as the hospital, before they can find their way to our community. From what I am told, the whole grid is more or less down, and even with help from power companies from other states, they are having a hard time getting through with all the damage that has been done.

"As for rebuilding our community, the construction crews are also working overtime and will get to us as soon as they can, I am sure. In the meantime, people must be aware that they cannot take the law into their own hands. You have to have a valid permit, and we cannot have people just doing their own thing and building things that are not in compliance with the rules of the Association and building codes."

"I heard a rumor that the place with the chickee house that those Haitians built is grandfathered in because it is part of Native American construction. Why can't we build something like that while we wait for the construction people to get here?"

Peabody saw us in the back of the room but did not address us directly.

"Native Americans are allowed to build things like that, but they have to have a project manager that is an Indian, and even if they do, the Association rules don't allow it." Peabody was looking around, trying to gauge the reaction.

Then another person shouted out loud what most of them were probably thinking: "Why don't you leave them alone? We have other problems to deal with aside from playing by Association rules. This is a state of emergency. There is another storm coming, and so far they are the only ones, other than that guy over there and his Amazon partner, that have a place that has a chance to hold up against the wind, rain and water."

All eyes turned to Harrison. He stood motionless.

"We still have to abide by the laws," Peabody said. He looked around anxiously. "What are we, if we don't stick to what the law says? Are we a bunch of savages? Besides which, there is no proof that that, that, *thing* this little boy built was under the direction of a bona fide Indian."

"It's not just that boy over there. We also seen your boy Larry there helping."

The lady who said that was motioning towards me, and then to Larry, who was standing on the side of the meeting room against the wall. He lowered his head.

"No one is above the law. The law is the law. 'No ticky no laundry' as they say in Chinatown. If he ain't got an injun, it ain't legal."

As if on cue Calusa entered the room, tall and proud as always. She walked slowly and deliberately to the front of the room. Behind her was a guy straight from central casting who had long dark hair, dressed in full tribal regalia, beads, braided hair – the works. If you wanted to hire someone to play the part, he would have been it. He was barefoot, to boot. I later learned he had not worn shoes.

Ever.

Since he was born.

Kate came in with them. She was similarly dressed.

"What have we here? A real live redskin? Just because he looks like an Indian doesn't mean he has the bonafides. How do we know he is real?"

"Oh, he's real all right." It was Kate speaking up, coming up to the front of the room, right in front of Peabody who sat there stunned. "He is a great medicine man that has come back with us all the way from the Everglades."

"Oh, and who might you be? Pocahontas?"

"No. My name is White Feather. But you can still call me Kate."

"What I am going to call is Child and Family Services. Where is your mother and father? Do they know you are out crawling around in a swamp with a bunch of savages?"

I think right about this point is where Peabody was really losing the crowd.

"I am her mother." My mom stepped forward. "Kate, could you please come back here with me?" She looked at Calusa. "Thank you so very much for taking such good care of my daughter and also for your help on behalf of our community." She turned to the medicine man. "Thank you, sir, as well, for your wise counsel."

"You must be tired from your long journey. Please allow me to offer you the hospitality at our humble home where we can provide shelter from the coming storm." Harrison had made his way a little closer to the front of the room but spoke in a booming voice I had never heard before. He did not need to get any closer.

Everyone heard him.

"Not so fast." Peabody's eyes were darting around, gauging the mood of the crowd, looking a little desperate. This whole thing was not going the way he had imagined.

"That place of yours is the only safe and secure building we have. You have running water and electricity, unlike the rest of us."

"And food," Kate added.

"As the president of the Association, I demand that you relinquish your compound to me and the other board members as a command center from which to operate. This community is sick and tired of your renegade ways, and it is time we take control."

Harrison tilted back his head and let out a roar of laughter. I never saw him laugh like that. Heck, I never heard him laugh, period.

Never had I seen him act this way in all the time I knew him.

When he stopped laughing, he lowered his head down and glared right at Peabody. "Why, Mr. Peabody, I am not a member of the Homeowner's Association. I suggest you make other arrangements, but you better hurry. That storm is heading right for us. Maybe you and your comrades here can bunker down in that house of yours? Certainly not this place; I wouldn't want to be anywhere near here when that storm hits."

Harrison turned to leave. The rest of us followed.

"Don't you turn your back on me! You and your, your harem!"

We all stopped for a second and turned to look at the sweaty association President. He pointed at my mom. "And you, you are a married woman shacking up with this weirdo renegade and his Amazon princess bride. Oh yeah, I know. I checked the records. Your husband is a deserter from the navy. Looks like he deserted you – and these two as well." He motioned towards me and Kate. "Can't say as I blame him."

My mom's face turned red as a beet.

"But he is still legally your husband. The law is the law. Here you are, all high and mighty, part of a harem shacked up in that illegal compound with a hermit and his African love slave, and two little children exposed to the whole sordid thing. You should be ashamed of yourself, and I mean it when I say I will call Children and Families."

Harrison came to her rescue, extending an arm to her, and with a slight bow said, "Would you please join us as my honored guest in my humble compound, along with your dear children and our new friends from the Everglades? I promise that you will all be very safe with Calusa and me, as will your children."

"Why, thank you, kind sir. You are, indeed, a gentleman and a scholar." She took his arm and glanced back at Peabody, her face no longer rose-hued.

Harrison looked at him, too, his jaw set.

"I think our business here has come to an end, and this meeting is going to be adjourned, I should think, so that the president here and the others here in this assemblage can get to work making ready for the approaching storm."

TWENTY

"Can I ask you something, Captain?"

This is how Angela started the day up in the Roost. We were poring over charts and histories of prior storms and models and graphics and so on and so forth, trying to get a read on which way No. 20 would be heading.

"Sure. If I can answer, I would be glad to."

"How do you know No. 20 is going to veer off at the last second?"

"I don't know. I just feel that that is what is going to happen."

"Are you some sort of oracle? People in the village talk, you know."

"Oh, what do they say? I am like the Wizard of Oz?"

"Who?"

"Never mind. It is an old story they made into a movie a long, long time ago."

"Tell me the story, Cappy."

"Okay, Little Pixie, but I will just give you the gist of it. A little girl and her dog get whisked away by a tornado and land in a magical place where she seeks out a wizard who turns out to be just a regular guy hiding behind some curtains while he works some machinery that creates this scary image of the great and powerful Oz. He really doesn't have magical powers and isn't really all that powerful, either. He is just really smart. Harrison has the book around here somewhere, down in the study."

145

"Harrison? Is that the guy who was the original Oz, before you took over?"

I stopped what I was doing and looked down on little Angela. I swear her eyes were twinkling. She had a nice smile on her face.

"I guess you could say that, but neither he nor I are the ones who could ward off the storms so that they would veer off at the last second. We had no power to do that."

"Someone had magic powers that have been protecting us all this time?"

"Not some*one*, some*thing*. It is a feeling, a way of being in tune with Mother Nature, of asking her for things and giving things in return because you are a part of her."

"Sounds like magic to me."

"For people who do not understand, maybe it looks that way. I cannot say I understand it completely myself, but I knew someone a long time ago who did, and who taught me and that Harrison guy you mentioned all about it. At least she tried to."

"She? It was a girl?"

"I suppose she was at some point, but when I met her, she was a tall, beautiful, powerful Amazon princess warrior."

"No way."

"Yes way. But her greatest power was the ability to speak to what she called the Great Spirit and to the Grandmother that she told me was the Earth. Even more than speak to them, she told me, was the ability to listen. When they were angry and not in the mood to spare the men who defiled the land, and the water, and the spaces where all living creatures were supposed to share with one another, she would ask them for forgiveness. Not for the men who had provoked them, but for the sake of the children."

"It's not their fault. The kids should not be punished for what the grown-ups did."

"Exactly. But what was done was done. The sins of the fathers are visited upon the sons and their sons and so on down the line – same with the daughters."

"That sounds like a really crappy rule."

"This is true, but it's not too late for you and your sons and daughters."

"I don't have any."

"Not yet. Now it is my turn to ask a question."

"Shoot."

"Did you know your father?"

She froze, pretending to look at the computer screen. I caught the glimpse of a little moisture in the corner of her eye. I started to regret I had asked the question.

"I saw him once. He lay dying in a bed. I was very little and hardly remember. All I can see in the picture I have of him in my mind was a sunken, sullen face with yellow skin stretched tight over his cheekbones and jaw." She was staring off into space as if conjuring the image of her father in her mind's eye, studying his features.

She snapped out of it.

"That's all I remember of him. I was little."

She went back to work.

I sank back down into a chair and pretended to look at the screens and consider which way Storm No. 20 was going to go. My mind was preoccupied with images of Angela's father who I could see clearly, maybe as clearly as she. Then I began to think back about my own father and the images I had stored in my mind about him. I was hoping Angela would not ask me to reciprocate by conjuring those images.

They came into my mind all the same:

I must confess that while I dared not show it at the time, I had a strong reaction to what Peabody said to my mom about my dad on that day so many years ago when we had the big meeting about the Big One, and the Little One that was bearing down on us.

We didn't have time to really talk about it at first. We had to get ready for the Little One, and I was eager to get the Chickee Clubhouse ready for the storm. I also wanted Mick Jagger's opinion about it before the storm hit. I brought him out to the chickee and showed him the place. Art, Cousteau, Merci, and some of the other boys were there, following him around like he was some sort of celebrity.

"Look, I'm not the real Mick Jagger," he told them. "Give me a little space." I shooed them away so he could inspect the place real properlike. He looked around, pulled at some of the thatch, and said "hmmmm" a lot.

"Well, what do you think? Is this any good? Is it going to stand up to this storm?"

"How should I know?" he said with a shrug. "I don't know anything about construction. Did you get a permit to build it?"

I have to admit I was crestfallen, probably visibly so.

He noticed.

"Look here, my young friend. I am not an engineer. I am a medicine man. This looks like you have followed all the ways in building this as did my ancestors. Calusa tells me you slaved over this thing and studied our ways until blood came out of your ears. Your heart and soul have been poured into this, which is the most important thing. Your spirit is caught up into what you have done, and you seek to honor the Great Spirit as best that that western brain and heart of yours could possibly manage to do."

"But I am not one of you, is that what you are saying?"

"No, that is not what I said. Did I say that? Is there someone else here talking that I should know about? Maybe you are hearing voices from the spirit world or something."

He gave me a big smile to let me know he was just having some fun with me. Then the medicine man came up closer to me. He put his hands on both of my shoulders, peering into my eyes, searching for something or someone inside.

"Ah, I see you in there. Yes, you are one of us. You are one with all that surrounds us, just like we are. You always were, always will be. All you needed to do was listen. Put your ear to the ground and hear what the earth was saying to you. But, alas, you could not hear her. Now, after getting the dirt out of your ears, you will be able to hear more clearly what Mother Earth is saying to you. Maybe you could do a vision quest like your little sister. That might help. Wouldn't hurt, that's for sure."

"What would my name be?"

"That has already been given to you. 'Captain' I think she said it was." He looked at my face, his eyes moving up to the ever-present cap on my head.

"Fitting," he said.

Dinner that night at the Hermitage was quite the occasion. The winds were starting to kick up, and I was anxious to get over to the Chickee Clubhouse before things got too rough. But I would not want to miss this for the world.

Mick Jagger was there along with some other people from his tribe. They had brought poles and their own teepee stuff but were persuaded to wait until after the storm had passed before setting them up. They were going to stay for a while and help us white people with dirt in our ears figure out how to make a real Indian village.

Kate and Calusa, of course, were there. Kate told us more about her vision quest and how she got her name White Feather, which was not that hard to figure out. We also found out that the cat had been renamed Black Thunder, which was not that hard to figure out either. Now we had a clap of Thunder to go with the Lightning Bolt.

Was it just my imagination, or had my little sister grown into a little woman?

I was surprised when the medicine man bragged about what a great chickee I had built. His buddies nodded in agreement. "You will do just fine in this storm," he said. "Besides which I am told the storm is going to veer off at the last minute."

"I want to thank you so much for agreeing to come help my son and the rest of the community, although they hardly deserve it." My mom was wearing some sort of beaded braid in her hair – courtesy, no doubt – of White Feather. "I am hopeful that all these efforts are not in vain and that we can survive this storm and the storm of the people around us who seem to wish harm to befall us."

"They do not wish it but invite harm upon themselves," said the medicine man.

"I have not mentioned this before, but I have what I guess is an announcement to make," my mom began. "The place where the Captain has made the chickee may withstand the wind and water, but I am not too certain it can stand up to the bank. We have a mortgage, and eventually they will foreclose and take it away."

"Maybe they will sell it to our tribe, and we can turn it into a casino." The medicine man was always trying to lighten things up.

"That could be, but what I have in mind is a bit different although equally radical. You see, a nice lady who gave up her life in the last storm was very dear to me. She was also very fond of the Captain here and White Feather. I found her Will in a safe in the wreckage of her house. She left us her house, and as it turns out, she owns the vacant lot next door and a couple of other properties in the neighborhood. Now that we have gained some experience in Native American construction, I think these would be good places to rebuild our community in a way that it should have been built in the first place."

I must say I was left rather speechless.

The medicine man wasn't, of course.

"We would be most honored to assist in whatever way that we can to make this vision into a reality, but it seems that you have others here that do not appreciate our skin color, much less our ways. We may have to make war against them." He turned in his chair to look at one of his lieutenants. "Did we bring any war paint with us?"

"I have some." It was Calusa.

The medicine man turned back around. "Oh, good, something tells me we will need to use some of it. Maybe a couple barrels full."

"I don't know," I heard myself saying. "I got a feeling about what happened at that meeting. We have reached a tipping point, methinks. Many of the villagers here are a lot more color blind than that Peabody guy. I can see it in their eyes."

"Pea-Brain, you mean." It was Kate chiming in.

"You would have to be blind, color or otherwise, to not see what is going on," Harrison said. "But I agree with the Captain. We won't have many more problems with the Pea-Shooter. His guns are not that big to begin with, and he is in way over his head."

"Be that as it may, I am concerned that I and my children may have overstayed our welcome here, and would not want to be an imposition. We have the opportunity to build a place of our own, one as strong and resilient as this one, and we should seize that opportunity not only for our own sake but to set an example for others, just like the one Harrison and Calusa have set for all of us. Will you help us?"

"Of course, Mother of White Feather. We have not come up with a good name for you yet, but maybe soon you can stop by our village and do a vision quest of your own."

"I would like that."

After a pregnant pause that seemed to last forever, Harrison spoke up.

"You should know that you are always welcome to stay here. I hope that the rude things that Peabody said are not driving you away."

"Pee-Pee Herman," White Feather offered.

"Is his Indian name Herman, and he goes in his pants?" The medicine man had taken the bait, and we were off to the races with all sorts of urination jokes, and new and inventive ways in which the venerable vegetable that grows in pods but is often much maligned became disparaged yet again in a conversation that lasted well into the night, the wind howling harmlessly outside.

My mom took me aside during the din of all the jokes and carrying-on.

"Son, what he said about your father being a deserter and all that . . ."

"Let's not talk about that right now. But I do want to talk about it later, after this storm passes. I think Kate needs to hear this, too."

She nodded her head in agreement. I excused myself and headed out into the storm. Bolt came with, as did one of the people in the medicine man's entourage. Pavlov Dog, I think his name was. They must have had a Rolling Stones album or two playing when they got their Indian names. That was none of my business. I was glad he came along.

Art was in the chickee as well as Larry and a crowd of people from Cousteau's clan. Seems they had nowhere else to go. We cheated a little because we were in the house with the cement walls to protect us, inside of the walls of the chickee. Things were boarded up pretty tight. Art and the other boys had gotten the instruments off the roof and stored them away in the trusty shed that had worked so well last time. We had candles and were hunkered down pretty good when there came a pounding at the front door which had been sealed shut. "Who goes there?" Art shouted over the din of the winds.

"It's me. I was at the meeting. We didn't have time to evacuate. Can we come in?"

Art looked at me. I shrugged. He pulled open the door, and there were at least a half-dozen people, clutching their windbreakers and rain gear. They had looks on their faces that I will never forget. Wind-whipped fear and rainwater etched their expressions. They started piling in, and I was not sure where to put them all. We all couldn't fit into the house itself, so some had to huddle in the spaces between the house and the Chickee, which seemed to be holding up just fine. We had a few more late arrivals wanting to check in, but eventually things got too hairy outside. People who had not already evacuated had either decided to stay put or were out there, lost in the darkness.

I was huddled next to Larry, Art, and some of the Haitians by a candle. I could tell the winds had reached their peak. Then they would subside. Then push again.

"About what happened at the meeting . . ." Larry started to explain.

He didn't have to.

"Larry, you are not Pudge," I said.

"Oui. Sak pase, mon ami?" Cousteau chimed in. "Sak pase" was about the only thing we really knew in Creole. It means "what's up with that?" more or less.

"I don't know. I guess I always had a real weight problem."

"Well, not anymore, man. That guy is a real jerk. Where does he get off talking to you like that? Is he your dad or something messed up like that?" Cousteau asked.

Larry didn't answer. He hung his head down real low.

"You are Ours now," said Cousteau.

"You mean I am part of your tribe?"

"No, no, 'Ours' is French for Bear. You are Our Bear."

"Well, it sure sounds a lot better than 'Peabody,' that's for sure," I said. "I can tell you that without a doubt – had enough peeing jokes tonight to last a lifetime."

Larry looked up. I don't think I ever saw him hang his head down like that for the rest of his life. He smiled and nodded appreciation to all his true friends.

"Thanks guys. That means a lot to me."

"Oui, Oui. Merci. Merci. Merci beaucoup Ours Bear."

There were a lot of "mercies" that night.

TWENTY-ONE

CL 20/0021
The Hermitage Captain's Quarter
Sunday

I woke up this morning in my own bed where I spent the night. I usually don't do that when there is a storm. I know what you are wondering. Was I alone? The answer is yes. We did not have guests for a hurricane party like we did for Lucky 13. No. 20 was not that big of a deal, at least not by our standards. Heck, did not even merit a nickname. Neither Maryann nor anyone else spent the night.

Not including Angela, of course.

I found her up in the Roost. Sure enough, she was in my usual spot, there on the cot, fast asleep. She was probably exhausted. I went back downstairs to fetch her a nice cup of hot tea. She does not drink coffee as much, but I do. I made some of the good stuff with Kid Carson milk, grabbed some bananas, and went back upstairs.

She was sitting up on the cot, looking a little groggy. I set down the tray and offered her some tea and a banana. She set down the cup of tea and held the banana, just sort of staring at it for a few seconds. Then she looked up at me.

"Who do I thank for this?"

"Why, bananas are complimentary here at the Hermitage, especially for hardworking volunteers who help with these constant storms."

"I wasn't the one who helped with this storm, someone else did. I do appreciate the banana, but what I am thankful for is how this storm veered off at the last second, just like you knew it would. Or, should I say, just like the Amazon warrior princess willed it."

I had sat down in one of the chairs, sipping my Carson brew and watching her carefully while she was talking. I had already explained these things to her just about to the best of my ability, but she needed to hear it from an expert.

She deserved that much.

"All right, I'll tell you what I am going to do. You have questions and want answers. The great and powerful Oz does not have all the answers. By the way, did you find that book yet?"

"Not yet, but I intend to. What's the name of it again?"

"It's 'The Wonderful Wizard of Oz.' I forget the author. You'll find it in the library. In the story there is a nice lady from one of the directions – I think north or south, I forget which – that they call a 'witch' but who was a woman with knowledge about magic and magical powers and so on. The little girl, her name was Dorothy, and her dog Toto go to this nice lady and she helps Dorothy find the answers to her questions."

"So all I have to do is check out the Oz book from the library, read the part about the non-witch from some unknown point on the compass, and then I will be able to figure out how the Amazon warrior princess deflects storms away from us. Do I have that right? That's all I have to do, and all my questions will be answered?"

"No, Grasshopper. Books cannot be checked out from the library. Nor are questions such as these to be answered like those on a pop quiz. You have to find the answers yourself, from in here." I patted my chest for emphasis. "I cannot tell you what to believe. A book can't either. Nobody can, but I can take you to some people who can explain things better to you than I can. Would you like to do that?"

She nodded her head so vigorously I got dizzy myself just watching her.

"Very well, then. Send a message to White Feather that we are coming to visit."

"White Feather? Who's that?"

I was at the top of the stairs, coffee mug in hand. I had to start down to venture out for my morning constitutional so as to survey the effects of No. 20 on the village. I paused at the first step down, mainly for dramatic effect. I turned slowly to Angela, trying to draw out the suspense. It was real suspenseful, I can assure you of that.

"Why, my sister Kate, of course."

I snickered a little on my way down the stairs, wondering if my little performance had sufficiently piqued her curiosity. We would make that trip, but first I wanted to take a look around, especially at the plaza. This talk of magic and wizards had piqued my own interest in revisiting where it really all began for us, back in the Roaring Twenties.

At the plaza I could see there was really not too much damage that Lucky 13 had not already done. People were already clearing the debris that was there, and one or two were already setting up their tables and tents for the day's market. They were bringing out their stuff from the Convention Center: the over-sized chickee that we used for gatherings, shelter from storms, and powwows. I didn't notice any damage at all to it.

No. 20 had veered south, so far south that even though we caught some of the "dirty" side of the storm, we were not hit very hard at all. The follow-on storm to the Big One back in the Twenties, the one I like to call the Little One, did the opposite.

That storm went north of us, but in many ways it had more than a little impact:

That must have been some sight back then, the morning after the Little One hit us. Imagine about two dozen or so people, packed like sardines into the Chickee Clubhouse, finally emerging into the damp morning air, the sun just managing to peek out of the cloud cover, just in one little crevice of a spot up in the sky.

There was a lot of stretching involved.

We looked around, and things looked pretty raggedy. Any semblance of order we had managed to make in the aftermath of the Big One was undone, for the most part. Sort of like having someone muss up your hair right after just getting back from a bad hairdo. The intention is not good, but maybe they are doing you a favor.

In our case the lone exception was the Chickee Clubhouse, which held up just fine, thank you very much, standing tall and proud, rising up from all the chaos and rubble.

Everyone was anxious to get back to see how their own places fared, knowing what was the likely answer to that one. You could tell just by seeing the sea of blue tarps scattered everywhere what they would likely find when they got to their own place. Lots of people came up to me and thanked me profusely. They shook my hand vigorously, eyeing Pavlov, who was standing erect right next to me, with his arms crossed over his chest, as if he was guarding some sort of chief from a new tribe. Most of them wanted to know if we could come by their places to see if there was something we could do for them.

In due course we did, and we did.

We ended up starting what you could call a "barn raising" program. For some people this meant we would build chickees in the style of the clubhouse. For others we would put up structures on an adjacent lot or maybe even several, depending on the situation. The structures were built up as much as possible. Canals and ditches were dug, in due course, with the dirt and debris used to build up the land or as fill for the posts.

Other spots that were a hopeless mess were cleared, with the debris and tree parts used as construction material. Once cleared, the vacant spaces were set to be no longer vacant. They would become spaces where new trees were planted of various species, including the fast-growing bamboo trees that we got from a nearby nursery. As it turned out, they were more than willing to barter with us for the things they needed that we had, in exchange for their bamboo saplings or other tree species we needed to reforest our village.

There was much bartering going on, not just for trees but for many other things. In time we found ourselves trading with other places that eventually turned into villages in their own right, just as we were starting to build ours. We had made fast friends with our neighbors from the other side of the Great Divide. They helped us rebuild into what eventually became our village. We helped them do likewise. Soon we had developed an expertise of village building. We traded this expertise and the labor to make it all happen with other people all around us and even in faraway places.

What later became a village-making "movement," I guess you could call it, really began in earnest at the Jacobs' place, although Chickee Clubhouse should probably be regarded as the first village-style thing that was created – not counting the Hermitage itself, of course. The Jacobs' site was the first really noticeable structure that drove home the point that we had made a departure from the way things had been done in the past.

We had to.

The roof had been crushed, and we decided to use the foundation, built up a few more feet, as the floor for the largest chickee-type structure that we could build, one of the largest known to exist, outside of the replica of the one built by the Apalachee at the San Luis Mission in North Florida. The surrounding area was cleared of debris, leaving the trees still left standing after the storms. We left them right where they were. We knew that we needed to restore as much land as we could to its natural state to absorb as much of the coming onslaught of rising water and rain as we could.

Our first big chickee, which later became known as the Convention Center, went up surprisingly fast. We had a lot of help. Mick Jagger presided, but as you may have heard, he really did not know much about construction. He did provide plenty of entertainment value, especially when the inevitable happened and Peabody showed up.

"Don't you *people* get it? This is all a big waste of time. You will end up having to tear this whole thing down once the authorities finally find their way here and see what a mess you are making. And don't tell me you have a permit. I know you don't." He was standing in his usual spot on the road, hands on hips, sweating as usual.

We let the medicine man deal with it.

"Great White Father of Sunken Building with Fans, we hear your words and seek only peace between our nation and yours. But we have been offered no treaty or – how you say in your tongue – 'permit' from the White Man to the North, South, East, or West so that we may find shelter from the anger of the Great Spirit here in these lands. Come, let us smokem peace pipe in yon wigwam and take counsel." He motioned towards one of the teepees that he and his entourage had put up in a cleared place in the space next door.

"I don't know what you are smoking in that pipe of yours, but I will have none of it, nor of you and your nonsense. That storm hit Palm Beach to the north of us real hard, and you may not know this, but there are a lot of very important people there. And as soon as the authorities, *including the armed forces*, by the way, are done being preoccupied with getting those poor folks back on their feet, you can be sure they will be here to deal with the likes of you and your wigwam and that, that *monstrosity* you people are making."

"I see, White Father with Sweaty Hands; that explains much, including why our smoke signals to the White Man have gone unanswered, as have our phone calls and email messages. We fear we have been abandoned, left to our own – how do you say – 'devices' which, for the most part, do not work very well around here. We are told that the people to the north who you say are – in your tongue – 'poor' are not so described in our own native language, and so we do not have a proper translation of the meaning of your words."

The medicine man sat back down, legs crossed, reaching over to pull out a doll that he found at the Haitian market.

"Excuse me, sir, but I am not done with you, yet. This is no time to start playing with your dollies." The medicine man looked at him, holding up the doll.

"Oh this? We took counsel from the wise ones across the Great Divide." He motioned towards Cousteau who was up on the roof and in the general direction of Little Haiti. "They have powerful medicine." He looked back down at the black doll.

Someone had sewn a bobble head of a white baseball player on top of it.

He held up the doll again. He looked at Peabody, then at the doll, stroking his chin in mock contemplation. Peabody looked startled for a second. Then he noticed one of the masks that had already been tacked up on a Convention Center support beam.

"You can't scare me with this Voodoo garbage either. I am a Christian with strong Christian values. I don't believe in that stuff, so you can take your Voodoo dolls and your African masks and your wampum and other foolishness and go back to the jungle where you came from. We don't want your kind around here. Same goes for *them*."

He was motioning with his head towards Cousteau.

"You speak with angry tongue, oh White Man with Fear of Pin Cushions, but this cannot be an image of you. See?" The medicine man held up the doll, waving it around. "The head is that of a white man but the body that of a black man. We know not of your ancestors, but surely you would not say you are half a black man, would you?"

"Certainly not!"

"Well then, this black body is not yours, except, well, maybe one part."

"What are you talking about? I don't have a black bone in my body."

"It is not your bones that are black." The medicine man paused for full effect. Peabody shrugged his shoulders as if to ask, "Then *what*?"

"It is your heart."

TWENTY-TWO

CL 20/0022
The Hermitage Study/Friday

Today was a first. For my weekly kayak outing, I had to trade in the kayak I was using for that old gheenoe Harrison has had around here for a hundred years. I needed more room for my passenger Angela who wanted to come along for some reason. My solitude was messed up some, but in the end I was glad she came with me.

Too much solitude is bad even for an old hermit such as myself.

We toured around and up through the Little River that brought us over to some of the villages on the other side of what used to be the Great Divide. Nowadays we just thought of the place where we lived as one village connected to another in a string of pearls, so to speak, gems of different places for different people that were all really the same on the inside. We had no time for trying to find something that made us different.

We had no inclination anymore to do such things anyway, once we had learned, a long time ago, that our survival depended on not making war against each other. I was going to make another one of my infamous mental notes, which I usually forgot about later, when I decided instead to share the thought that had crossed my mind with Angela.

"Was it Benjamin Franklin who drew that picture of the colonies as they existed hundreds of years ago with the caption 'Join or Die'?"

"Yes. Supposedly, Franklin drew that as a crude sort of political cartoon. He was trying to unify the colonies to fight the Europeans who had colonized them and – ironically enough" she paused and turned around from the bow to look at me, obviously learning how to create dramatic effect from someone – "their Native American allies."

I stopped paddling for a moment as well. "True enough, although the image I have in my brain is of a snake cut into pieces. I guess that means that, aside from almost electrocuting himself with a kite he flew in a lightning storm, the old boy wanted to put together a real viper of a creature to slither forth and wipe out the native inhabitants."

"I will have to check the manuals when we get back to see what Harrison had to say on the subject." I said, finishing my lecture.

"Do you think someday you will let *me* read some of the manuals?"

"All in due time, Grasshopper." I had started calling her "Grasshopper" instead of "Pixie" for some reason. I think it was because Harrison called me that sometimes.

"'Grasshopper?' Why do you call me that? Is it my legs?" She stretched her little legs out to their fullest length. Good thing gheenoes are hard to tip over.

"Uh, well, I can barely remember, but there was some old TV series a long, long, long time ago set in the Wild West that had this ninja character who learned stuff from a Buddhist master who used to call him 'Grasshopper' for some reason. I am not sure why, but I don't think it had anything to do with his spindly legs. Not that yours are spindly, nor anything other than a splendid example of the most beautiful of arachnids."

"Are you sure? Aren't arachnids spiders?"

"Not sure about that – we might have to check the manuals – but what I am sure of is that your legs are not spidery or spindly. They are just plain beautiful and plenty long enough. Why, they stretch all the way down to the ground when you are standing up."

I thought I finessed that whole thing wonderfully.

She put her legs back in the gheenoe where they were supposed to be. Good thing she didn't try to prove that her legs really did reach all the way to the ground when she was standing up. We would have gone for a swim for sure if she tried to check out that theory while we were still paddling around in the gheenoe.

"Not to fret, She-Who-Does-Not-Like-To-Be-Called-Grasshopper. Soon you will be on a vision quest and will have a new Indian name bestowed upon you."

"What do you mean?"

"Patience, She-Who-Is-Not-Grasshopper. All will be revealed when we cast off for that voyage to see my sister White Feather."

As we continued along the Blueway, we passed through communities, most of which embraced the idea of being called villages. Villagers waved to us as we passed by.

"Boy, you must be some sort of celebrity."

"To be honest, people like to wave to people in boats. Happens all the time. Most of them don't know me from Adam, but they all sure knew Harrison. The legend of Harrison grew far and wide, even though I'm sure he hated the notoriety."

"I have heard of him, but who is that guy 'Adam'?"

"Never mind, it's just an expression. We can look that up in the manuals when we get back. Either that, or maybe the Book of Genesis."

"I'd rather hear more stories about Harrison the Hermit. You know, from back in the olden days when he was doing all these things that made him so famous."

So I told her:

Back then the medicine man, along with his entourage, usually took nightly meals at his campsite where his teepees were, next to the Convention Center. Every so often he would hold forth by a campfire, a crowd gathering to hear his words of wisdom, but more often than not they liked to hear the stories, jokes, and parodies he would spin.

But on the night of his unforgettable scene with Peabody, it happened that there was a dinner party, so to speak, at the Hermitage. All the main characters were there, including myself, of course. The biggest character was the medicine man, at least at first.

After he retold the story and we went through a number of new vision quest style names for the hapless Peabody, things turned more philosophical.

"I can't help but think," Harrison began "that I have been at war with the Peabodys of the world for such a long time, and only now have begun to realize why. This may sound odd but by going 'off the grid,' so to speak, Calusa and I have made a break from much more than just the way people like him were doing things. Their ways not only did not make sense to us, they were downright abhorrent. But while we thought of ourselves just wanting to be left alone, that was not good enough for them. We were doing things differently than what they demanded, and that bothered them."

"Perhaps there is a good reason for that," the medicine man said. "You severed your ties to the 'grid,' as you put it, but you also severed yourselves from the ways of the white masters who conquered this land, pushing my people out of their way. They were intent on exterminating not just my people but our way of life."

"A cultural and spiritual genocide," Calusa added, much to my surprise.

I had never thought of her as a leader in a cause of such depth. I was beginning to see her and a lot of other things in a whole new light.

There was a silent pause for a moment. Then Harrison continued. "Perhaps what we are witnessing is the end of one revolution and the beginning of another or, rather, a return to a way of doing things as they were done in the past, that hold better promise than the way of the conquerors of this land. We are witnessing the end of the Industrial Revolution and all the horrors visited upon us by it, and the undoing of how that horror destroyed the balance of the natural world which now is to be restored."

"You are not a witness to that." The words came from my mom. "You are the catalyst that is making it happen, at least in this corner of the world."

"I am no revolutionary. I am just trying to mind my own business."

"But don't you see you can't do that anymore? People look up to you and the example you and Calusa have set, the example set by the people who have come into our community with open hearts and open minds that are following along a path that was laid out by the two of you. And that includes me and my children."

I felt a little put-on-the-spot by that last part.

Not sure about White Feather.

"I am a hermit, remember? Hermits make for bad revolutionaries."

"She speaks wisdom, oh Harrison the Hermit Crab. Do not let such crabbiness lead you back into a hole where others can no longer see you."

I never got over how well Mick Jagger came up with stuff like that on the spot.

"Okay, fine. I will crawl out of my hole, mainly at night when there aren't so many people around, do some scavenging on the beach for stuff to bring back into my hole and maybe let people come to the library and read some of my books, but there will be no checking out of books from the library anymore."

He looked at me for some reason.

"I'm afraid it's a little late for you, oh Crabby Man of the Hermitage." My mom was breaking some bad news for him. "There is a reporter on the way. She will be here tomorrow. She is from the national radio station and is doing a story on the spread of the village concept or whatever you want to call it. Seems that there is a lot of chatter on the Internet about what we are doing, and she wants to learn more about it. Perhaps, through her efforts, we can spread the word to other communities that are suffering."

Harrison liked to about choke on what he was eating.

"I am perfectly fine pontificating here, among friends, or at least people who I regard as trusted friends, about all of these things, but going out there and broadcasting these ideas to the world is not a good move at this point. We can deal with small people like the guy with the pea-shooter, but if we draw too much attention to ourselves, we are going to find that bazookas are being pointed at our heads. I don't know about you," he continued, looking at the medicine man, "but I am neither bulletproof nor bazooka proof."

"Wise words these, my friend, who I trust and know is a trusted friend. We can always retreat to the swamp and avoid the bazooka fire, as we have in ages past, but I find that I kinda like it here. I would like to come and visit whenever we please, provided the invitation is always extended," he said, leaning towards Calusa with a smile that she actually returned. "It's not as cozy here as the swamp in the Everglades, but it is nice as a change of pace every once in a while. Besides we have an investment here we need to watch over."

"You mean we might finally get a casino here?" I thought I would add to the conversation, maybe lighten things up a little more, taking a cue from the medicine man.

"We have an investment in *you*, Young Warrior with Hat of a Leader, who has brought us here to help build bridges and other useful things."

"Oh, I see where this is going," said Harrison.

"My dear," he said, turning to my mother, "there are sure to be many useful quotes from Mick Jagger, Pavlov Dog, White Feather, and a host of other interesting people with names people will think are a little off, but please leave Hermit the Crab out of it. And, while I understand why you are doing what you are doing, please don't let this reporter do a story that identifies who we are and where we are. Can't we do this in a way where we are anonymous? There is no reason we need to be called out with a big target on our backs.

"Do we have an accord?" Harrison was nearly pleading with her.

"That is a good idea," she replied. "I will get her to promise to leave out the names of the people involved and where we are. It will make the story more intriguing and emphasize that we are at risk from retaliation by the bad guys and their pea-shooters."

"Then we have an accord. She is welcome to stay here at the Hermitage under those conditions, unless, of course, she wants to bunk in the teepees."

"Or at the clubhouse," I offered.

His protestations to the contrary notwithstanding, Harrison was the perfect host, ushering around the journalist to points of interest, giving grand lectures to her, showing her books and how the Hermitage functioned independently of the grid, proudly showing her how the community turned their refuse into building materials and had become so self-reliant, having no need of lame hand-outs from relief workers and the government, showing her how the village had become one and had joined with the Haitian community and tribal members who had grown in number while she was visiting, building their own little village next to the Convention Center while she was there.

When it came time for her to bid bon voyage, boarding the boat that would take her back to her studio to do her story, Harrison was there, along with my mom and the rest of us at the dock. He reminded her again not to use his name and to protect their location, so as to prevent reprisals against what they were doing, which was just trying to survive.

"Funny you should mention that," she said, waving her recorder in the air. "I just got an earful from that guy Peabody, most of which I can't air due to the content and the fact we are committed to diversity and not inclined to give a platform to people who have, hmmm, shall we say, ideas that are less than inclusive. I understand your concerns. I will check with my editors, but I can assure you we will do all that we can to make sure that you will not be identified and targeted for the views you have expressed."

She paused for a moment and turned to look at the gathering of people at the dock who had entrusted so much to her on faith that she would protect them. She no doubt saw the anxious expressions on our faces.

"Let me tell you why your story is so important to be told. There are so many people out there that are lost. They are afraid. They do not know what is happening to them. They see no light at the end of the long, dark tunnel they have found themselves in. There is no leadership to help them understand what is happening to them, much less see that they are even in a tunnel to begin with, let alone see a light at the end of it. You have shown them a light. Something they can cling to, something they can believe in.

"That is a story that is worth the risk to tell."

"We hear your words, oh White Woman with Recording of Rants from the Dark Side," said the medicine man. "Although perhaps telling people to 'head for the light" sounds like they are close to the end of the road, we trust you to say the right words to your people in your story. Our fate is in your capable hands."

"We just hope that you do not have butter fingers."

She smiled and boarded the boat.

"Well, Hermit not of Frogs but of Crabs, you have survived your interview. Now we shall see if you can do the same with what will surely be your celebrity," the medicine man said, turning to his good friend.

"You are much too modest, Mick Jagger Who Really Isn't. I am sure you have many more quotable things she will use than my anonymous rants."

We all drew closer together to watch as she departed as if we were posing for a group picture. The lady actually took one from the boat.

My mom was standing next to Harrison.

I swear I could see them holding hands.

TWENTY-THREE

CL 20/0023
The Hermitage Foyer/Thursday

After my morning constitutional today, I took up a position at the big, old table in the foyer area with my big mug of Carson coffee, which was great as usual. I had spread out a bunch of oversized charts and had notes of the float plan the Arts had shown me for our trip over to the west coast. Turns out they already had a plan for a journey in that direction that was part of our regular trade route. We would load food, herbal medicines, bamboo, fuel we had distilled, parts, or other things we had to trade onto one of our bigger vessels so we could stop in at the villages or towns on our network of places on the trade route.

Probably the most valuable thing we had to trade, when we were not giving it away, was knowledge. Sometimes I would allow books to be traded, as long as I got some back in exchange. But by far the knowledge that had the most demand was the Harrison Chronicles. People just loved to get their hands on an authentic copy, straight from the famed Hermitage, printed on actual paper, bound in book form the old-fashioned way.

There were chronicles on all sorts of topics of use to people in this day and age.

That reminds me, we need to trade for more paper and binding.

At first I just wanted to spread the word, like my mom always wanted to do. But after a while, I thought the best thing for the village was to trade copies of the Chronicles for things that we really needed, things we could only import from somewhere else and could not make ourselves.

Like paper.

We were about as self-reliant a community as they come. But as they say "No man is an island," and we had discovered many, many years ago that each community had at least one thing that others did not have, something different to offer to other communities. Banding together to barter with one another made each village that much stronger.

Our bond became stronger, too.

Angela came down when she saw me at the big table. She more or less lived at the Hermitage full-time nowadays, which was a good thing. The village needed her.

I needed her.

"What's all this?"

"These are charts showing our route when we go to visit White Feather and do that vision quest of yours. See here?" I placed a finger on one of the charts. "We are going to go up the coast to this point here where we will enter the Okeechobee Waterway, then cut across the peninsula to this big lake, then hug the coast of the lake southward until we get to this point here at Moore Haven, then go down the Caloosahatchee, eventually coming out the other side of the state, where we sail north up to Pine Island."

"They did email the route to me and I mapped it out on the computer already. What do we need all these big paper charts for?"

I think I may have slumped a little at the question.

"I think it is good to get a bigger perspective than what you see on a tiny little computer screen. Besides which, these eyes of mine are not as young as they used to be, definitely not as youthful as yours. I can see this more clearly on these big charts. I like to have a real good idea of where I am going before setting sail."

"Why are we going through the middle of the state? The worst part of the hurricane season is over, and we should be safe out at sea."

"It is not to avoid the hurricanes or other things out there that may pose a threat to us. It's part of our regular trade route. We will be making a lot of stops on the way."

"What other things out there that are not hurricanes are a threat?"

Her eyes were getting a little bigger than usual. She was not big on boating and nautical stuff, but up until now she had showed no fear of such a long trip on the water.

"You can meet all sorts of people on the water and at a port. Almost all of them are friendly and will offer help if you need it or ask for help if they are in need. It is part of the code of mariners going back centuries, but not everyone abides by the code."

"You mean there are still pirates out there?" Her eyes were getting even bigger.

"Throughout history there have always been pirates and people like that. There aren't any more out there now than there has always been. Don't worry, we will be very safe. Besides which, we are small fry. We are not worth the bother. And if they ever did accost one of our vessels, which they never have, we would give them what they want – excepting the women, of course – and they would leave us alone."

Not sure why I put in that part about not giving them our women.

Not too smart.

"You mean they might want all our booty and mine to boot?" I had to laugh at that.

"Not to worry, we would never give you up. Your booty and the rest of you is way too valuable, even if they had a library full of books to trade." I smiled at her. "Don't forget, you are under the protection of the legendary Harrison Hermitage, known far and wide as the guiding light showing us all the way through these dark ages."

"You mean we also are under a magic spell to ward off pirates that might otherwise be coming for us as well as the hurricanes? That's reassuring."

"Well, Grasshopper, a life of not taking risks to explore the world is barely worth living. Have faith, ye who has so little.

You will no doubt learn more on your vision quest about these things. Remember the Rime of the Ancient Mariner. Pirates are a superstitious lot. They have never attacked a vessel flying the flag with the Mask of the Ancient Ones."

She looked down at her legs. "I sure hope I get a better Indian name than 'Grasshopper.' That one is really starting to annoy."

I didn't give her the full story. At some point I would show her that part of the Chronicles, or maybe just tell her the story, seeing as how I was there when all these things happened. They were not the best of memories:

I remember the first sign of trouble was the day I saw the Coast Guard cutter at the docks back behind the Hermitage. I knew it was a smaller vessel in their fleet, but it looked massive and intimidating, tied to that little dock. When I went inside there was Harrison, sitting at the big, old table, talking to that Coast Guard guy I had seen at the big meeting we had. You know, the one when Peabody tried to commandeer the Hermitage.

"Come on in, Captain," Harrison said when he saw me walk through the door. He turned back to his guest. "There's no need to stand up and salute. The Captain here has not enlisted yet, on account of the age restrictions mainly. I think you still outrank him."

"What's going on? Are we in some sort of trouble?"

"No, not at all. Quite to the contrary." The Coast Guard guy — I forget his name — was looking over at me. "We were chatting about a few things, and Harrison here was giving me a briefing on all the good things you-all have been doing here. And I have been going over a few things going on out there." He nodded his head towards the water.

He paused for a moment, shooting Harrison a questioning look.

"It's okay, he needs to know this, and he may as well hear it from you."

"Very well then, as I was saying, we are aware that your community has been underserved by the state and federal response to the disasters that have hit Florida and elsewhere these past months. We are also aware that your community and the others in this area have, shall we say, taken matters into your own hands."

We both looked at him, and then at each other.

"Not to worry, as I said, there are a lot of good things you are doing here, and it is a good thing that you are doing them, because I am here to tell you that any real help from the outside will be a long, long time coming, if it ever gets here at all."

"Why is that?" I asked.

"Those storms that hit Florida in rapid succession ravaged the peninsula, leaving a swath of destruction the likes of which we have never seen before and from which we may never fully recover. Even if we had the resources to put these communities back together again – which we do not – we have been advised by our superiors at the highest levels that there are more to come. Anything we rebuild up will just be knocked right back down again. Let's face it, you are in hurricane alley. We have it on good authority that the best thing to do is to retreat from the coastline and move further inland."

"You mean we should just give up and leave our homes, our whole neighborhood, just like that?" I was in shock at what he was saying, and it probably showed.

"You don't have to bug out if you don't want to. What I am saying is that you are now on notice, if you were not already, that you are in harm's way. We cannot protect you from what is to come next or even give you a good idea of when the next storm will rip through here, but we do know that eventually this will happen again, and when it does, the federal government is not going to be able to be of much help to you. We are stretched thin, to the breaking point really, with our other commitments."

"You mean like fighting wars overseas? Like the ones my father was sent to fight?"

"I don't know anything about your father. But you are right, we are fighting battles all over the world, and we now have to contend with battles closer to home."

"What do you mean?"

"I cannot get into details, but it seems some of our enemies have decided that being overextended the way we are has made it feasible to launch attacks closer to our shores, and even inland. The whole world is becoming a battlefield, including our country."

"What he is saying is that we are basically on our own." Harrison was sitting erect in his chair, his hands on the table top, fingers interlaced. He was staring straight ahead with what appeared to be a faraway look in his eyes.

"Exactly," said the Coast Guard guy.

Harrison snapped out of his trance.

"Okay then, looks like we have our work cut out for us."

"There is one more thing."

"More good news?" Harrison was fully back to his usual sardonic self.

"During the storm some prisoners managed to escape from the brig."

"Were any of them deserters?" I blurted out.

"There may have been some of those, but for the most part they are hardened criminals and killers. Very dangerous men you would not want to cross paths with. We have reports that they have commandeered at least one vessel and are out on the high seas, terrorizing passing ships and boaters, plundering, and generally making life even more difficult than it already is for us. You have to be on the lookout for them."

"You mean, they are like pirates?" I couldn't believe what I was hearing.

"Yeah, I guess you could call them that. They are renegades. And unless and until they are caught, no one is safe. For the most part they stay out at sea, but sooner or later they will show up at a port of call and wreak havoc." He looked out the window. I followed his eyes and saw what he saw: the cutter bobbing up and down at our dock.

He stood up and shook Harrison's hand.

"I cannot say anything official, of course, but I want you to know that I have heard many rumors about the things you have been doing here, how you have taken matters into your own hands and have decided to fend for yourselves without asking for help," he paused for a moment, a sly grin spreading on his face – "or asking permission."

He turned towards me and gave a salute. "Captain!"

I saluted back. He opened the door to head out to the dock but then stopped, turning back to look at the two of us, standing side by side near the doorway.

"Was that you I heard about on the radio?"

We both looked at each other. Then we looked at him.

We shrugged our shoulders.

TWENTY-FOUR

CL 20/0024
Pahokee, Florida/Saturday

We set sail early this morning. The sun was not up yet, and Angela wanted to know why we didn't wait until it was light out so we could see where we were going. She learned pretty quickly to not ask the young Art much of anything if she wanted more than a one-word answer. He was not her type of conversationalist, she being a real chatterbox and all and he being – well, you know. Still, she kept eyeing him appreciatively, it seemed to me.

I must admit I was a little concerned about that. Art did not need any distractions on a long voyage such as this, and we needed no more drama than necessary, especially since we would be confined in a limited space for that many days.

Fuel always being a scarce commodity, we decided to head out a bit offshore and sail north rather than motoring up the Intracoastal Waterway. I think Angela got a little spooked as we ventured out into the dark Atlantic, what with the pirate stories and all, but the clouds cleared up, and the moon came out. The seas were calm and the wind strong enough that we made good time heading up to our point of entry to the Okeechobee Waterway. When we got there, near Stuart, we lowered the sails and dropped the mast down. We would be motoring our way for some distance before we got to Lake O.

I noticed after a while more than the usual number of people were standing at the edge of the waterway, waving to us. Some were waving flags of some sort. I took out binoculars and saw they had an image of the Mask of the Ancient Ones on them, but it wasn't until we rounded a bend and pulled into a dock near Indiantown that I began to get an idea of what was going on. There was what looked like hundreds of people waving those flags and smiling and waving at us enthusiastically. Some were wearing Native American-looking headdresses made of feathers or dressed in similar garb.

There were some hand-painted signs.

One said "How Now Hermitage?" Another, "Harrison Where Are You?" When I saw "Bon Voyage Vision Quest!" I had a pretty good idea of what had happened.

"Angela, my dear, how did all these people know we would be floating this way and that our boat is named Vision Quest?"

She shrugged her shoulders. "I dunno."

"ANGELA?" I said through a smile of clenched teeth, waving to the throngs.

"It's all over the Internet," Art said, obviously on such an important occasion that he actually strung all those words together, all at the same time.

"Oh, *really?*"

Angela shrunk down but kept waving. She was clearly enjoying this.

We spent more time than I would have liked, signing copies of the Chronicles and shaking people's hands and trading stories about the Roaring Twenties and fielding questions about whatever happened to Harrison that I was unable to answer. We were finally able to wrest ourselves away, but a similar scene played out wherever we stopped.

Once we made it into Lake O, we found our way to Pahokee, a small community that had quite the history of its own. I noticed there were a few tepees set up near the shore. We did some good trading there and also had some stories to swap about Mick Jagger, the medicine man, Pavlov Dog, and how the lost tribes of Florida had found their place among the white man and people of color during our hour of need.

Angela took all this in in wonderment. Her vision quest was turning into a real adventure, and we were not even halfway there yet. Later that night I was dozing in a teepee, nearly in a dead sleep when she came in. She sat down with an audible thud and had a frown on her face. She was holding one of the Chronicles in her lap.

"What happened? Are you and Art-2-D3 not getting along?"

"Oh, he's just a jerk, at least as far as I can tell. He doesn't say much."

She no doubt had no idea that I was making a joke about a really old series of movies that had some space travelers and robots in it. They were always having some kind of war in those movies. The robots had names consisting of just letters and numbers.

"Is this your first boyfriend?"

"He's not my boyfriend. Why would you say such a thing?"

"And why would you avoid the issue? How many boyfriends have you had?"

"Is that any of your business?"

"I guess not."

She was quiet for a moment. "I seem to have problems with boys. They don't seem to understand me very well, and I sure don't understand them. That's why I like books. They are a lot more understandable and a whole lot more dependable."

"That must be hard, especially without having a father around to talk to. Fathers are not much use for much, but that is one thing they are supposed to know something about: how the male of the species thinks or, more to the point, fails in the endeavor."

"How would you know? Your father deserted you from what I read." She held up the Chronicle book that she had, apparently, snatched from the inventory on board Vision Quest. She had, it would seem, helped herself to the one about me and my father.

"I guess that is true for the most part, from what my mother told me. Plus, of course, I have never been a father myself, so you're right, I don't know much about it."

Her look softened a bit. Her anger was subsiding.

"What did your mom say to you?"

I told her:

It was a few days after the big meeting, the one where Peabody said my dad was a deserter, and my mom was, well, part of a brothel of some sort, I guess you would call it. I was sitting out at the dock by the bay. It was near sunset. I let my legs dangle over the side and let my thoughts float around aimlessly in the air.

"Whatcha thinking about?" My mom came out to join me. She sat down next to me and let her own legs dangle. She stared off into the sunset, too.

"Oh, there was this song I remember hearing once when Dad took me to some sort of place where there was a guitar player and, well, people drinking a lot of beer."

"Was it something about sitting on a dock of the bay?"

"Yeah, that was it. You know it?"

"Yes, and I know your father. He knew better than to take you to a place like that."

"I wish *I* knew him."

"Me, too."

I looked over at her. "Why did he desert us?"

"Despite what that awful man said, he was not a deserter, at least not as far as we were concerned. He enlisted in the Navy and was sent off to fight those stupid wars that are constantly being fought, wars that nobody seems to ever win. From what he says in his letters, it took him a while to figure that out. Once he did, he realized that he made a mistake, and now he had blood on his hands." She paused, just for a few seconds, taking in a long breath of air. "Blood of a lot of innocents, women and children included."

"What happened to him? Why didn't he quit?"

"A soldier is not allowed to just quit like that. That includes sailors. Then one day, when he was at a port halfway around the world, he went AWOL."

"Absent without leave."

"That's right. He spent a lot of time trying to keep from getting caught and got into a lot of trouble trying to keep from being found out, but eventually they hunted him down and caught him. They put him in prison and brought him up on charges."

"Was he in the brig?"

"Yes, I guess that is what you call it." She turned to me with an earnest expression. "I'm sorry I didn't tell you these things sooner. I just didn't know how to tell you, or really even if I should have told you at all. I'm still not sure. A boy needs a father, and he needs one he can look up to. So does a daughter. Both you and Kate deserve a better hand than the one dealt to you as far as your parents are concerned."

I put my arm around her. "Well, at least we ended up with a decent mom. You have worked your fingers to the bone to take care of us, and now that we are in this predicament, I think we have all made out pretty well, considering."

"Thank God for Harrison – and Calusa. I know I thought they were strange at first; I didn't trust them. But now I see how wonderful they are, how wonderful both of them are for both you and Kate – er, I mean, White Feather."

"Sure, they are swell, but you are our mother, and you will always be our mother. As for our dad . . ." I stared out, looking at the distant horizon, my words trailing off.

"I know he is out there, somewhere."

"Sweetheart, he is in prison."

"There was a prison break. A bunch of guys in the brig escaped. The Coast Guard guy told me."

Her face turned white.

"Where?"

"I don't know, but the guy said there may have been deserters mixed in with a bunch of killers and bad criminals. If he is with them, I hope they don't hurt him."

She must have smiled to herself at the naïveté.

"One thing about your father is that he knows how to take care of himself. In that way, at least, you are like him, which is a good thing."

I smiled at her.

That was good to hear.

"I was worried there for a while when I saw that Captain's hat you are always wearing. I was worried you would end up in the Navy like your father."

"Nah, Harrison always tells me I'm a lover, not a fighter. I sure don't have any desire to go off and kill innocent people, especially when there is no reason for it."

"Good old Harrison. I'm glad you two became such good friends. I think he gave you some things you really needed that your dad was not able to give you."

"Sort of like the father I never really had?"

"Something like that."

"Mom, can I ask you a question?"

"Sure."

"Are you in love with him?"

Boy, what a question. Can't believe I asked her that.

"I am very fond of him and very grateful for what he has done for you and our family and, although he wouldn't want me to say this, for this community. He is a great man, and I respect him and all that he stands for."

"But?"

"No 'buts.' Let's just leave it at that for now. I am, after all, technically speaking, still a married woman with a husband who is apparently floating around out there somewhere, in the clutches of a gang of bloodthirsty pirates. Besides, Harrison has Calusa, of course."

We sat for a while at the dock until it got pretty dark. Then we headed in, she to the Hermitage, and I to my beloved club-house to hang out with the other lost boys.

It was late by the time I was done telling Angela that story, and I was tired and ready to get some sleep. We had a long journey the next day.

"I think I am about ready to turn in," I said to Angela.

"I'm sorry about what I said before."

"What was that?"

"About how your father deserted you, and implying you didn't know anything about being a father since you were never one yourself."

"Well, the truth hurts, as they say. I guess I deserved it, seeing as how I brought up your own situation, you not knowing what it is like to have a father and all that stuff."

"Oh, but that is not true." She had nestled into her corner of the teepee, pulling the covers up over her shoulders, snuggling warm and secure into their embrace.

"How so?" I asked.

"I have you, don't I?"

TWENTY-FIVE

CL 20/0025
Aboard Vision Quest
Fort Myers, Florida/Sunday

This evening we finally made it to Fort Myers. There was a ticker tape parade atmosphere all around us. Maybe it was more like a flotilla. Plenty of boats surrounded us as we made our way to the docks, slowing almost to a crawl. People were waving those flags, holding up all kinds of signs, and carrying on like we had just won the World Series.

I hated it.

I understood that there was a lot of curiosity about Harrison and the Hermitage and all the things that had happened, starting back in the Roaring Twenties, but this was too much. Being the hermit that he was, I doubted Harrison would approve. Being somewhat of one myself, I know I was not too keen on all the fuss these people were making.

When we reached Fort Myers, we had officially made it to the other side of Florida. Here we found ourselves in the land of legendary pirates, like Gaspar, who was more legend than an actual person. We were also in the land once dominated by a fierce tribe of indigenous peoples. They and their culture were eventually decimated by invading Europeans. At least they got a few licks in before they were driven to extinction, or so we all thought at first. Not too far from where we docked, Juan Ponce de Leon met his fate, having been hit with an arrow in his backside more than five and a half centuries in the past. He turned tail, what was left of it, and ran back to Cuba.

He died from his wounds soon after he got back there.

We did some good trading in Fort Myers before settling in for the night. I decided not to take the townspeople up on their offer to stay at one of the hotels that were still standing despite the hurricanes and rising tides that had pummeled their community over the years. I stayed on the boat with Angela and the rest of our small crew. I did not feel the need to guard our stuff necessarily, except maybe from Angela. I knew she wanted to poke her nose into more of the Chronicles, especially ones about pirates and whatnot.

She came out to the dock where I was sitting. I guess all this talk about pirates and Indians and Harrison and so on made me more, well, more nostalgic than usual even for me. That is why I ended up sitting on a dock at the bay, like that stupid song goes that I can never remember. You remember, that one the guy with the guitar was singing during a few of the moments of quality time spent with my father.

In a honky-tonk bar.

With a bunch of drunken people – mostly sailors probably.

But as lousy as that sounds, it is a lot better than my other memory of him.

"Whatcha got there?" She had noticed the thin bound manual at my side.

"Oh this?" I lifted the thing up like I was brandishing it. "Nothing much – well, not to most people. It is part of the Chronicles. The part you most want to read about."

"How do *you* know?" She could not take her eyes off of it.

"Oh, just a feeling." She snatched it out of my hand and went running to find her battery-powered reading light I had given her.

"It's just a loner – I need that back," I called out after her. I suppressed a feeling of regret at letting her read that particular book. I don't think most people are aware of what happened that day, back in the Twenties.

I know I don't like to think about it . . .

There I was, sitting on a dock again, back behind the Hermitage. Art and I were fishing. Larry came running up to us. I have never seen a person with such an intense look of fear on his face. He was trying to talk as he was also trying to catch his breath.

"We have, uh, big trouble ... Peabody, uh, is . . ."

"Trouble with that guy? I'm not sure I am that interested."

" . . . is, is . . . he's dead."

"What?" Larry finally caught his breath enough to tell us what happened.

"There were these men, they were escaped convicts or something I heard. They docked out near the community center. Their boat was running a flag that looked like some version of a Jolly Roger, skulls and that sort of thing, I was told."

"They killed Peabody?"

"Yeah. He was talking tough to them, you know how he is, and one of them gutted him with a bayonet on the end of a rifle. But that's not all."

"What?"

"The leader of the gang, he looked like that one psychopathic guy who had that cult back in the sixties that stabbed all those people, what was his name?"

"Charlie Manson?" Larry snapped his fingers and pointed at me.

"Yeah, *that* guy. Anyway, he said, 'Take me to your leader – the *real* one' or something like that. Real scary looking guy, gives everybody the creeps. I was told that they didn't know what to do, but eventually one of the people told them about Harrison. I think they are planning on heading over there. It's going to be big trouble."

We were running down the dock, back towards the front of the Hermitage, before Larry even finished talking. We barely made it when we saw the gang of men marching down the street in our direction. There must have been at least a dozen or more of them. They made a motley crew but did look pretty menacing. The Charlie Manson guy was dangling something in his hand as he walked. The others were clustered behind him and on either side of him as he walked. He stopped at the edge of the road, positioning himself and his crew just on the other side of the moat. We stood on the other side.

"This your cat?" He held the dead animal up by the tail.

"Thunder!" Kate came out and started to run towards the road.

We held her back.

"Seems somebody done shot your cat all up." He swung her backward and then, with a heave, tossed her forward in our direction. She landed with a thud.

"No! No! What did you do to her?" Kate was crying. I held her closer.

I could see a blur of motion that flashed in the corner of my eye and looked up. Bolt had emerged from the walls of the Hermitage, Calusa not far behind him. He crouched forward towards the men and his good friend Thunder, growly menacingly at Manson.

"Would someone please put down this rabid animal?"

A man came forward and trained his rifle on our dog. Then I saw something pass by like another flash. Actually, I heard it more than anything else. There was sort of a "whoosh" sound, like an arrow flying through the air.

That's because that is exactly what it was.

The rifle was ripped out of the man's hand, blood spraying outward. He fell to his knees, holding his injured hand, howling in pain. Manson walked over and retrieved the arrow that had fallen not far from where he was standing. He studied it for a moment. He looked at Calusa. She was standing stock still, but her bow and quiver were still slung over her shoulder. Then he looked at the mask tacked up outside the Hermitage.

"Well, I guess they were right after all. There be a bunch of injuns around here."

There was a whistle. Bolt retreated back behind the moat. Manson peered into the recesses of the vegetation in the direction of where he heard the whistle. Harrison came out slowly. He was holding a cross bow aimed right at Manson.

"Ah, I heard there was a real White Man in charge over here. That must be you."

"I'm in charge of nothing except keeping my people from being harmed."

"So you are the mighty leader of all these women and children; is that right?" He motioned towards us all, including my mom, who had come out of the Hermitage. She took a position next to Calusa. Kate held onto her hand.

"You have quite the harem there, my man. Even a mighty fine slave woman to keep you occupied. Hope I didn't interrupt anything." His men snickered.

"Forgive me, sir, but I am not your 'man,' and, as far as I know, I have no beef with you or these other fellas. Why don't you-all just go back to where you came from?"

"Well, now, I see you are real good with that thing." Manson looked over at the man with the bloody hand, who had managed to stand up and move closer to his boss. "But I doubt even you would be able to take us all out, even with the help of that injun lady." He nodded his head in the direction of Calusa, who had slowly brought her bow around and in front of her, an arrow from her quiver already nestled in her bow string.

"Oh, I only need to take one of you out to finish this little problem we seem to be having here." Harrison took clear aim right at Manson's head.

Then there was a rustling sound in the vegetation. I could see the medicine man, Pavlov, and a group of about a dozen or so braves from his entourage emerge from the bushes. They fanned out near the edge of the moat, the medicine man unarmed, in front. The braves pulled out their bows and trained their arrows on the motley crew.

"Hold on there, Geronimo, we just came to pay a call on you is all; we didn't mean to get you all riled up. Just looking for some provisions and maybe have a little fun with some of your fine ladies and them squaws you have around here." He looked at my mom.

Calusa raised her bow and drew back the string.

"Okay, okay, I get the message. We will be on our way."

"That will be just fine," Harrison said, "except for one thing."

"Oh, and what might that be?"

"Leave behind the guy who killed our cat. We will deal with him in our own way."

Manson had a look of shock on his face for a moment. Then he threw his head back and gave a long, loud, mocking sort of laugh.

"I'll tell you what I am going to do. I'll trade you the dead cat for the man with the bloody hand that you shot, and call it even. That seems fair, don't it?"

Harrison was frozen. He did not flinch. Neither did Calusa. They were aiming their arrows right at Manson and his gang, who were clustering closer behind their leader.

"By your silence, I assume we have an accord. We will be taking our leave then, provided, of course, you don't shoot us in the back when we turn around. But you and Pocahontas here should make no mistake. Men like us have long memories, and there will come a day when we return to this place. When we do, we will remember what you did to this poor lad and his hand, and we will also take what we came here for."

He looked at my mom. His lips parted in a leering smile.

Harrison still had his arrow pointed at Manson's head. I saw him glance at my mom, then back at the sneering face of Manson, then he glanced at me. He knew I was watching him carefully. He was thinking. He was carefully calculating what sort of impact killing Manson would have on me. He was thinking what would happen to her if he didn't.

I looked over at Manson. He still had that sneer on his face.

Right at the moment when I thought Harrison was going to let go of his arrow, the sneer on Manson's face froze, his eyes bulging. He had a curious expression on his face all of a sudden. It reminded me of how Mrs. Jacobs' face looked when I found her dead. A look of surprise, I guess you would call it. But I heard no swoosh, no sound that told what had just happened. That became apparent when Manson himself fell to his knees and then plopped forward, face down on the pavement.

Behind him was a man holding a bloody bayonet on the end of his rifle.

He was my father.

Harrison trained his weapon on the man standing there with a bayonet that he had just used to dispatch the immediate threat to us all. The other men backed up a few feet, some of them gasping at what had happened to their former leader.

"You were right, we have no beef with you," my father said. He set the butt of the old rifle on the pavement, pulling out a kerchief of some sort from his pocket to wipe the blood off the bayonet that was affixed at the top. He glanced around a little at his surroundings. "Our beef is with the government. And from what I see, and what I have been told, the government is no friend to you, and vice versa." He looked straight at my mom. He looked down at my sister. Then he looked straight at me.

"There is nothing here for men such as us."

He started to turn away, to walk back to where their boat was moored. "C'mon boys, we have overstayed our welcome and need to get going before the Coast Guard gets here and we have some real trouble to deal with."

"What about him?" One of the men wanted to know what to do with Manson, who was still lying face down in the street.

"Didn't you hear what the man said? We have to leave behind the culprit that killed that poor defenseless cat." He looked at Harrison. "Ain't that right?"

Harrison lowered his weapon. Calusa did likewise.

"A deal is a deal. We will give him an honorable burial at sea, which sounds like a sight more than he may deserve. But there is another thing left unresolved."

"What is that, pray tell?"

"When should we expect another visit from you and your men?"

My father looked at my mom one last time, then at me.

"We will never set foot in this place again. I swear to you on my honor, such that it is, should our paths cross again, you will be given safe passage, and no harm shall come to you by my hand or any of my men." He looked back at them grimly. "Isn't that right, boys?" They nodded in general agreement. Then he pointed an outstretched finger at the Mask of the Ancient Ones tacked up against the Hermitage.

"That goes for anyone else upon the high seas who fly the flag of your tribe."

He turned away again, and the men started to head towards the bay and their waiting ship. Then he stopped, turned around and walked closer, standing at the edge of the street, standing erect, right in front of me. He stood at attention and gave me a salute.

"Captain!"

My mouth had to be gaping open, but I managed to return a weak salute.

Then my father turned around and walked away.

I watched the figure of my father grow smaller, the silhouette etched against the sunlight glittering off the waters of the bay. This may sound strange, but what I remember most was how bowlegged he was. I guess when you see your father maybe for the last time, you pick up on trivial details such as that.

Bowlegged.

My father is bowlegged.

Just then, the face of a full-blown Native American medicine man consumed my entire field of vision. He had a serious expression on his face. I can even remember each line and wrinkle on his weathered countenance. He turned his head to look at the disappearing figure of the bowlegged man, walking with his crew towards the bay.

Then he turned his face back to my own.

A smile crossed his lips.

"Well, I think that went rather well, don't you?"

TWENTY-SIX

CL 20/0026
Tarpon Lodgings
Pine Island, Florida/Monday

By the time we reached the pass, the sun had already started to peek over the horizon. I could see it just over the treeline way off in the distance, past the expanse of waters that is Charlotte Harbor. I was thinking how I had missed several days of my morning constitutional, and if I was not careful, would also miss my weekly kayaking if I didn't get someone to give me a loaner at Kate's village.

Angela had come out and was sitting quietly near to me at the bow.

"I put the Chronicles book I read last night by your bunk."

"Hope you found it illuminating."

She said nothing. I was relieved. There was no sense getting into it at that moment, and I certainly wasn't in the mood. In fact, I might not ever be in the mood.

Yes, never would be a perfect time to get into all that stuff.

"Is that it up ahead?" She asked, pointing to the docks at Pine Island.

"Yep, there she blows," said Art No. 3 in a rare blast of chit-chat.

I was glad for it.

"That must be the lodge back behind the docks," said Angela.

"Cap'n?" Art said. He had apparently run out of words.

"Technically, I guess you could say so. It had been washed away quite some number of years ago, but they rebuilt it back up pretty much almost the way it looked way back in the Twenties. Looks almost the same as when I first saw it. They built it up a lot higher, of course. Docks are higher, too, and closer to the lodge than they used to be."

Art throttled back on the engine as we got closer.

"I haven't seen the Chronicles of that first time you pulled into this place."

"Something tells me you will, just not on this trip. When we get back to the Hermitage, I will make sure you get your hands on that one and some of the other ones I know you would like to see. For this trip, you will have to make due by listening to stories from my sister and some of the other old-timers who are still around."

Art cut the engine, letting Vision Quest drift, the port side eventually nuzzling up alongside the dock. I had a line securing the bow while Angela took care of the aft. There was little fanfare dockside as we tied off. Actually there was none, for which I was grateful. We had already started pulling our gear and other stuff we needed out of the cabin, tossing it up on the dock when a man I did not recognize at first approached. He was grinning broadly. He had a metal skull cap on his head with horns sticking out of either side.

There must have been an early start to the festival last night.

He stopped a few feet away from our boat. He stood at attention, cocked his arm out to the side, and held up his hand, palm facing us, Indian-style.

"Greetings. I am son of Erik and White Feather. You may call me Erik's Son if you must, but I am known within this tribe as Leaf-That-Turns."

"Let me guess: That boat over there that is outfitted in the style of a Viking ship, the one that says 'Leaf Erik Son' painted on the side, is yours. Do I have that right?"

Masks of the Ancient Ones were affixed to either side at the bow, near the cheeks of the mermaid that looked outward from the ship, chin jutting forward.

"Yes, Captain-Over-All-That-Moves. You are indeed wise even beyond your many years to have perceived such things, having just now arrived." By then my wise old bones had clambered up onto the dock and stood upright, giving a bear hug to my nephew.

"Good to see you," I whispered in his ear. "It's been too long."

"Me, too," he said as he pulled away. "Mom's waiting back at the Institute." He turned to the gawking Art and Angela. "Let me help you with those things. You have accommodations at the legendary Tarpon Lodgings, which, despite all that Mother Nature had to say about it, is still standing, even after that storm 'Lucky' that came to visit."

"Don't worry about the cargo," I said to Art. "We will meet with them to do some trading later. Everything is safe here. We are among friends."

After we got settled in, Angela and I paddled our way from the docks towards a canal leading inland. The storm had damaged the boardwalk that would have otherwise brought us on foot from the lodge to the "Institute," as it was called. It was just as well. I now had a canoe to take on my next regularly-scheduled Blueways tour, only this time I would have quite the change of scenery. I might even bring young Pixie Girl along for the ride.

There was a lot for both of us to learn about this place.

But as promised, I told her the story of when I first came here:

Many years ago when I first arrived, we docked at the Tarpon, just as we did this morning. But the similarities pretty much end there. The water level was not nearly as high as it is today, and the Institute was just a research facility operated by a university, set in what was basically one giant archaeological site.

That site had been transformed after we arrived. In a way, we breathed life back into this space, once occupied hundreds of years ago by an extinct civilization.

The main building that housed exhibits and a lecture hall where people could learn more about the ancient people that had their headquarters there at the site had been demolished by the Big One. The building looked a lot like our house back home right after the storm: barren walls with no roof and lots of debris scattered everywhere.

I had first learned about the Institute as we were having one of our nightly dinners at the Hermitage. We were all in a relaxed mood, laughing and telling jokes. The medicine man had decided to drop by that evening. He was returning to his own people the next day with his entourage. He had helped us so much to rebuild the Village, even though he knew next to nothing about construction. Heck, he knew less than nothing, but what he lacked in construction know-how, he more than made up for in other forms of knowledge.

He shared with us his sense of humor – and of proportion. He helped us to gain better insight into the larger purpose of things, without getting overwhelmed by them.

Things looked bad, but they could be worse – a lot worse.

"Whenever I break bread with friends, I like to have a toast," he said, raising his water glass, "especially if it is at breakfast. But I digress." He looked around the table at all of us, his gaze finally coming to rest upon Calusa.

"I have a proposition to make."

"You are propositioning Calusa?" My mom had made a joke of her own. My sister and I were way too young to know what she meant. We were to learn in due time how prophetic was both the humor of what she said, and what he had to say.

"In a manner of speaking, I suppose so. You see, my people often travel to places on the far side of the peninsula, a land where ancient peoples once ruled this entire vast countryside before being subjugated and then annihilated by the White Man." He paused for a moment to nod towards Harrison and then at me. "No offense to the white guys at the table." Then he looked at my mom and little sister.

"The women and girls, of course, are almost completely off the hook."

"That seems chivalrous enough, I suppose," Harrison chimed in.

"Yes, I suppose so, although we do not have such a word in our native tongue."

"What, pray tell, is the proposition of which you speak?" Harrison asked.

"We have arranged for an expedition." It was my mom who answered. "A 'mission' you might call it. Only instead of the white people sending in missionaries to change the ways of the indigenous people, we are doing the reverse. We want to return the land more to the way it once was, and in the process learn the ways of those who were here before the white man came. Then we will teach those ways to others."

"You want to do the same thing there that we are doing here," I heard myself say.

"Exactly, He Who Has Cap to Hold in Overflowing Brain," the medicine man said. We have learned that the sacred place where our ancestors had, well, built their "headquarters," in a manner of speaking, has been nearly destroyed by these storms. These sacred places were being managed by one of the White Man's big universities, but now they are in trouble and cannot rebuild without our help."

"So we will show them our ways, just as we did here," said Calusa.

"This will never work," said Harrison. "There is a very important, missing ingredient you have all forgotten to take into consideration."

"What would that be, oh White Man with Heavy Heart but with Really Strong Crossbow that Shoots Arrows like No Indian Can?"

"Who will there be at this Ghost Town of Dead Indians you are talking about to give the white woman, seated here now before you, her name on this vision quest?" He motioned in the direction of my mom. He said this with a smile, but I could tell he was bothered by something. I am not sure he was that thrilled with the idea.

"Oh, I didn't think of that," said the medicine man, stroking his chin.

"You must come with us," said Kate, er, I mean White Feather. She was looking earnestly at the medicine man. "We can take her to the places, like you did with me, where she can see what is there, the way you did with me. Places that have no footprints except for the creatures who honor each other and the Great Spirit."

She was so earnest, the medicine man decided not to make another quip.

"Capital suggestion," Harrison interjected. He lifted his glass of water and with some flourish said, "We shall christen a vessel *Vision Quest* and you will set sail for the left coast of our besieged peninsula, laden with provisions for those poor lost souls who cling to a past that will now become their present, on a mission of mercy – and survival."

We all reached forward to clink each other's glasses, but, judging from the looks on their faces, I am not so sure how confident everyone was with this proposition.

That included me.

The next morning the medicine man set sail for his village in the Everglades. He would later join the expedition. Pavlov stayed behind to guide us to the left coast and the land of the forgotten tribe. Later that morning Harrison helped to load our provisions and other gear onto the newly christened Vision Quest. He was sending his beloved Calusa on an adventure into a land that was barren and lifeless, the land of her ancient heritage.

I had a distinct feeling that he knew he may never see her again.

That went for the rest of us.

He had, for all intents and purposes, let her go, sending her off on a quest of her own, with what little semblance of a family he had.

He embraced her as she boarded the Vision Quest.

I had never before seen tears in either of their eyes.

Once on board Harrison waved to us from the dock as we departed. He looked a little sad from what I remember. I had an urge to jump in the water and swim back to him, but he had told me the night before to keep watch on our people, make sure nothing happened to them. We were flying the flag with the Mask of the Ancient Ones, but once we reached our destination, we would be on our own.

I saw my mom choke back a tear, I think. She had her hand to her mouth as she watched the loving embrace of Harrison and Calusa and the image of the man who had saved us all become smaller and smaller and then disappear from view.

Two days later, when we finally pulled Vision Quest into the docks at Tarpon Lodge, there was a scene of destruction with which we had become all too familiar.

The task did not seem too daunting.

We had seen this before.

We knew what to do.

TWENTY-SEVEN

CL 20/0027
The Institute, Pine Island, Florida
(Monday)

Today was a red-letter day. I was able to do both my weekly kayaking workout and morning constitutional – sort of. Hope I don't feel it tomorrow.

Angela and I got to explore around the inland waters that had inundated the area around the northern parts of Pine Island before heading into the system of canals at the Institute. The canals had, in fact, been there all along, centuries ago.

The gradual advance of erosion had filled in the sides, making them shallow ditches at the most defined parts. That is how we found them when the expedition from the Hermitage first landed here, back in the Twenties. Today, from our vantage point in our canoe, we could see them fully restored to their former glory.

We also could more clearly see the shell middens and mounds that rose up high above the lower-lying areas of the Institute's village. When the original expedition from the Hermitage arrived, most of the research material about the Ancient Ones who had originally settled here were still intact, preserved by the scientists and archeologists who had valiantly safeguarded them, despite the ravages of the storms.

We had blueprints on how to rebuild the lost civilization of the Ancient Ones, including the canals. We put those blueprints to good purpose.

As Angela and I paddled through the canals, villagers smiled and waved to us.

I still had a faint recollection of the blueprint research. I recognized some of the sights we had seen this morning along the canal route. Eventually, over the years, the village at the Institute had restored the northern section of Pine Island to the way it had been hundreds of years in the past: an array of courtyards, clutches of dwellings, circular plazas, tide pools, and other living or working areas interconnected by the canals.

We disembarked from our kayaks near one of the larger shell mounds, walking around a bit to stretch our legs. An artificial tide pool linked to the canal was not far from the entrance to the trail up to the big shell mound we were about to climb. I remember from the blueprints how the pool was designed to fill up with the incoming tides that would capture and hold the water after the tide ebbed. Live fish and other critters from the seas would be stored in the pool for future reference.

Nothing like fresh fish for breakfast, I thought to myself.

I was starting to get a little hungry.

I rounded out what I decided to deem my usual constitutional by hiking up the short trail to the big mound, the biggest one in the complex. According to the blueprints, the chief built his place, larger than all the others in town, at the top of the biggest mound.

Naturally, that is where Kate's living quarters could be found.

She had been sitting outside and rose to greet us as we approached. She was wearing a flowing white sarong-type gown that stretched to her feet and a light shawl wrapped loosely around her shoulders. Her long gray hair was braided, framing a face weathered by time and the elements, but still distinguished, very much befitting her station in life as the chief of one of the most important communities in the network of villages.

She still looked like my kid sister to me.

"Ahoy there, Captain and big brother of mine," she said, leaning forward for a hug.

"White Feather, we meet again at last," I said to her.

"This must be our favorite correspondent from the Hermitage," she said after she pulled away from our embrace, looking over at Angela. "Well, how do you like our little village?" She stretched out her arm in a sweeping gesture towards the maze of canals and other features of the sprawling grounds of the Institute below. The mist from the sky that had been cooling us off had begun to turn into a very light rain.

Kate did not seem to notice. She was smiling from ear to ear. Drops of rain water began to accumulate on her head, and then began to roll down her face.

"I am very honored to meet you," Angela said, giving a slight curtsy. "Is Mr. White Feather around?"

"Oh, no, he is on a trading mission to the north. We are running low on coffee, and up there in the mountains they have the richest kind."

"Except maybe in Jamaica," I interjected. "How about showing us inside your place, little sister?" The light rain was starting to turn into a near downpour.

We bent down and entered her home.

Inside, one could see the typical building method we had adapted from the chickees that indigenous tribes were still building, even to this day, and similar structures that had been built by other tribes in the distant past, such as those the Apalachee to the north had built centuries ago. From the inside you could see the beams holding up the thatched sides of her house, arrayed in a circular pattern, forming an open-air cone at the top. A few drops of rain sprinkled the fire pit, just enough to create a little smoke that ascended up and out through the skylight, but not enough to snuff out the fire.

That was good news to me as I saw breakfast grilling on the fire.

"How about a cup of cacina before we break our fast this morning?" Kate ladled the dark brew into a wooden bowl, offering it to Angela.

"What is it?" she asked, sniffing at the steaming bowl before jerking her nose away.

"It's called the 'Black Drink' or 'Indian Tea.' It's made from yaupon holly. I think there may be some caffeine or something in it," I explained, looking appreciatively over her shoulder at the bowl she had cupped between her hands.

She took a sip, grimaced, then handed the bowl over to me.

"Excuse me, I don't mean to offend," she said to her hostess. "I am not a big coffee drinker, and that has to be the strongest tea known to man."

"How about some goat milk to go with that?" Kate asked of me. "Makes it go down a little more smoothly for the faint of heart."

After breakfast we had a nice powwow, forming a circle around the fire. The flames cast a glow upon our faces, giving the gathering a mystical, eerie feel to it. Angela looked content, sipping regular tea Kate had scrounged up for her. Mostly there was a lot of shop talk, so to speak, until Angela decided to change the subject.

"I have been reading some of the Harrison Chronicles, the ones about what life was like for you and your brother back in the Twenties. You know, at the Hermitage."

"Oh, is that so? He must be very fond of you. Why, I don't think even I have seen most of those, and I am mentioned in them, I should think."

She looked over at me with a smile that didn't look like a real one.

"Oh, you're in there all right." Angela said, leaning over and gently placing her hand on Kate's knee. She had an earnest expression on her face. "Sorry about your cat."

Did I mention she was an animal lover?

"My cat?" Kate sat with a perplexed expression on her face.

"Thunder was her name, I think. It was all in the manual I read. You know, that day the pirates came to the Hermitage? That Harrison guy kept them from killing Bolt, the border collie and made the pirates give up the guy who killed the cat named Thunder."

"Oh *that* cat. Yes, now I remember. That was so many years ago I had almost forgotten all about that cat of mine – well actually, she was Mrs. Jacobs' cat."

"Did I bring up a subject I shouldn't have?" Angela had a look of concern.

"No, not at all. You are practically one of us. There are no family secrets that we would want to keep from you. I just forgot all about that part of the story."

The flap to the door swung open, and a man stooped down and in, drawing near to where we were seated. When he straightened up to his full height, Angela looked up at his face, towering up somewhere seemingly in the clouds. He was shirtless and was wearing some sort of buckskin and no shoes. His black hair was pulled back into a ponytail.

"Greetings, Jack. This is my brother and his protégé, the one we spoke of." She turned back to us. "Jack will be escorting you to Useppa where you will be completing the vision quest that has led you on your long journey all the way to us."

"Jumping Jack, or just plain Jack, at your service." He bowed at his charges.

"Thank you. I am most grateful," said Angela. "Is 'Jumping Jack' the Indian name you were given? Did you see an amberjack jumping around during your vision quest?"

"I'm not sure; that could be. But my brothers are always teasing me, saying that I was named after a song that was playing at the time. It was by an old rock band."

"That wouldn't be the Rolling Stones, by chance?"
I had to ask.

"Could be; I don't remember. They are all long since dead. I will pick you up at the docks over by the lodge tomorrow morning. Would dawn be early enough for you? You want to start early to get a really good vision quest, you know."

"Dawn sounds fine. We'll see you then."
Jack bowed again and then left.

"Was he given his name by the medicine man that I read about in the manuals? The one that came over here with your mom and the Captain? Is he part of that tribe?"

Did I mention Angela asked a lot of questions?

"Well, yes and no. He was named by the medicine man, and because he is the son of the medicine man, he became part of that tribe. But his mother technically is not part of that tribe. She and her son, and his brothers and sisters, are really part of a new tribe that was started here many years ago, back in the Twenties. You may have heard of her in some of the manuals you have been granted access to by the Captain over there."

"It's Calusa, isn't it?"

"That's right. She was the driving force behind everything that we have been building here in this part of the world. She still is, but she is getting on in years and doesn't leave Useppa that much nowadays. Her children and grandchildren and great-grandchildren are part of her legacy. She is the one who has resurrected a proud tribe of peoples who once inhabited these lands and waters, and their ways that have kept us safe all these many years, and, we hope, that will sustain us for many years to come."

"But what about your mother? Didn't she come here with you on a vision quest of her own? Did she get an Indian name of her own? What was it?"

"She asks a lot of questions. That is why I call her 'Grasshopper'."

"That's a horrible name. I am sure you will get a much better one tomorrow."

"But what about your mom?" Angela asked.

"Hasn't he given you the manuals to read about that part of the story?"

Angela shook her head. I got up to stretch. I had been sitting too long, and my knees were starting to get a little stiff.

"Looks like it stopped raining. I'm going to take a little walk, get some fresh air," I said as I leaned down and out the opening at the front of Kate's house.

"We'll join you. I'd like to hear the story myself," said Kate.

So I told the story as I remembered it:

We had spent several months at the Institute helping pull things together after the Big One. We had used materials on hand and scavenged for others, just like we did back in our own neighborhood. The locals were rallied and taught this new way of rebuilding in the wake of the last storm, but more importantly, how to do that in a way that would help them better withstand the next one. They were taught the ways of being self-sufficient, knowing that there was no Calvary on the way to save them.

The medicine man eventually joined us, just as he said he would. This time he brought an even bigger entourage than he did last time. They were great teachers. More importantly, they taught teachers how to teach, how to spread the word all around the islands that were being brought back in time, but back to the future.

My mom was one of them.

We had been working hard to get the Institute back up and running before the start of the hurricane season, a date that was fast approaching. I knew the time had come for me to return to the Hermitage. I had a sense that we had abandoned Harrison, although he never would admit that he felt that way. He didn't have to anyway. I myself felt that way and, to be honest with you, I really did miss him.

I thought my mom did, too, although she didn't show it very much.

When the day came to depart, I walked over from the docks to the main building at the Institute. We had rebuilt it to be fully functional and secure, even managing to get solar panels, wind generators, and cistern systems installed. Work continued on digging out the canals that had eroded over with time. We had already dug a canal that linked the interior of the compound to Big Pine Sound. The place was well on its way to becoming the great village it was destined to become.

"Where's Mom?"

Kate was at the front desk, doing homework of some sort. "She left." Kate did not look up from her studies.

"Where'd she go?"

"She went to Captiva. Said there was some sort of brouhaha over there about the islanders getting with the program. They are not prepared for the storms this season." She looked up from her book. "'Brouhaha.' I like that word. What does it mean?"

"It means she is not here to see me off. Vision Quest is all loaded with supplies and my stuff, and she is ready to set sail – and so am I." I didn't tell her at the time, but I had never heard 'brouhaha' before. I would be looking that one up later. I liked it, too. It sounds like laughter when you say it. Try it some time. You'll see what I mean.

"Here, she told me to give you this." She handed me a bottle. "What is it?"

"What does it look like, silly? It's a message in a bottle. She said it was for Harrison's only eyes – there is to be no peeking." She wagged her finger at me. I am pretty sure my mom told her it was for Harrison's eyes only, but I didn't feel like correcting her.

Back at the dock I met up with Vince. His nickname was "Skipper" which posed no conflict with "Captain" as far as I could tell, especially seeing as how we both would be on different vessels, making this trip as a tandem. I would be sailing on the Vision Quest with my first mate, Pavlov. Skip was on a boat called "Minnow" for some reason. The thing was anything but a small fry. Minnow was built for long voyages at sea.

"With all due respect to the Mask of the Ancient Ones – and there is plenty of respect to be had, make no mistake about that – but there are plenty of scary people out there, and folks need to be extra careful these days. We need to sail together so we can better watch over each other in case something goes amiss." He had given me this lecture earlier when we were out at the docks, making ready for this voyage.

The Minnow had the mask prominently displayed.

There was already an early storm brewing that looked to be heading west but was expected to turn in a northerly direction. Our float plan was to head south and keep a "weather eye" on it, as they say, to see when we could turn towards making a more northeasterly heading. We were hoping to avoid the rainbands and swelling seas.

I wouldn't say that little storm had a bead on us, but it was not doing what we were hoping it would do as we made our way south towards the tip of the Florida peninsula. The Skipper was extra cautious and radioed to us that we would have to dip further south, just to give that thing a wide berth. We planned to rendezvous if we lost sight of each other at the Cayman Islands, just south of Cuba. Skip didn't want to go anywhere near Cuba, at least not as near as he absolutely had to. We were not technically at war with Cuba at the time, as far as I know, but things were not exactly peaceful either.

Seems like almost everywhere things were a little crazy.

People took to calling people flying our flag the "Crazy Americans."

We flew the Mask of the Ancient Ones to even things out somewhat, in case we met up with someone not too happy with having bombs dropped on their heads or whatever crazy thing the national government was up to at that moment in time.

The Skipper felt comfortable enough near Guantanamo Bay on the east end of the island of Cuba where there was an American military presence. But even there, Skip himself was worried, seeing as how that place had been turned into a concentration camp of sorts. The military had filled the place up with folks that the American government called "terrorists." Other folk said they were "revolutionaries."

We really did not want to be on either side of that losing argument.

Skip had us dock at a place he knew about on Little Cayman Island, near Booby Pond at the Blossom Village development. They had been largely spared by the Big One, and the Little One, but were always spoiling for a fight. The little island was off the beaten track and far enough from the more well-to-do main Cayman Island to help us keep a low profile. We did not want to draw any kind of political consequences, if you know what I mean. Things were hard enough avoiding a storm without having to deal with that kind.

He was not too enthusiastic at first, but Skip eventually let me and Pavlov come with him to a place he knew about, an "unofficial watering hole" he called it. We left enough crew behind, with promises we would bring something back, to make sure our stuff was safe. It was in the early afternoon, and there was plenty of daylight.

I, at least, felt safe enough – Pavlov maybe not so much.

I got the feeling he had been designated as my unofficial bodyguard by the medicine man. He was way out of his element in that watering hole but didn't show it.

Neither did I.

The only other experience like that for me was when my dad and I were at that honky-tonk bar I told you about. You know, the one that my mom said he never should have taken me to. Only here there was not even any music playing.

Pavlov and I were sitting at a table. A waitress came by, and I was relieved when she didn't tell him, "We don't serve your kind here." He ordered us some beer. She looked at me for a second but said nothing, then went to fetch a pitcher of beer.

It tasted awful.

"Well, seems like we have a celebrity in our midst." Skipper slid into a seat at our table. "Seems we are entitled to a round or two, thanks to you." He clinked my almost completely full mug of beer with his own almost empty one.

"What are you saying?" asked my bodyguard.

"Well, our boy here is a descendent of the legendary 'Crazy Legs' pirate. He was the one who granted clemency to all who fly the Mask of the Ancient Ones. Authentic reproductions of which, of course, adorn our vessels out yonder." He motioned in general towards where our boats were berthed. Obviously he was drunk but gets credit for using big words like "reproductions" and "authentic" in a complete sentence.

"'Crazy Legs'?" Pavlov ventured.

"Yeah, well, there is an old legend of a pirate who took over Margarita Island, just off the Venezuelan coast which, as you may have heard, is in an unofficial war with the United States." He looked around to see if anyone was listening. He lowered his voice.

"There is now a new guy that is running things down there that was named after the original pirate, sort of. From what I am hearing, he commands all of his people – and there are quite a few – to recognize all those who fly the colors of the Ancient Ones. Why? Because one of his relatives, who is known as 'the Captain,' is part of the tribe that flies the flag of the mask of the aforementioned Ancient Ones. I think that be you, my friend."

We clinked glasses. I felt all eyes upon us.

"Let's get our crazy legs under us and out of here," was what I came up with.

"Sure, but one last question: Do you know why they call him 'Crazy Legs'?"

"I really can't say for sure, but I have an idea."

The next morning was clear and crisp, but we got a late start as Skipper had to nurse a bit of a hangover. We had more than a few people waving at us enthusiastically as we departed, which made me feel a little self-conscious. Once out to sea, we had little trouble, traveling east and then northward through the gap between Haiti and Cuba, right past Guantanamo Bay, Cuba, with not the slightest bit of difficulty.

Minding the gap, we turned westward just south of the Bahama Islands and then due north towards home. I was so glad to see the familiar sights of Biscayne Bay and the Intracoastal Waterway that brought us right up to the docks of the Hermitage.

I could scarcely wait as we tied off. I raced down the dock and towards the entrance to the Hermitage, past Larry and Art who had their hands up, trying to tell me something. I ran right past them. It sure felt good to be home. That was all I could think of.

Once inside, I plopped down on the chair in the study.

How good that chair felt.

Larry walked in. Art was behind him. I looked at both of them.

"Where is he?" I asked.

"He's gone," Larry said.

"Here" was the one-word statement from Art.

He handed me a bottle.

Inside was a letter.

TWENTY-EIGHT

CL 20/0028
Useppa Island, Florida
Tuesday

Just before daybreak Angela and I stumbled out to the docks. Jumping Jack was already there with his boat. Art emerged from Vision Quest as we approached. He could have stayed at the lodge as well, but for some reason preferred to sleep aboard. It wasn't that he wanted to guard the cargo, he just liked to sleep on a boat more than on terra firma.

"Jack, is that you?" The sun was about to come out, but it was still pretty dark, even with the moon as full as it was. "Hard to see you in the pitch dark night."

"I like to get an early start. So does the medicine man," he said, flashing a smile.

Okay, I admit I did that on purpose.

"Jumping Jack Flashed" a smile. Clever, don't you think?

The four of us piled into Jack's boat. We were silent on the ride there. Angela looked a little nervous, but I decided not to ask her if she was. Jack slowed the boat down as we approached the docks at Useppa. They fared much better than I expected. The storms ended up passing by quite a few miles to the north yet, still this island was very vulnerable with the rising sea having reclaimed a good portion of it.

"Welcome to Useppa, land of the Ancient Ones," Jack said as he extended a hand to help Angela onto the dock. "Be careful, as there are some planks missing."

Useppa was a classic tale of how over the years the sea gradually rose up to swallow islands, some of them whole. With others, like this one, the sea patiently lapped away at the retreating edges of their shorelines, beckoning them to surrender to the inevitable.

But this island was exceptional. Measures had been taken to preserve what was left of the island and the treasures she held. Archeologists from long, long ago had unearthed evidence of the ancient inhabitants who lived there going back thousands of years in the past, including the remains of what became known as "Useppa Man."

Later, the remains of "Useppa Woman" were also discovered. I could not help but think that many years in the future, people would read the story of the Amazon warrior princess who had taken up residence on Useppa. She had added another chapter to the history of her people and to the island. She had become the next Useppa Woman.

Jack brought us up to the main house on the island. It was an inn many years ago when the island was still being used as a private resort. The structure had been rebuilt after having been leveled by one of the many hurricanes that passed through this part of Hurricane Alley. Calusa and the other inhabitants of the island had decided to preserve the inn and a few other historic structures on the island. The rest of the island, where there was buildable space, was occupied by the traditional round, thatched structures, most of them elevated by poles to heights well above sea level.

Jack brought us into the main foyer inside the main house. "Wait here while I go tell them you're here," Jack said. We wandered about the foyer, taking in the Native American art and artifacts that adorned the walls. I heard the rustle of beads hanging from a doorway being pushed aside. A tall, slightly stooped woman emerged. Jack followed close behind and then swiftly came to her side. She was walking steadily but with the help of a walking stick studded with emblems from various islands around the world.

I approached her as she extended an outstretched arm to embrace me. I gave her a good long hug. I was afraid to let go of her – and not because I thought she might fall.

"Hello, my Amazon warrior princess," I said softly.

"She can't hear too good so you might have to speak up, Captain." The voice came from a man who had also just walked through the door and into the foyer. He was quite a bit older than when I had last seen him, but I recognized the medicine man instantly.

"You must be the medicine man," Angela said, extending her hand to him.

"You'll have to get closer; he is as blind as a bat," said Calusa. She was still holding my arm to steady herself while she repositioned her walking stick. "Let me have a look at you," she said, peering into my eyes. "Yes, that's the Captain alright. I can see the boy I knew, trapped in there, inside the body of an older man he has grown to become."

"Where? I don't see him," said the medicine man.

"You can't see much of anything these days," she told the medicine man.

He stepped towards Angela. "Please forgive the foolishness of a foolish old man and my manners, young lady. She's right, these old eyes don't work so good like they once did. You must be the young lady here for a reading." He gave her a slight bow of the head.

She looked puzzled for a second. "Why, yes, I suppose so, if that is what you call it. I am here for a vision quest and, hopefully, a nickname that is better than 'Grasshopper'".

"That is, indeed, an awful name. And, as luck would have it, there are very few, if any, grasshoppers around here, human or otherwise. Incidentally, at the risk of sounding rude, allow me to correct you on something. You are not *here* for a vision quest, you are *on* a vision quest and have been for some time. You have come here to a waypoint along your path. Here you will open your eyes and your heart to what is around you, what is part of you, what is part of all of us. Then you will tell me what you see, and I will try to interpret the meaning of the visions that have come to you, to help you understand them."

"He's right, but don't let him get near a radio or stereo playing rock and roll music, or you will end up being named after one of his favorite songs," Jack added.

"Thank you, Jumping Jack Who Flashes His Brilliance. But what really is in a name? A rose by any other name smells as sweet, as the White Man used to say. The only problem, of course, are the thorns, so you have to take the good with the bad."

"Shall I bring them to the sweat lodge?" asked Jack.

"'Them'? You mean there is more than just the one? Are we running a two-for-one special on readings today that I did not know about?"

"I don't need a name. The one I have is fine." Art No. 3 stepped forward and spoke up, I guess so that Calusa could hear him, too. Either that or he got confused and thought the medicine man could see him better if he spoke louder.

"Ah yes, No-Ha, I remember now. I should have guessed that the breathing I heard over there, and not much else, came from he of the No-Ha clan – those that can be seen but not heard so much, except, of course, for those of us with poor eyesight."

"This is the son of the son of No-Ha, as you called him back in the day. I was remiss and should have introduced you more properly," I decided to say. Art had a real confused look on his face. I decided I would try to clear things up for him a little later, if Angela didn't herself. By now she surely had read all about No-Ha in the manuals.

"Why don't we head out to the sweat lodge? Jack, please jump through the doorway and lead the way. Young man, please follow my first born. Young lady, if you do not mind guiding an old half-blind man, would you let me take your arm?" He felt out forward with his hand. She took his hand and placed it on her arm, guiding him towards the open door through which Jack and Art No.3 had just gone through.

As they were leaving, the medicine man called back over his shoulder, "Captain, you stay here and visit with the Amazon warrior princess for a spell. But don't forget to speak up so she can hear you."

"He is right, I do not hear so well, but that is just as well. I have many things to tell you. Maybe, for a change, I will do a lot of talking so that you do not have to as much. Come, let's go into the study." We walked into the study. The room reminded me of the one back at the Hermitage. I helped Calusa ease into a chair and then sat down myself.

Her story was of a time well before those chronicled in these pages and those kept by Harrison in his own journals, at least as far as I am aware. He was a merchant marine at the time he met Calusa in Cienfuegos, Cuba. He was on leave from where his ship was docked at Kingston in Jamaica and chartered a boat to take him to Cienfuegos.

"He was always searching for the same thing at every port of call where he found himself to be and all throughout the islands here and even in the Pacific. That is how he came to have such an affinity for the islands and the people of the islands. He saw that they were slowly sinking into the sea. He saw that with each passing storm another piece of their lives was being washed away. He saw this and saw he could do nothing about it.

"That is why your mother's missions to the islands touched his heart so."

"What was he searching for?"

She started to get up but then thought better of it.

"In that drawer, over there, there is a drawing."

I went to the desk drawer she was pointing to and pulled out a sketch she had drawn. I held it up for her to see. "This?" She motioned to me to bring it to her.

"He had a faded photograph of this boy that he always kept with him. He would show it to everyone and anyone who would listen, asking if they had seen this boy. Someone had told him my mother might know someone who might know something. I made a sketch of the boy from the photograph." She studied the sketch for a moment. "I tried to age the image of the boy in the photograph. A number of years had passed since the photo was taken. I thought that might give us a better chance at finding the boy."

She handed the sketch to me, turning her gaze to the garden just on the other side of the window. "He is a man now, long in years but not that long, about your age."

I looked at the sketch. Calusa was always a good artist. She had made a very realistic, detailed image of the lost boy. Light bulbs finally went off inside my head.

"Is this a picture of his son?" She didn't hear me.

"This is his son, born of an island woman he had taken up with before joining the merchant marines. She disappeared with the child, and he never heard from them again."

"That explains a lot." She looked at me quizzically. She couldn't hear me. I waved off my comment as if to say "never mind" in my best effort at sign language. Turned out, that probably was the best way to communicate with Calusa after all.

She continued with her story.

Her mother thought she did recognize the boy as being with a woman she had met in Cap-Haitien, but she was not sure. She could not offer anything else to help him find her and the boy except maybe for one thing: Calusa herself.

Her mother knew that Calusa had a much better chance of finding the boy than a white seaman stumbling around port cities with an old faded photo in his pocket. Plus, she spoke the language of the islands, including Creole. There was just one catch. He had to bring her with him when he returned to America so she could have a chance at a better life than what was in store for her there in the islands. He came back for her not long after, when she was of age and he could credibly claim her as his bride.

In time they grew to love each other, to be sure, but they were not lovers.

There were many things that began to come into focus for me. I had questions to ask. She would not be able to answer them. Her hearing was not that great, but even if it was, I am not sure she would be able to answer all of them.

I picked one.

"Why did my mother forsake him?" I nearly shouted.

She was taken aback.

"Oh, no, my child. She did not forsake him. She loved him very deeply. I know this to be true. Why else would she bear his child?"

Her words cut straight through me.

She saw my look of confusion but still did not seem to understand.

"Did you not notice she was full with child when you left us those many years ago? Did you not read the note she placed in the bottle?"

My face went white, I am sure.

Truth be told, I never did look at the message in the bottle. It was still sitting, still corked, in a cabinet back at the Hermitage, next to the bottle Harrison had left for me. They sat there side-by-side all these years, like urns holding someone's ashes. I was told the message was for Harrison's eyes only. "No peeking" I was told. Being the good little Boy Scout that I am, I never peeked. I left it unopened in case Harrison returned for it.

"I have a sister? Or maybe a brother? Where?"

I am not sure she could hear me.

"She is most beautiful and graces us with her presence every day. 'Mourning Dove' is her name. She is here in spirit all around us. She is here, with us, always." She held her hand to her breast and closed her eyes in thoughtful contemplation.

"Can I see her?" I said the words, but they were not loud enough for her to hear them, at least not in the ears that were failing her.

"You can see her, feel her, here." She patted her breast yet again.

In the months that I was here as a boy, helping the people of Pine Island get their sea legs under them, my mom was gone most of the time, visiting the islands in the Pine Island Sound area as part of what became her mission work. I was beginning to wonder if part of her mission was to conceal the fact that she was carrying Harrison's child.

The child that he never knew he even had was stillborn. After that, my mom threw herself with even more vigor into her mission work. She became somewhat of a celebrated figure in island lore, making treks to nearly every single island nation in the Caribbean basin and beyond. She was known as White Hawk, the Missionary. I always thought that she was hoping she would run into Harrison in her travels. I became convinced of that when she embarked on her last voyage, this time to Easter Island.

White Hawk was never heard from again.

"How did White Hawk get her name?" I asked loud enough for her to hear.

"That was not the name she was given. She became Wounded Sea Hawk during her vision quest. The legend was she had a vision of an osprey, who swooped down upon her prey, sinking her talons into what she had seen in the waters, something that was more than what she had expected. When she tried to ascend, her talons, inextricably imbedded in her catch, held her down. She was unable to lift her burden and was slowly pulled down into the waters where she succumbed. She became, in a sense, wounded by the size of what she undertook, which drove her into the sea – a sea that consumed her."

The story of Wounded Sea Hawk.

The metaphor fit perfectly.

TWENTY-NINE

CL 20/0029
Tarpon Lodgings, Pine Island
Wednesday

This morning I headed out early, Jumping Jack style, with a steaming mug of cacina I rustled up from the downstairs kitchen. Outside I headed towards the docks. There was a breeze that stirred up the warm air just enough to cool things down ever so slightly.

Halfway to the docks I realized I would likely miss another morning constitutional.

Dang, that would be two days in a row.

Art was asleep on a cot at the stern. He probably wanted to take advantage of the breeze. He and Angela were brought back late last night from her vision quest. By that time I was already asleep. I had gotten a loaner kayak and came back while they were still with the medicine man, getting renamed and such. I guess that would make up for today's lack of a constitutional. It was a fairly solid workout to paddle from one island to the other.

I let the poor boy sleep for a little while longer. He was probably exhausted. I made my way to the Minnow to check in with Skip, who was already busily making ready for our voyage we would be making together. Skip was the son of Vince, who had shepherded me down to the Caymans and then over to the dock at the Hermitage all those many years ago.

I could see some stirrings over at the Leaf Erikson boat as well.

This time we would be taking three boats on the way back. We would be heading offshore and then south, around the tip of Florida, past where what is left of Key West is still sticking up out of the water. Then we would head east and then due north. The weather forecast looked good. There was little chance of weather forcing us southward into seas where there is more of a risk of pirates. We did not want to tempt fate with all the cargo we were hauling. Bringing three boats would improve our odds.

This would be like the Nina, Pina, and Santa Maria all over again. Leaf's and Skip's boats would be bringing cargo of their own stuff that they would be offering to trade at points along the way. Vision Quest might do likewise.

I walked back over to the Vision Quest and sat for a spell, watching Art sleep and sipping the rest of the cacina in my mug. He finally stirred, sat up and stretched, letting out a yawn. He looked over at me with bleary eyes.

"How'd it go yesterday, Art – or is it No-Ha or some other name you will be going by from now on?" He said nothing. "How about Angela? Did she get a new name?"

"Not really. He started calling her 'Angie.' Some old rock song got him going."

"I bet she's not too happy about that." Art shook his head.

"Mornin' Cap'n. Is that more Black Death you have there, or are they serving something else today that won't dissolve the enamel on your teeth?"

"Morning, Angie." I instantly regretted calling her that, especially when I saw her face fall. "C'mon, let's go see what we can scrounge up in the kitchen. We'll leave this for the mechanics to degrease the engines." I tossed the rest of the cacina in the drink, happy with how I had cleverly changed the subject.

"Art, you coming?"

He shook his head again.

We sat in the small dining area at the lodge. She was sipping her tea. I had switched to orange juice, locally grown of course. I was getting hungry.

"Here, let me know what you make of this." I pulled out the drawing Calusa had let me have of the lost boy of Harrison. She studied the picture carefully for some time while I told her the story of what had happened to Harrison and the boy.

"You know, I bet we could find this guy," she said, holding up the drawing.

"How so?"

"We have this thing you may have heard of, although you rarely use it except to chase storms. It's called the internet. Plus they have this thing called email."

"Oh, well, I'm not very good at that sort of stuff, being a hermit and all."

"Yeah I know but I am. Can I hold on to this?"

"Sure." She bolted from the table and went upstairs to her laptop she had brought with her. "That's just a loaner," I called after her.

After a big breakfast I checked in at the docks to see how things were going with the Nina, Pina, and Santa Maria. I saw a canoe rounding a bend and heading in my direction.

It was my sister.

"Ahoy, Captain!" She pulled up alongside the dock. "Care to help paddle this thing? I know you are missing your morning walk and thought you might want to work off whatever you had for breakfast this morning. Knowing you, it was a big one."

"I'd love to." I clambered aboard and took the seat at the bow.

We paddled north to the area around Jug Creek where some of the little specs of land that used to be islands were still sticking out of the water. Many had been preserved in their more natural state. That made them better able to survive in an environment of rising sea levels. Calusa Island was one of them. We headed in that direction, pausing to catch our breath when we pulled near the mangrove-laden shoreline.

"She told me about Mourning Dove," I said, after a short pause. Kate kept gulping down water from her canteen without flinching, as if she hadn't heard me. She wiped the moisture from her lips with her sleeve and screwed the cap back on the canteen.

"She's out there somewhere," she said, nodding in the general direction of the Gulf of Mexico. "Our mother thought that was the best place for her. Can't say as I could question her on that point. She put her out to sea before she herself did the same."

"Do you think on her missions she was looking for him?"

"That may be true. But after she never heard back from him about Mourning Dove, and he just sailed off into the sunset like that, she got the message that he didn't want to be found. It seems like, between him and our father, she saw a pattern developing."

I stopped short. We stared at each other for a moment.

"He didn't know anything about Mourning Dove, nor did I."

She had a look of surprise. Her mouth fell open.

"What do you mean? She sent him a note in that bottle I gave you to take back to him. Didn't you guys read it?"

"He had left by the time I got there and, no, I was told it was for his eyes only. No peeking, remember? He never knew he had a daughter, and I never knew I had a sister. All he knew is that we left him. In his mind, there was nothing for him to leave behind when he ventured out on his own, sailing into the sunset, as you say."

"Oh my God," she said, drawing her hand to her mouth.

I realized then that back at the Hermitage sat two bottles, side by side. Inside each were messages from two people to each other, never having been read by the other. They, indeed, sat like urns bearing the ashes of what was their love for one another, each thinking the other had been forsaken, again, by those whom they had loved the most.

Those thoughts kept echoing in my mind as we paddled back to the lodge in silence. I climbed out of the canoe and gently shoved it into the still waters of the basin.

"I didn't know," she said, tears welling up in her eyes.

"Nor did I," I said. "It's no one's fault, really. Maybe what happened to them was part of each of their destinies. Maybe . . ."

". . . maybe they found each other out there somehow," she said.

"You finished my thought. Are you sure we aren't twins?"

I smiled. She smiled back.

Then she disappeared around the bend.

Later that afternoon I was in the dining area, looking at charts and going over the float plans. I had a hard time concentrating. The thought of Harrison out there, thinking he was truly alone and virtually forsaken by everyone who he let get close to him. The thought haunted me. Could it be my mom, who thought he had forsaken her, had ventured out herself on her missions, thinking in the back of her mind she may find him?

I was standing over a chart splayed out on the table, staring at the circles and depths and shorelines and islands but not really seeing anything. You know how that goes. It's like when you are reading a book and find yourself halfway down the page, but your mind is elsewhere – you don't know what you just read and have to read it all over again. Angela walked in while I stood there like a zombie looking at nothing. She placed Calusa's sketch of the boy on top of the charts I was not really looking at.

"I think I found our boy. Or, man, I guess I should say."

"Oh?"

"I can't say I pinpointed where he might be, but I think I found someone who can, or at least knows of someone who can. It's a good thing you let me see some of those manuals. They have a lot of information that helped to fill in some details. Although, to be honest, I still don't know if Harrison is his first or last name."

"I can't believe it. After all these years of searching, you were able to find him just like that." I snapped my fingers. "You are an incredible woman, whatever your name is."

"Well, thank you, but don't thank me yet. I have a source and a lead. That's all."

"Well, tell me what you have."

"I went all around the World Wide Web and ended up right here." She pointed to the floor. "It was your sister."

"My sister knows where Harrison's son is? I didn't know she knew he had a son."

"She didn't. But one of the people from the Institute told me that your sister knew about Calusa's mother. They were doing some background research into Calusa's past and whether she was part of a tribe from Florida. From that research I was able to find a woman who was the daughter of Calusa's mother's sister."

"Let me think for a second. That would be Calusa's cousin?"

"Precisely."

"Calusa's cousin knows where Harrison's son is?"

"Patience, Grasshopper."

She smiled at that one.

"We don't know that yet, but what we do know is that the sister was a friend of the lady that was the boy's mother. There is a rumor that they eventually moved to Cap-Haitien, where the sister had been living back in the Twenties. Seems that the island where they had been living, Antigua, had to be evacuated, so they moved to Cap-Haitien."

"I remember that story. Antigua was being swallowed up by the sea."

"That's how I was able to track them. A lady with the same or similar-sounding name as the cousin was quoted in a story about the evacuation and how friends of theirs had to stay with them as refugees in Cap-Haitien."

"Is the cousin still alive?"

"I am not sure that she is, but I was able to establish contact with a guy in Haiti who is part of the village network. His dad knows about Calusa. He also knows *you*."

"His name is Cousteau, isn't it?"

"Yes – how did you know? Oh yeah, I forgot, it's in the manuals. Anyway, the guy from the network is venturing up a mountain near the town to see if they can locate the cousin. He said he would let me know what he comes up with."

My head was swimming. Angela just told me that the long-lost boy of Harrison might be sitting on a mountain top in Haiti. The whole thing was bewildering, but at the same time, things were starting to make a whole lot more sense. I was beginning to see the connection between Calusa, the Haitians who lived on the other side of the Great Divide, and how we ended up becoming such good friends.

Cousteau himself had gone on a mission to Haiti many years ago, back in the Twenties. He brought with him the knowledge we had gained about how to rebuild after a major storm, how to reforest the land, how to, well, save the islanders from themselves.

I started to make an alternative float plan, just in case.

CL 20/0030
Key West, Florida
Thursday

The next day the three ships set sail. I sat down next to Angela at the stern, where she was gazing out at what would soon be a dwindling horizon. She didn't look sad exactly, but I got a sense her vision quest was not quite what she expected.

"I guess being called 'Angie' is not a new and exciting thing for you."

"Not really. But I guess if the shoe fits, you have to wear it."

"Sounds like another one of those old sayings, like some of the other ones I keep saying all the time. You are, indeed, becoming wise, Soaring Falcon."

She gave me a strange look as if to say, "What kind of crazy talk is that?"

"Look, over there. See that Peregrine Falcon flying up into the air? She reminds me of you. Compact, full of energy, on her way to ever-expanding new heights she will soon reach. Yes, that is you. Soaring Falcon. You'll probably be one in your next life."

"Plus, I like animals, especially birds. Do they mate for life?"

"You'll have to research that one. But something tells me you will someday. That is, if you don't end up being such a hermit like some people I know."

We pulled into the main docks at Marco Island. Angela hailed a ride on a skiff to the community building to meet up with the people stationed there that were part of the network. I was not in the mood for some reason and stayed with Art and the boat. We didn't have much trading to do and ended up watching Leaf and Skip wheeling and dealing at the docks with the good people of the island, who were among the first to understand some time ago to change the way they built things. Lucky 13 spared them this time, but they knew their island was right at one of the corners of Hurricane Alley.

Their turn would come again soon enough.

They were as prepared as anyone could be for when it hit.

We had finished our business, and the flotilla of three boats was about to set sail when Angela climbed out of the skiff and onto the dock. Back out at sea we sat together at our usual spot at the stern of the Vision Quest, looking out at the Gulf of Mexico. My thoughts again turned to my mom and Harrison out there somewhere. Maybe they were together, maybe not. Most likely they were both long gone, one way or the other.

"I heard back from that guy in Cap-Haitien."

"Oh? Do tell."

"'Do tell'? I have never heard that before."

"It's just another one of those really old sayings I keep trying on you to see if you have ever heard them. It means 'tell me about it.'"

"Well, I figured out that much. Just hadn't heard it before. I will put it in my list of idioms for future reference when I want to really confuse people."

"Just the youngsters. Us old timers have heard it before."

"Anyway, the guy found Calusa's cousin – well, actually, her daughter. The cousin apparently passed away. She said she might know the man we are looking for. At least, he seems to fit the description. There is a chance we have found our man."

I had to ponder the meaning of what she was telling me for a few minutes. There was a possibility that with Angela's help, we had finally found the person Harrison had been looking for all these years. Did he know his father had been searching for him? We fell silent, and I looked out across the waters, as if searching for something myself.

Our next stop was at the floating docks of Key West. They had resumed construction on the docks after letting Lucky 13 and No. 20 pass by way to the north of them. They were lifting the gangways to the floating docks up a few more feet before the rising tides put them all under water for good. This time we were greeted at the docks by the chief of the island by the name of Speckled Trout. He was sitting at the helm of the old Boston Whaler he used to get around in the stilt village the key had become, inviting us aboard to take a tour while the others were busily trading.

"You must be the one they call 'Captain,'" Speckled Trout said. He had freckles on his face which gave me a pretty good idea how he got his name.

"That's him alright. Hi, I'm Soaring Falcon." She gave him a slight bow.

"Speckled Trout," he said, bowing back.

Like most of the structures on Key West, the chief's house that he brought us to was built on stilts. It was constructed in the usual fashion of the people of the island network, thatched with rounded edges and a domed roof. We pulled up in the wide canal that ran along the side of his place and went inside to visit for a spell and get something to eat.

You know me, starving as usual.

"You are heading back to the famed Harrison Hermitage, I am told. Tell me how you are faring there these days."

"Same as here, pretty much," I said. "We keep rising up, trying to keep our feet from getting wet, and the tides keep pace, rising up to meet where we are, right before we rise up again. Not sure how long we can keep that up before we become as much of a stilt-ville as your village. But I will be making a bit of a detour."

"Oh? Do tell." Angela had decided to try out the new phrase she had learned.

"Skip has agreed to take me to Cap-Haitien in his boat. You and Art will be continuing on to the Hermitage. Leaf will escort you in his boat."

She was stunned at the news.

"What about the pirates?"

"You should be safe enough with Leaf to get you home."

"I'm not worried about us."

"I will be fine. Skip and his vessel are well known in those waters. His boat has the Mask of the Ancient Ones – two of them, in fact. Plus, of course, I have a personal connection to the guy who started the whole pirate thing back in the Twenties."

"You knew the one they called 'Crazy Legs,' whose pirates are said to have set up their headquarters on Margarita Island?" Speckled Trout's eyes had widened.

"I can't say as I knew him, but he was my father."

"But do you know why they call him 'Crazy Legs'?"

I sighed at the question. "I have an inkling but don't know that for sure either."

"The legend has it that the original pirate down there, going back a couple hundred years ago, was known as 'Red Legs,' but the new guy had legs that were not red." Angela decided to jump in and give a dissertation on pirate lore. "Maybe he was about as nutty as the Captain here turned out to be. Thus, the appellation 'Crazy.'"

"'Appellation'? Isn't that a mountain range somewhere? You sure do use funny words, Soaring Falcon. Are you sure you do not speak with forked tongue?"

She laughed. "No, I just read a lot."

CL 20/0031
Cap-Haitien, Haiti
Friday

At the docks the next morning, Speckled Trout bade us bon voyage. He had offered to send a ship to go with us, but I told him we would be fine. I did give him our float plan and asked him and Angela to keep track of us.

"You know I will be checking on you every hour on the hour," said Angela. "Are you sure you want to do this? It's not like you to do something reckless like this."

"I know I may sound as crazy as my old man, but I am quite lucid, I can assure you. This is something I have to do. I think you understand why, but if not, if I don't come back, you can look at the message Harrison left me in that bottle in the cabinet back at the Hermitage. I think that explains things better than anything else could."

"That's what I am afraid of."

"What? It's just a message in a bottle."

"No, not that. I'm afraid you won't come back."

I held her, then looked into her eyes.

There were some tears in them.

"Not to worry. You are not something I would want to leave behind."

There was, as they say, smooth sailing to Cap-Haitien. The weather was near perfect, almost as if to invite us along our journey. But a few miles off the coast of the island of Hispaniola, we spotted three ships heading in our direction. They did not respond to our hailing. We started to get a little worried. Then they tacked to either side, giving us a wide enough berth that I could not make out their markings with my spy glass.

Then they turned around and started following us.

They were making lots of ground, gaining on us. Then they got close enough to where Skip could make out the flag they were flying.

"They're pirates," he said grimly.

"Can we outrun them?"

Skip and his two-man crew looked at me with serious expressions.

"We'll never make it. The best thing to do is cry 'Uncle,' and let them raid our cargo. If we play nice, maybe they won't kill us."

We slowed down enough to let them pull along either side of us, but they kept their distance. I could see them standing along the sides of their boat. They were a scruffy lot. Images of what had happened with that Manson fellow and my father at the Hermitage when I was but a boy came into my head. I stood there, watching them.

Then, suddenly, in unison, they gave me a salute.

I saluted back.

Then their boats peeled away. They remained in the distance but never too far away that we lost sight of them – or they us.

We were greeted at the port in Cap-Haitien by a throng of people waving to us, some with those flags with the Mask of the Ancient Ones on them.

"What's this all about?" Skip wanted to know.

"Looks like Soaring Falcon sent a bunch of emails soaring all over the place."

An older man stood in the midst of the crowd, his arms folded. He had a big, wide grin on his face. Hadn't seen him in years, but I could tell it was Cousteau.

"Well, the prodigal son returns, so to speak."

His English was really good these days, as was his use of the language.

"I have someone I think you are going to want to meet."

He took me to his chief's house. I lowered my head to enter. My eyes had to adjust before I could see the group of people seated around the firepit at the center. They all stood up as I entered, except an elderly man on the other side of the crackling fire.

"Bon jour, Capitaine. Bienvenue a Haiti," a young woman said, bowing slightly. I knew enough French to know what she said, and enough sense to know to bow back.

"I am sorry, but my French is not as good as yours. Parlez vous anglais?"

"Oui – I mean, yes, a little."

"Did you know Calusa? The one we called the Great Amazon Warrior Princess?"

She looked at Cousteau with a puzzled expression at first. Then she turned to me and said, "I did not know her, but she was my great auntie."

I pulled out the now-crumbled sketch Calusa gave me and thrust it at her.

"Do you know this boy? He would be an old man now. This is what he looked like when he was a boy. His father was named Harrison." For some idiotic reason I thought she would understand what the heck I was talking about.

Turned out she did.

"Henri? Oui, oui, of course I know him."

"It's all over the Internet, Cap'n," said Cousteau. "Somebody calling herself Soaring Falcon has been sending out messages like a multitude of arrows, flying all over the Caribbean, telling us the story of Harrison and his lost son."

"I'm sure he would really appreciate that."

Harrison would surely cringe at having his private life splayed all over the Internet like that. "Does anyone know what happened to his son?"

"Why, of course. He stopped by for lunch." He motioned towards the fire. The people standing there parted to reveal the old man still sitting there. His eyes were downcast at first, until I sat across from him. Our eyes met.

"You knew my father?" he asked in perfect English.

"I knew him well. He was a great man. He never stopped trying to find you. He searched all of the islands looking for you."

"You are the one he named 'Captain'?"

"Yes. How did you know?"

"He told me."

"He *told* you? I don't understand." I looked up at Cousteau and the other faces of the people gathered there. Some looked like they were crying.

"Yes, he told me all about you and the story of the Amazon Warrior Princess and White Feather and, of course, Monsieur Cousteau." He glanced up at Cousteau, who had that big grin on his face again. "He had come to Antigua, where I used to live with my mother. He taught us many things on the island, but the waters were rising, and we had to leave. But he did not come with us when we left."

"Where did he go? Where is he?"

"I do not know. He said he needed to find someone else he had lost. He wasn't sure if she wanted him to find her, but he was going to try to find out."

"But what happened to him? Where did he go?"

"I don't know exactly." He paused for a moment, stroking his chin.

"He said something about Easter Island."

"TWENTY-TWENTY"
(Epilogue)

Falcon's Log
Volume 40/#0001 (Book 84)
The Hermitage/Tuesday

T his morning I sat out on the veranda, sipping my favorite
tea, looking out at the waves and the rising sun peeking
over the tree line off in the distance.

We had attached the veranda to the Hermitage some years
ago when we hoisted the thing another few feet into the air
to, well, keep our feet from getting wet. At this point it had
become the main stilt house in a veritable sea of stilt houses still
left standing from the old, historic Hermitage Village that once
graced these shores.

This place, and the few others remaining, stood like bulwarks
against the rising sea, not so much defying as reaching an accom-
modation with her. The manuals were right, as were their authors.
The global climate had changed, and even after the industrial
revolution had run its course and we had all learned to return to
a simpler way of life, learning to live in nature instead of trying
to conquer her, the tide had, so to speak, already turned.

The scientists tell us that the temperature of the planet had
leveled off. We might even be experiencing a little bit of a decline
in temperatures if trends continue. That is good news to hear, to
be sure, but we are not about to return to the way things were,
even if the seas receded and we actually had some land to build

one of those god-awful houses they used to have that I read about in the manuals.

Did you know they actually built houses out of concrete right up to the shoreline? They had roads that the water could not go through that flooded everywhere when it rained. Then when it stopped raining, there would be a drought, and they had no water. I know that sounds crazy, but that is what people used to do way back then.

I swear I am not making it up. It is all right there in the manuals.

Oh, wait, I just remembered something. Funny how things start to slip your mind as you get older. Except memories from the past it seems these days. Good thing I started writing things down myself in these manuals. Falcon's Log I call them. I learned to start doing that from him, you know: the guy for whom the Captain's Log is named.

For all I know, by writing these words I may as well be talking to myself. I will maybe never know if you or anybody else will ever read them. Come to think of it, I think that is exactly what it says in one of the Captain's Logs. He was wondering the same thing.

Well, as things turned out, he did come to know at least one person would read the words he had written down in that journal of his. Come to think of it, the same thing happened with Harrison, his predecessor.

Now, what was it I was trying to remember that I forgot again?

Oh, yeah, now I remember. You haven't read the pages from the manuals – the Chronicles as we call some of them, the ones that tell the story of what happened that time, way back, many years ago, when the Captain left me and went to Haiti. Well, okay, that is maybe a little over-dramatic. He did not really "leave me," and, true to his word, he came back to the Hermitage where I was waiting for him. I knew he would.

But, still, I did get nervous for a while when he went off to Haiti like that.

When I saw his boat coming up to the dock with Skip, I ran down to the cabinet, got out the two bottles, and set them on that old table. You are not going to believe this, but that table is still right here, high and dry. I swear that thing will outlast us all.

I know what you're thinking, but, no, I did not uncork that bottle and look at the message his mom had sent to Harrison. "No peeking" was the rule. The Captain may have been a Boy Scout, but, well, I am somewhat of a Girl Scout myself. That thing was sitting right there on the table, unopened, right beside the other bottle, when the Captain came bursting into the room. I have to admit I started balling like a, well, like a girl I suppose, but I don't care. Heck, he was crying himself, although I am not sure it was just because he was happy to be home – and happy to see me, seeing as all he had been through.

You see, we had grown pretty close. He was like a father to me. I think I was like a daughter to him.

My own daughter is in the next room, still sleeping. Poor thing is still wrung out from that long boat ride to get over here to the Hermitage. These days she keeps asking me why I keep telling her about the old days and using these old expressions she never heard of before. I don't know why I have been doing that lately. Seems like there is so much I want her to know about before she will have to take up where I eventually will leave off.

Maybe I should let her read some of the manuals like she keeps pestering me to do.

Speaking of which, where was I?

Oh, yeah, the two bottles.

He uncorked that one bottle and slowly sat down as he read the message in it. He had a real dour look on his face as he handed it over to me. At some point, after I read it, I wrote down what it said and put that into the Chronicles for posterity. Later it went back in the bottle, and we put it back on the shelf with the other one.

They are both there, by the way, in case someone wants to take a peek.

My Dearest Harrison,

I think of you so often and miss you so terribly. I can't put that one image of you out of my mind. You were standing on the dock as we were leaving. I had a premonition that I might never see you again.

The thought of that is tearing away at my heart.

I will never forget the last night we spent together.

There is something you should know. I am not sure how you will feel about this, but I am now carrying our child.

I think it's a girl.

I am frightened of bringing another child into this world. The last time this happened, the prospect seems to have driven away the man who was in my life. I do not understand why this is so, but I guess I will have to try and understand it, especially if having your child is much more than a man like you had bargained for.

I know that you think of yourself as a man who has made it in this world alone for the most part, except for Calusa, of course, but I hope you can accept me and this child as a part of your world, as you have with my son.

But if not, I will try to understand.

I hope my premonition is not real and that we will see each other again, maybe on an island somewhere.

I love you and miss you.

Wounded Sea Hawk.

"I don't get it. Why did he just leave like that? Oh, wait, that's right, the bottle was never opened until just now. He never read this message," I said to the Captain.

"That's right; you and I are the first people to ever read it. He was already gone by the time I got back here. He didn't know he had a child on the way."

"Maybe he also didn't know how she felt about him."

"You presume well, She Who Used to Be Called Grasshopper." He pulled the message from Harrison out of the other bottle and handed it to me.

"Knowing you, you probably read this already."

"Of course I didn't. You said to read it only if you didn't come back, remember? I knew you would come back. You said you would never leave me like that."

"And now you can see why."

He motioned in the direction of the letter I was holding in my hands.

I have to admit they were shaking a little.

Ahoy there, Captain.

I don't know if you or anyone else will be reading these words. If you are, then there are a few last things I need to explain to you.

In the desk drawer there is a deed to the Hermitage made out to you. There is also a Will giving everything I own to you, except for Bolt, of course, and my boat. I am taking them with me.

You are in charge now, and I know you will do a fine job of taking care of the village and all the villagers, even the ones who are a little idiotic. You have the manuals and all the books in the library to help you figure out what to do next.

I must admit I felt pretty sad to see you and everyone else, especially your mom, leaving for the west coast, but I understand why you had to go. I wish it were otherwise, but I know I am not really a part of your family. Don't feel sorry for me and don't think I feel sorry for myself.

This is the way things have always worked out for me. When it comes right down to it, I am alone in this world. I am used to it.

Maybe out there, on an island somewhere, I will find my own family.

But if not, at least I have grown to feel as though the islanders I have met in my travels are kindred spirits. I have something in common with them. They live out their lives, isolated and alone, floating around on worlds that can be of their own making, if they could just learn how.

Theirs is the story of Easter Island, but it doesn't have to end that way.

There is still hope for them and the rest of us.

Maybe even your good friend,

Harrison.